Praise for *How All This Started*

Winner of the 2001 Pacific Northwest Booksellers Association Award

"Pete Fromm beautifully weaves the themes of baseball, fidelity, aspiration, and madness into an intriguing and thought-provoking novel. . . . Gripping."
—2001 Pacific Northwest Booksellers Association Book Award Committee

"Pete Fromm's memorable coming-of-age novel is about baseball and mental illness, but those are mostly plot devices. It's really about the mystery and terrible beauty of families. . . . This is a grown-up novel, creating a family worth caring about."
—*USA Today*

"A fine debut novel . . . lean and vital . . . A tight, moving tale."
—*Spokane Spokesman-Review*

"Vivid and disturbing . . . a real 'fireballer' for those who like their fiction fast and tumultuous."
—*The Bellingham Herald* (Washington)

"Tension and tenderness . . . carry this emotionally rich and often emotionally wrenching tale."
—*Library Journal*

"Beautifully written and well thought out, Fromm's debut novel captures the bond between a brother and sister. With subtle humor and complete honesty, he portrays the heartbreaking reality of a family dealing with manic depression and a young boy's struggle to come to terms with his hero's failings."
—*Booklist*

"A gripping debut. . . Baseball lovers will want to read this book, but so will anyone who has loved a difficult sibling."
—*Publishers Weekly*

Also by Pete Fromm

How All This Started

Pete Fromm

PICADOR USA   New York

www.picadorusa.com

Picador® is a U.S. registered trademark and is used by St. Martin's Press under license from Pan Books Limited.

For information on Picador USA Reading Group Guides, as well as ordering, please contact the Trade Marketing department at St. Martin's Press.
Phone: 1-800-221-7945 extension 763
Fax: 212-677-7456
E-mail: trademarketing@stmartins.com

Frontispiece photo by Photodisc, Inc.

Design by Amanda Dewey

Library of Congress Cataloging-in-Publication Data

Fromm, Pete.
    How all this started / Pete Fromm.
        p. cm.
    ISBN 0-312-20933-9 (hc)
    ISBN 0-312-27697-4 (pbk)
    1. Manic-depressive persons—Fiction. 2. Brothers and sisters—Fiction
    3. Baseball players—Fiction. 4. Texas—Fiction. I. Title.

PS3556.R5942 H69 2000
813'.54—dc21   00-034696

First Picador USA Paperback Edition: October 2001

10 9 8 7 6 5 4 3 2 1

*For my brother, Joe, who survived his younger-brother
days with stubborn valor and grace*

✤

And my sister, Jean, who sat through even the rain delays

Acknowledgments

I would like to thank the staff and students of Pecos High School for their generosity and willingness to answer what must have seemed pointless questions. In particular, I thank the Armstead family for welcoming me to Texas and showing me their ranch and their life, in and out of baseball.

I'd also like to thank Dr. Rennae Johnson, who gave of her expertise freely and graciously, as did Dr. Thomas Key. Thanks as well to the people of the Great Falls Dodgers organization and Tattoo York's.

And a final thanks to my editors, Diane Higgins and Patricia Fernandez, for their tremendous help in bringing this story to its final form.

How All
This
Started

one

Howling gusts ripped at the corners of our house, tearing at the roof, shaking the windows, and I lay open-eyed in the dark, listening. Blue northers Dad called these storms, and through the gravel BB-ing the house, the occasional scratchy thump of a creosote bush shot against the siding—the wind itself, moaning and keening—I strained to hear the first trace of Abilene's return. I'd even left my jeans on, so I wouldn't be naked when she came.

She'd been gone over a week, without a word, Mom and Dad in a quiet panic, their voices trailing off whenever I appeared. But Abilene and I had never once missed a norther.

When I was little, still wearing pajamas, before Abilene's disappearing this way was something anybody could ever have pictured, I'd sneak into her room as soon as the wind started. Wrapped under the same blankets, we'd giggle as the whole world got turned upside down by something as deadly normal as wind. There wasn't a thing out there to stop it, even slow it down, only, as far as any eye could see, the endless, level horizon of stubby, drought-brittled creosote and head-high mesquite. The wind would roar through that thin cover, tearing loose anything broken, dusting the skies for days. But we used to open all her windows, shivering against each other in the dark, feeling the strange, wet cold, the scorched smell of the desert turned pregnant, like no other time at all. Abilene said if Mom and Dad found us like that, we'd tell them the storm had woken me, had scared me. Burying our faces in her pillow, we laughed like crazy at the idea of us being scared of anything. We laughed till our ribs ached, till we had to throw back the blankets for air. Then we lay still in the cold, holding on to each other for the warmth, and we listened to the wild wind, raging wherever it cared to go.

But that'd been when we were just kids, and Abilene was too old now—*I* was too old now—to go tiptoeing into her room no matter how much I might have wanted to. Even if she had been home.

Outside the wind kept up its battering, whistling through the loose shingles, but as I lay staring at the dark, it turned into as much a lullaby as anything, and instead of dashing from beneath the covers and opening the window, the way we used to, I ended up dozing off. It would've been too lonely anyway, having the desert all wet and cold in the room with just me.

I woke to the window screeching back and forth, stubborn in its frame. I sat up smiling, picturing how excited Abilene would look, shooting her fists up first in one corner, then the other, zigzagging the window up, letting in the wind, maybe even jumping in with me like the old days.

But the window, though half-open, was empty. A pale light flooded in with the cold, like maybe there was a fire somewhere out there. It was bright enough to look around, but the only person in my room was Nolan Ryan, my old poster ghostly in the outside light, his leg caught chin high, about to uncork his scorching fastball, the word *Fireballer* arcing over his head.

Then, even louder than the wind, I caught the bleating rumble of Abilene's broken-muffler truck, smelled the creeping fog of blue exhaust. "Ab'lene?" I whispered.

Something hit the bottom edge of the window then, from outside, shoving it up the rest of the way. A two-by-four or something. Some kind of big stick. It clattered in the yard, and before I could think, Abilene's hands shot up over the sill, her head poking into my room, her elbows clawing at the ledge, feet scrabbling against the siding.

"Ab'lene?" I said again, louder, my smile growing.

She hooked her waist over the sill and slithered inside.

When Abilene leapt up, quick as a snake, the light outside left nothing but a long, lean, black shadow of her, wider through the shoulders than anywhere else. Not much different from Nolan Ryan, really, if Nolan Ryan had been a girl. A perfect one.

"Hey, Ab'lene," I said, my smile huge. We'd used her window forever; our escape hatch, crawling onto the porch roof and dropping down between Mom's flowers. Abilene had even waxed the frame for silence. But there was no roof under my window. There was nothing out there at all. It was as if she'd been off somewhere learning to fly, and was just back now to share the secret.

Abilene blew out a big breath, barely holding back her laughter. "Hey, Austin," she whispered. "You awake?"

"No."

A snort escaped. "Do you hear this *wind!*"

"I've been waiting for you." I poked a leg from beneath the blankets, showing her my jeans.

Abilene paused, then grabbed my leg, giving it a shake. "You *were* waiting!" She stooped and tossed my shirt to me. "Come on. We're burning daylight."

"It's the middle of the night, Ab'lene," I said, drawing the shirt over my head, poking my arms through, hiding my scrawny self as quick as I could. I couldn't help a shiver at the cold touch of the cloth.

"Night. Day. Same thing." She was looking around the floor. "Where's your jacket?"

"Downstairs."

Abilene shook her head. "Poor planning, Austin. What with a norther and all."

"I wasn't sure you'd come."

Abilene jerked to a standstill, her shape dark against the watery light of the window. "Of course you were."

"I know," I said fast. "It's a good norther, isn't it?"

"You got that!" she cried, smacking at my shoulder, her fist balled up tight. But then, serious, she asked, "You knew I couldn't stay away with that going on, didn't you?"

"We didn't know where you were," I whispered. "We didn't have any idea."

"Hell," Abilene said, laughing again. "Neither did I!"

I stood up from the bed, but didn't move away from it.

"But I came back for you," she answered. "Just like you knew I would. Now let's go."

I eased toward the door, listening for any trace of Mom and Dad.

Abilene tugged me around, pointing at the window.

"But . . ."

"Follow me," she said, grinning.

Darting feet first out the window, she clung to the sill like a spider. "Just kick off a little," she said, and that fast she was gone, smacking down in the bed of her truck, backed up tight to the house. "Presto!" she called.

She clapped her hands, waiting for me. "Child's play!"

I poked my head out instead of my feet.

She clapped again, not so patiently. "Turn around. The other way."

Afraid to tell her I'd meet her at the door, I wormed my legs out and dangled down the side of the house, the wind slapping at me just like everything else out there. Me in my T-shirt. I craned to see beneath me and Abilene said, "For crying out loud, Austin."

Then, back in my room, I heard a tiny, soft tapping: the ratchety click of my doorknob. I pushed off the wall of our house and let go.

Abilene caught me tight, keeping me from falling out of the truck. Her chest pushed up against my shoulder blades. I turned into her. "Mom and Dad are up," I whispered.

Abilene sprang over the side of the truck, bouncing behind the wheel and calling, "Time to go!" The engine roared and I jumped too.

The crushed white rock Dad kept raked smooth skittered out behind us, pinging in the wheel wells as Abilene scorched out of our driveway, blowing off into the desert, leaving our yard— the indistinguishable patch of nothing surrounding our house— far behind.

I knelt up on the seat, looking back, seeing my room light up like a beacon, a shadow so thin and small in the window it could only have been Mom, watching after us. Billowing in the icy wind of the norther, the curtains blocked more light than she did. Dad, of course, would have been like an eclipse up there.

two

Abilene wound the engine out, bouncing us through the washboards and across the potholes as I dropped down to face forward. A box on the floor took up all my legroom, and I sat scrunched with my knees above the dash, digging for my seat belt. All I came up with was a stub of webbing, the fresh cut soft and frayed against my fingers.

Catching me, Abilene howled, "No moss on our backs!"

In the backglow of the headlights I could just see the old seat-belt buckles lying on the box at my feet, scribbles of webbing trailing away like kite tails. An open razor knife slid around with them, then dropped to the floor.

"No moss!" I answered, tilting my head back to roar like she did, but clinging to the door handle and what was left of the seat belt all the same.

We reached the pavement before I'd started feeling anything

beyond that leap out my window, landing in Abilene's arms, her rare warm softness pressed hard against me. "Where are we going?" I yelled over the roar of her truck.

She turned west and sped down the highway, her lights dim and wavery, rolling out a tiny patch of the sun-blanched pavement before us. We were headed for Pecos, maybe, in that direction anyway, instead of the shorter run east to Pyote and the bomber base, and Abilene just kept smiling.

"Where were you, Ab'lene?" I asked again, as quiet as I could considering the noise.

She gave a toss of her head toward the box at my feet. "Got those for you."

I glanced down, thinking of the open razor knife rattling loose down there. Across the top of the box I saw the Rawlings label. Official Major League. "Baseballs?"

"Now you can really throw some smoke."

"Where did you get them?"

But Abilene wagged a finger. "Gift horse," she warned.

We drove in silence then, the old truck wobbly with the speed. She turned into the south edge of Pecos, the truck lights flashing across the old Shell station's sign propped against the pole that used to hold it up in the sky, where people could see. The gas station had been abandoned before I was born, the yellow seashell now tanned with grime. Like usual, Abilene detoured through Maxey Park, the dusty, tiny zoo she swore would close down the instant the last animal died. She leaned out her window, braying at those dejected zebras, the dark hump of the lone buffalo.

She hooked north out of the zoo then, cutting by the shut-up Woolworth, the big For Lease sign in the old Safeway, the red letters long ago faded to pink. I was pretty sure I knew where we were going, but Abilene wove through town, past all the empty buildings, the sun-frayed plywood covering the windows, the movie theater still sporting its handwritten Opening Soon sign, though the doors hadn't been cracked in ten years.

As we sidled down the quiet, empty streets, I didn't have to yell anymore, and I said, "Mom and Dad were pretty spooked, Ab'lene. About you disappearing."

Abilene nodded, but said, "Couldn't be helped," then, "I'll make it up to them."

How? I wanted to ask, but Abilene pulled in beneath the mulberry trees along the high school's outfield fence and was out of the truck before I knew she'd killed the engine, the slam of her door loud in the still town.

As soon as I opened my door, though, the wind nearly tore it from my grip, the stillness gone. Pushing it shut, I walked around to stand beside Abilene, gazing out at the field, squinting against the grit blown off the diamond. The wind pushed me around, made me adjust my balance, but Abilene stood like a pillar. I hadn't been out here with her in five years, since she was my age, the year she forced her way onto the team.

During the years since that horrible season neither of us had ever mentioned her brief baseball career on this field. We had never said a thing about how, though she could have pitched with the best of them, she'd had to fight through everything the teachers and the athletics office could throw at her, only to get shunned by the team. The boys, her teammates, refused even to step to the plate for her to throw batting practice. Mom and Dad too only kept telling her it was best not to keep setting herself up for disappointment. They asked her, "Why not play softball?" like that was one bit like the real thing.

Abilene had sat through the entire season without throwing a pitch, without giving in. Afterward, though, she wrapped up school in a blaze of credits, graduating a year early, talking of nothing but getting out of here. But then she was back again after only three months of junior college. Another thing we never talked about.

"So this is it," Abilene said now, waving her arms toward the field. "The site of all your glory to come."

I shivered and looked out across the grass, even in the dark the greenest thing in Pecos. The pitching mound's hump was hidden in the night, though you could make out the light patch of the infield dirt, kind of glowing way out there. I was a sophomore this year, but Abilene had redshirted me last year—something she said they did all the time in college. "Give you a year to grow," she'd said. Adding size to raw talent. Size, talent, and overwhelming training, which Abilene had been supplying since before I could remember. Appearing out of nowhere, she always said, we'd take the world by storm, this incredible phenom bursting onto the baseball scene, hurling pure, blazing fire. But I knew she wanted me to start when she had, to be the sophomore who would, this time, blow everyone away.

And because of all her talk of secrecy, her dream of me storming in and leaving the jaws of every baseball player in Texas gaping in stunned surprise and awe, I'd slunk through school without hardly saying a word, without making a friend, just going through my classes, not even playing a game of catch. I'd grown six inches in the last year, Abilene's plans as dead-on as ever. During the season I'd left school by the back door so I could at least walk by the field and watch the team practice for the few seconds it took to circle around to the cemetery, where Abilene sat waiting beneath the water tower, her truck idling, that ready to get out to the abandoned bomber base and work on my pitching.

Now Abilene squeezed through the gap in the left-field corner of the fence and I followed after her. I thought she'd want me to bring the balls, have me pitch off a real mound, call balls and strikes, but she didn't say a word about them. Instead, as I hustled to keep up, I saw her pull something from the inside pocket of her jacket: a stick or a gun or something.

Abilene twirled whatever it was around the end of her finger, gunslinger style, and catching a quick steely sheen, for just one second I thought she might really have a gun. But then, in the faint glimmer of the far-off yard light, I made out a wrench, though not like any wrench I'd ever seen before.

Without a word of warning Abilene dropped to her knees in the grass. I nearly walked over her. "What?" I asked.

She worked her wrench in the grass and then leapt up, waving the long pipe and ratcheting end of one of the field sprinklers high above her head. She ran off, dropping down over the next sprinkler head she came across, and the next. I don't know how she found them in the dark.

"Ab'lene?" I asked, chasing after her.

She looked up and grinned, tossing the latest sprinkler to me. I barely managed to catch it, surprised by its heft, by the cool touch of metal uprooted from the ground.

"We are going to spread a swath of greenery wherever we go, Austin," she said, all rushed and breathless, like the very idea was too much to hold in.

She was already off for the next head, and I was starting to say "What?" again, like some kind of dim-witted parrot, when all of a sudden a rush of air came up out of the grass, and then, before I could even duck, the water gushed into the sprinklers. They began their *chicka-chicka-chicking,* arcing around great rainbows of water, but wherever Abilene had been, only sloppy geysers erupted from the field, huge fountains of water here where nothing could be more rare.

Abilene flashed past me, hugging her sprinklers to her chest, laughing like mad as a sweep of water caught her full on.

I ran after her, waving my own single sprinkler head, laughing with Abilene. I couldn't help it.

Slipping through the fence, we fell against the side of her pickup, both of us splattered with water, the wind whipping our clothes around us. My teeth chattered as we caught our breath, still staring out at the field, the glitter of the sprinklers making their steady rounds. The fountains of the missing heads sprouted from the field, outlining Abilene's crazy, wobbly path.

Even with the wind, the promise it brought of rain, the sprinklers were something to stop and listen to. And the smell of the water, on top of the norther, made you almost think anything was possible here.

Abilene turned away from the field first, and I heard the shivering hiss of metal sliding into metal. I looked around to see her dropping the posts of the sprinklers into the side-rail sockets along the truck's bed. The heads stuck up that way, looking ready to water our trail wherever we might go. I slid mine in too, but we were one short. Three on Abilene's side, only two on mine.

"Never mind," Abilene said, "it'll work just fine."

"Work?" I asked, hopping onto my seat as Abilene jumped behind the wheel.

"Imagine, Austin," she said, cranking over the engine. "All this place needs is water. Remember the cotton? Everywhere we go we'll leave a strip of green about a hundred feet wide and forever long. Nobody will be able to miss us."

I grinned. "You plan on driving forever?"

"What else?" she asked, edging around the cemetery on the other side of the school, then out of Pecos altogether. In the desert the long-abandoned cotton fields, if their fences had held out the cattle and the mesquite seeds they shitted, shone white in the night, packed hard and dry as the dirt of an infield, as empty and barren as the day the farmers left.

Abilene kept checking the rearview, kept glancing back over her shoulder like she was making sure all that greenery was really springing up behind us.

But what I pictured was the outfield, the patches surrounding our theft drying out, crinkly and brown and hard in all that spongy green. Finally I had to say, "Ab'lene, it's just a joke."

She glanced at me like she hadn't heard right.

"It can't really work, Ab'lene," I said, still waiting for her to spring her punch line, but with a creeping little niggle of worry that she wouldn't. "We don't have any water. Not really."

"If I want it to work, Austin, believe me, it will."

I kept my eyes forward after that, afraid that if I did turn, I might actually see the beautiful lush swath sprouting in our wake.

three

I was sure Abilene was heading back toward Pyote, to the old Rattlesnake Bomber Base, that we'd pitch a game with the new balls after all. I was picturing us starting in the dusty glow of the headlights, pitching wild against the fury of the norther's driving winds, hopefully soon the driving rain, when all of a sudden Abilene pulled over onto the shoulder. She let the truck idle a second before shutting it down. Then there was nothing but the wind, rocking the truck a little, pelting us with dirt and gravel, the dawn dull and low in front of us.

I waited for whatever she'd do next, but Abilene just sat there.

Then, without a word, Abilene pushed open her door and walked away down the old highway. I shoved my own door open, throwing the seat forward to pull her extra jean jacket out from behind it. Soft and worn, I buttoned it shut as I hustled after her up the overpass climbing across the interstate.

At the top of the bridge, Abilene stopped and leaned over the railing, staring down at the miles and miles of empty road.

The bridge pavement was bleached as hard as the old runway at the bomber base, white in the first gray light of day. A lizard hoping for sun shuffled off, kicking up a dry rustle.

My steps on the bridge sounded hollow, and I looked out around the huge, flat nothing surrounding us. Far as you could see, there wasn't a thing but this bridge, a big chunk of concrete connecting one side of nothing with the other; a few motionless pump jacks from the oil days, a few of the abandoned cotton fields—bright sections of dirt glimmering in the shadowed drab green of the dusty creosote and mesquite.

I stopped next to Abilene, who hadn't so much as breathed, far as I could tell, since I'd left the truck. She still hung there, bent over the railing at the waist, her braid, thick around as a baseball bat, pointing straight down at the road. In the light now the red of her hair was starting to show, so much brighter than my own donkey-butt brown. "What are we doing here, Ab'lene?"

"You tell me," she whispered.

I glanced up, the clouds so low they seemed within reach. "Standing in the geographic center of nowhere."

"So why'd you ask?"

I set my elbows on the rail beside Abilene, looking down at the interstate, then out to where it shrank and vanished in the distance, flat and gray and tiny way out there.

"You ever stop here?" Abilene asked.

"Why would I have done that, Ab'lene? When?"

Abilene shrugged, making her braid swing. I folded over the railing the way she did, dropping my head so low my toes tee-tered off the pavement, only inches from pitching forward, falling free to splat onto the interstate like a Pecos cantaloupe. The wind tattered at us, getting under my jacket, covering me with goose bumps.

For a second Abilene looked at me, our heads a foot apart, our elbows touching. "Weird, isn't it?" she said.

"What?" My lips felt fat, the blood rushing to my head.

"Look at that road, Austin. Tearing right through the middle of this place."

"Like it can't get away fast enough."

"You got that."

We listened to the wind moan through the railings.

"Look at this place, Austin." She didn't make a move to look herself. Neither did I. Neither of us had to look to know what lay around us.

"Can you believe there's such an easy way out?"

That fast she made the bridge just about the loneliest place on earth, hanging over an escape route so empty you could hear its seashell hum. "I can believe it," I said.

"Yeah, I guess I can too."

We watched the interstate, out of reach down there, until Abilene said, "I come here a lot."

I glanced at her again. "What for?"

She smiled, whispering, "You tell me," but before I could roll my eyes, she shook her head, taking back her words. "Sometimes . . . sometimes, Austin, I feel like if I could only give myself the push, the one tiny push off of here, I could fly. Really fly."

I thought of her landing in my room, only hours ago. The steel railing under me was shivery cold. "Fly like a cantaloupe," I said.

Abilene swayed a little. Back and forth. "I suppose."

She swung so far forward I almost grabbed for her, but she only lifted her head to spit, a big gob. She stopped rocking, holding herself rigid, watching it fall. I did too.

"Count the seconds and you'll know how far."

"That's lightning, Ab'lene."

"Whatever."

When her spit landed, Abilene whispered, "I never thought we'd leave a trail with those sprinklers, Austin. I was never so far gone I thought we could really make anything grow here."

I stopped working up my own gob of spit. I looked down the highway to where it faded into the blur of desert, the squash of clouds. When Abilene didn't say anything else, I said, "I bet it doesn't even rain, Ab'lene. Even now."

Abilene nodded, not paying attention. It hadn't rained in a year.

She just kept staring out at nothing. Then, without warning, Abilene pushed back away from the railing. I barely heard her say, "Why on earth didn't I keep going?"

I raced to catch up with her, but we'd stood too fast, the blood draining out of our heads, and Abilene staggered, falling into me. I held her up and she hung on to my shoulders, both of us wobbling there in the middle of the road. She laughed once, and before letting go she gave me a tiny squeeze.

Back at the truck I wedged in above the box, my knees in my face. Abilene twisted us through a three-corner turn, pointing toward home, and beyond that, the bomber base. As soon as we were rolling, Abilene took a hand off the wheel, waving at the box beneath my feet. "Baseballs."

I glanced again at the box. "I know. Thanks."

"A whole box."

I peered around my legs, nodding.

"With a whole box you won't have to run after them every few pitches."

"We collect them for each other, Ab'lene," I said, like it was something she didn't know as well as me.

"If I'm not there."

I thought about her one stab at college. Those endless three months alone, the worst time in my life. I didn't touch a baseball till she came back. "That never happens, Ab'lene."

"It will."

"But, hardly ever."

"Austin!" she shouted, taking both hands off the wheel, slapping the sides of her head. "You've got to listen to what I'm telling you."

I sat quiet.

"It's just . . ." Abilene started worrying at her braid, unwinding it until her hair flew around her head like a living halo. "Austin, do you think I'm always going to be here?"

I stayed quiet.

"I'm not," she said, sounding exhausted.

I glanced at her, then tugged her coat tighter around me. "You always pitch."

Now Abilene turned to look at me, watching me close as we barreled down the highway blind. "Austin, even I don't know how long I can stick this out."

"What are you going to do?"

Abilene only looked back to the road.

Once, when I was little, I asked her if she was going to marry Nolan Ryan. She'd laughed so hard it about killed her. So now I said, "You and Nolan finally getting serious?"

Abilene's jaw dropped for an instant, then came up in a grin. Her laughing, the best sound in the world, burst out for just a second, leaving the truck's rush emptier than ever once it was gone.

"Can we go to the base now, Ab'lene?" I whispered.

She nodded, the last of her smile disappearing, and we drove away from the sunrise, which wasn't much more than a smudge on the unbroken horizon. The wind kept howling, but it didn't smell like rain anymore.

four

As we drove along, Abilene quiet now behind the wheel, I couldn't stop going over the day she'd left, wondering if I should have seen all along that she was about to disappear. That afternoon, same as any other day, we'd gone to the bomber base to work on my pitching. But before we were halfway there, Abilene had jerked the truck off the pavement and rocketed straight through a cotton-field fence that had withstood everything but Abilene for more than twenty years. When we hit that hard, barren field, we sent up a rooster tail of bone-white dust that must have been a mile long, a mile high. Maybe that had been the first clue.

I'd gaped back at the stain of our trespassing laddering up the sky while Abilene kept up the speed, blowing through the fence on the field's other side, its old wire giving a last ricocheting twang before curling limp and dead around its weathered posts. Back in the scrub, Abilene had lurched the wheel this way and that, dodging the tire-piercing thorns of the mesquite, the creosote and catclaw only blurs we flashed over.

And, even though I'd waited for it, there was the surprise second of smoothness as we bolted onto the base's ancient runway, which you can never see till you're almost on top of it. Then Abilene took the mile and a half with the gas smashed flat, the truck feeling like it'd shake itself apart long before reaching takeoff speed. When the broken, roofless hangar walls at the far end loomed white against the sky's tired blue, Abilene stomped the brakes, slewing us around, crushing me against my door.

The truck idled roughly, the runway glittery with broken chunks of wire-mesh glass torn from the hangars. The pair of concrete walls themselves, their huge doors or windows or whatever gaping blankly, blocked off half the sky.

"The plane that took out Hiroshima stayed here," Abilene had said, all breathless. "Did I ever tell you that?"

I nodded.

"There hasn't been a soul here since. Nobody but me. Me and you." Pushing the truck into gear, she inched forward, crunching over the broken glass and the rubble of crumbling concrete until we were inside the hangar, between the two towering walls. She stopped beside the faded mural of the dead soldier, the words *Because Somebody Talked* still arcing over him, just like *Fireballer* over Nolan Ryan. Bringing her face right to mine, Abilene had whispered, "Not a word about this place, Austin. Not one. Not ever."

"Okay," I said, though there wasn't a person around here who didn't know about this place. It'd be like not noticing a mountain in the plains, a lake in the desert.

"It's our secret," she said.

We'd rolled out of the hangar again, back onto the runway, a straight, white path narrowing to nothing out in the distance. Abilene checked her mirrors, fiddled with the stick shift. "Preflight check," she murmured, then slowly began to accelerate, until finally we were tearing down the runway again, shaking and rattling, just trying to hold on.

When she didn't ease off the gas as we neared the takeoff end, I grabbed at the seat belt, buckling it down tight over my clenched stomach. Abilene shouted, "Next stop Hiroshima!" launching off the pavement as if she really expected to take flight, roar off above the dusty desert, the faded mountains, loaded down with just that one fat bomb.

But we crashed back down in the scrub, me holding on for all I was worth until Abilene finally slid to a stop inches shy of our secret place: the great steel cylinder of the fuel tank. Dust billowed through our open windows and we held our hands over our mouths, gasping as if we'd run that whole way. Finally Abilene said, "What did you expect? Hasn't been a flight out of here in fifty years."

"Almost had it, though," I answered, afraid to look at her. "Practically airborne."

"If only we had a B-29."

I nodded. "We'd be out of here for sure."

"Be quite a shock for the poor Japanese."

"No rule that we'd have to go there."

"True," Abilene said, grinning. "We could pick our own targets." She shook her head. "But where would we start?"

I remembered the way my seat belt release had clattered in the sudden stillness, Abilene's sneer as I pulled it from my lap. Then I'd opened my door to get away from that look, falling out into the staggering heat. Now I shifted away from the cut stub of webbing she'd left poking up out of the seat, where she knew I couldn't miss it.

Other than the runway and the hangar walls, the odd empty fifty-caliber shell casing, the tank's all that's left at the base. That day, I'd hurried inside and out of habit touched one of the impossible bullet holes: clean, finger-sized punctures outside, jagged, flared edges in, their stars of light the only thing piercing the blackness.

Scuttling my feet around for snakes, I'd retrieved the set of mitts we kept there, the armload of balls we'd collected over the years, some of them practically coverless, the string and yarn poking out of holes scraped right through the leather.

Stepping back out, knocked almost backward by the blinding brightness, the breathless heat, I saw Abilene already beneath the old power pole, the severed wires drooping from its crossbar. She pushed at the tire, our strike zone, swinging from one of the wires, and said, "Did I ever tell you this was a B-29 tire?"

"That?" I said. "Pretty small."

"Tail wheel."

It looked like any old truck tire.

"Maybe off the old *Enola Gay* herself."

I dropped the balls behind the pile of dirt and caliche we'd scraped together for a mound and stepped onto the splintery scrap of weathered two-by-six we'd hammered in with railroad spikes from the abandoned bed, our pitching rubber, exactly sixty feet six inches from the tire.

Tossing Abilene her mitt, I lobbed a warm-up throw and we began the day's work, Abilene swinging the tire for me, calling strikes, singles, and doubles, even the occasional home run. Once she decided I was ready, Abilene said we'd play a scrimmage, instead of her just coaching me, so during her innings I swung the tire.

Standing on our mound, her brows scrunched down like a hawk's, the muscles of her jaw standing out like ropes, Abilene would kick her leg as high as Nolan Ryan's. No matter how hard I swung the tire, making up for not having a McGwire or a Sosa to drive the pitch into another time zone, she'd let go pure smoking heat, right through the center of the tire. Sometimes I couldn't help screaming, "Fireballer!" After her first inning, nine straight strikes, Abilene whirled and fired a victory pitch at the tank itself. The way she made it ring, the bullet holes that pierced the steel seemed more possible. Like, if she really concentrated, she could make a baseball go clear through too. Nobody who saw Abilene pitch would ever again say *You throw like a girl*.

But I was throwing my best ever too, and by the end of the sixth we were still tied up at nothing apiece. It was further than I'd ever taken her.

We worked quick, without talking, our sweat dripping off our faces before it could evaporate, our shirts turning dark with it, clinging to us.

Then, in the top of the seventh, Abilene missed the tire completely—a home run. I gaped. It was my first lead ever.

Abilene broke the rocky set of her game face. But, instead of bearing down harder, she grinned. She took this exaggerated swipe at her forehead with the back of her wrist and said, "Hot enough to fry an egg on a skillet."

I smiled, but didn't laugh. It was something Dad always said, goofy on purpose, but the way Abilene said it made it seem stupid, Dad like a fool. I waited for what else she'd say, what she meant to mean, but Abilene just stood there. Then in one sudden swipe she peeled her T-shirt off over her head. She mopped her face with it, then dropped it down on the back of the mound like a rosin bag, bringing her game face back.

She'd done that plenty of times before, always wearing the same heavy, gray sports bra, but she hadn't done it in a long time, and I found I couldn't look at her normal anymore. And I knew that somehow she knew I wouldn't be able to look at her, that I wouldn't be able to concentrate with her like that. It seemed like cheating, Abilene pulling out all the stops just to beat me. I looked at the mound, not her, hoping I'd still catch the tight little nod she'd give when she was ready for me to let the tire fly.

But Abilene waited and waited, until finally I had to glance up. She smiled and gave me a wink. She didn't nod for the tire until my whole face had gone flame red.

Just like she always told me, I worked at putting everything else out of my mind, and even with her half-naked I was still up one—nothing in the bottom of the ninth. Abilene's silence now was like a wall, something ominous in it. She'd struck out the side in her halves of the eighth and ninth, and I remembered all her old speeches: "You can't control what your opponent is going to do, only yourself. Control yourself!" She was pitching like fire, but she'd made that one mistake. I was shutting them out from my side. I only needed three more outs.

But my first pitch ricocheted off the outside edge of the tire— a double. At the tire Abilene said, "Man on second," not cracking a smile. I bore down, getting the next two outs, but on my next batter, with one strike already against him, I nicked the inside rim, a single.

Without a second of hesitation, Abilene said flatly, "Single. Runner scores from second. Tie game."

The ball had barely touched the tire, an infield hit if there ever was one, runner maybe not even advancing, let alone scoring. But Abilene was the judge. She always had been. I stepped up to the rubber and struck out the last batter.

"Extra innings," she said, taking my place on the mound. She struck out her side in nothing flat.

So did I.

When it was my turn at the tire again, I watched Abilene pitch. She was grunting with each delivery, her leg kick as high as ever, maybe even higher, her hair undone and matted, sticking to her back, her shoulders, slapping across her face each time she fell off the mound in her follow-through. She shucked it away after each pitch, taking it in as part of the magic routine of her motion, but she wouldn't break stride long enough to rebraid it or even tie it back.

The sweat soaking her bra made it like a second skin, heavy and dark. As she reared back, firing so hard, so wild, I tried to watch only her motion.

When I pitched, I concentrated on everything she'd taught me, making every motion the same, the same as any day: one long, even fireballing roll.

By the twelfth, Abilene was overthrowing like crazy. She reared back like an outfielder, her pitching hand looking like it'd scrape the back of the mound. As if just the force of her throws could push me into a mistake, as if she could over-whelm me with pure heat—everything she would have killed me for doing. But I didn't dare say a word. Somehow her pitches were still going through the tire, strikes every one, and watching her fly apart, I began to be afraid I might somehow actually win.

And then, her grunts now nearly screams with every pitch, Abilene missed the tire clean. Nearly a foot over the top. An-other home run. She was home team, same as ever, and I still had to pitch the bottom of the inning, but I had a run again.

Not letting myself think, I shut my side down in order.

I won.

Abilene caught the tire, stilling it, its black rubber rotting to gray, cracked and fissured by the sun. I heard the swipe of gravel as I whisked up her shirt and tossed it to her, her steps quick as she retreated to the tank.

I stood stunned on the mound. In front of me, behind the tire, the balls lay scattered through the dirt and thorns. Collecting them was the loser's job.

"Well," I finally said, taking a step toward the tank, its last sliver of shade, leaving the balls where they lay for the first time in my life. "Looks like we dropped that bomb after all."

I could feel Abilene watching me, and sure enough, when I dared to look, she was staring straight through me, that tiny

I-know-something-you-don't-know smile curling the corners of
her mouth.

I slid down in the shade beside her, maybe just a little farther
away than normal.

Throwing her shirt over her shoulders, she pinned it to the
tank with her back to keep the steel from burning her skin.
Settling in, Abilene said, "Nice close."

I nodded, whispered, "Thanks."

Suddenly Abilene clapped my thigh with her big, hard
pitcher's hand. "It's high time. What kind of coach never lets
you know the feel of winning?"

Lets me know, I thought. There was absolutely no letting
about it. If you counted that ridiculous call on the infield single,
I'd beaten her twice.

My jaw must have dropped, and suddenly Abilene was laughing. "Feels good, doesn't it?" she asked, clapping my thigh that
way again, giving it a squeeze.

I jerked my leg away.

"Come on, Austin," she said, laughing harder, grabbing for
me again.

I stood up, out of her reach.

Abilene got quiet. She stared at me. Finally she blew out a
sigh. "Don't worry, Austin. Once you throw your first pitch,
they'll be all over you at Pecos High. Big-boobed, featherbrained
cheerleaders rubbing against you every which way."

"What?" I blurted.

"You'd like that, wouldn't you?"

"What are you talking about?" I was red and hot even in the
shade, even more careful not to look at her, her bra, the sweat
already dry, white with salt.

"So soft," she cooed with a shiver. "So juicy."

"Ab'lene!" I cried.

"Once you get under those sweaters, Austin, up those skirts," she said, her voice going suddenly hard on me, "you'll forget this place ever existed."

I shouted, "Ab'lene!"

And then she laughed and laughed. "You'll be all right, Austin. Just keep your head in the game, out of your jeans."

She pushed herself up, pulling her shirt down over her head, tucking it back into her jeans. "Ready?"

I stared. "The balls, Ab'lene," I said, leaving it at that.

She kept right on for her truck.

I watched her go, then trotted into the desert after the balls, no longer sure whether it was the loser's job or just mine.

That night she left. After coming home and having dinner, I was drifting off in bed when I heard the sudden coughing start of Abilene's truck, the almost simultaneous spit of rock from beneath her tires. I scrambled to the window in time to see her taillights going away down the road, a murky red blur through the dust in her wake.

I stood in the window a long time after the lights were gone, the night closing over every trace of her. I had no idea where she was going, but I was surprised most at being surprised she'd left. The way she'd gone after me at the base, the sting of her voice when she'd said I was going to forget all about the base, about her, she'd made it pretty clear. But she was so wrong. How could I ever forget any of that?

I walked out of my room and down the hall into Abilene's. She'd yanked down all the pictures of her high school friends years ago, thrown out her yearbooks, her valedictorian's graduation braid, her Pecos Eagles' team cap. Her room was the same as ever: bed unmade, clothes on the floor, a scattering of baseball books and coaching manuals through it all. As if there'd only ever been the two of us. As if she'd be right back. I wondered for a second why I hadn't just shanked one pitch, let her have it, but then knew that no matter what was happening now, that would have been a hundred times worse.

Back out in the hallway, I stopped at the railing, peering down the empty hole of the stairway. The house was so quiet without her it seemed to buzz, Mom and Dad having their last easy sleep, not knowing yet that she was gone.

five

Lost thinking of Abilene's leaving, I didn't even notice when she cut off the highway short of Pyote, driving straight on toward home. When we crested the last bulge of ground before our house, the white surprise of it jutting from the endless spidery scrub as if dropped from a tornado, I could hardly believe it. And Dad's car, though he should have been long gone to work, still sat solidly in the drive. Peeking at Abilene, I caught her squinting toward it, pushing the unraveled red of her hair away from her face.

She said, "This could be worse than I thought."

I whispered, "What's he still doing here?" though I already knew.

Abilene idled the rest of the way. Dead-stick, she called it. Shutting off the truck, she coasted onto Dad's white, crushed-rock driveway, grinding to a stop, the engine knocking and dieseling awhile. The window in my room was closed, and I pictured Mom up there, watching Abilene and me tear off into the night, slowly closing the window between us, her fingers white with the pressure. Then she'd flick on the baseball-player lamp Dad had given me years ago, the one Abilene never quit teasing me about, just long enough to straighten the curtain and tuck in my empty bed before going to tell Dad what she'd seen.

Abilene blew out a breath and butted her door open with her shoulder. "Time to pay the piper," she said, but then waited, one leg dangling outside the truck. "Do you remember Dad hauling in all this rock? Were you old enough to remember that? To know why?"

I shook my head without trying to remember anything so long ago.

"I wanted to build a baseball diamond here." Abilene laughed. "I wheeled and dealed. Wheedled and needled. Thought I had him pinned down to a compromise—only the infield, a scrap of backstop just big enough to keep the creosote from gobbling up our pitches. I thought I had him."

She stepped down, doing a quick shuffle-step on the ankle-breaking, bad-hopping rock. "Came home from school one day and there's this pile of glittery white rock. Looked like Michelangelo's scrap heap. But the big masterpiece himself had scrammed. Probably on his way to Wrigley Field. Fenway. No baseball here, that's for sure."

Now I could vaguely picture the trucks bringing the rock. Watching the deafening white cascades when they dumped, the clouds of dust—Abilene coming home later, so furious she followed Dad's directions the instant he gave them, wheelbarrowing rock and raking it out like a groundskeeper gone mad, more dust flying.

I said, "I don't remember any of that, Ab'lene."

Abilene shrugged, stepping toward the house, but then she whirled, suddenly sweeping her arms wide, like a ringmaster surrounded by wonders. "Just one more chapter of How All This Started!" she blared.

Under the sky's low, roiling black billows—more like ruptures than clouds—the white rock glimmered beneath Abilene, as if some sort of energy were simmering away inside all that shattered stone.

How All This Started was Dad's favorite story—about our names, Abilene's and mine. Not where we were born, but where we were conceived. "How all this started!" he'd always say, waving his arms around like he had a kingdom to show off. He'd tell the story at the slightest excuse, to anybody who asked, and some who didn't. "We were young, newlyweds, you know, and we were only in Abilene for the night!"

Back when Abilene was in high school, before the baseball disaster, when her friends were still always filling the house, Dad would sometimes start in on it right in front of them. But Abilene got good at derailing him, saying things like "What if you had done it in Marfa, Dad? What then? Would you have launched me into life sounding like I had a harelip?"

The story made most people blush or change the subject, something Dad, so happy and proud about us all, could never see. After Abilene told me about The Facts, I could hardly believe we'd been born in the first place—that they'd ever done anything like that, not once, but twice. As huge as Dad was, and tiny as Mom, Abilene said it was something you could have sold tickets to. "Fay Wray finally quits teasing the poor ape," she said once in front of all her high school friends, though I think Dad and I were the only ones who got it. We'd just watched the movie. It stopped him cold, the word *newlywed* still only half out of his mouth. It got to where whenever Dad'd start in on it, I'd try sneaking away.

Abilene stood a moment more on Dad's white rock, waving her arms at our lives, then, laughing a little, she jumped to the porch and leapt across it, swinging the door wide open. I ran after her. The wind put a new shiver into me even wrapped in her old coat, and when I reached her, I stood close for the warmth.

Dad sat at the kitchen table. He took up half of it, just staring at the steam wisping out of the coffee in front of him. His great, wide fingers were splayed out on the wood, one hand braced on each side of the cup, as if it, like Abilene, might just up and vanish. Slowly he looked up, looked right at Abilene. "You're back," he said.

"And better than ever!" she answered, like it was some grand reunion. But in the quiet that followed I could hear the humming buzz of the stove clock, the murmuring babble of the television in the living room.

Mom stood at the sink wiping her hands on the towel she'd tucked around her tiny waist, the cords and muscles standing up in her bone-thin arms. Her hair, still almost as red as Abilene's, was pulled back off her face with one of her headbands. She worked up a little smile. "Are you all right, Abilene?"

She was staring at Abilene. They both were.

Abilene smiled. "Fine. A little frayed at the edges, but fine."

"We're tired," I said.

"Think you can get some sleep?" Mom asked.

Abilene shoved herself away from the door like she was setting out to sea. "I might sleep for a week."

"Abilene?" Dad asked, pushing back his chair. He stood up, looking like he didn't know what to say, only that it had to be something. Standing there, he blocked Abilene's way.

Dad's so broad, so solid, and Abilene so long and lean, it's always a surprise to see Abilene not looking down at him, always a surprise to see her have to look up at anybody. But they locked eyes for a second before breaking off, both of them glancing around, taking things in, like maybe they'd both simultaneously discovered that they weren't in the same old kitchen as always.

"I know you're an adult, Abilene," Dad finally said. "But you live here with us."

Abilene nodded. "I know I should have called." She took half a step to get around him. "Sorry about that."

Dad stepped back, in her way.

Abilene stopped, her eyes narrowing for an instant.

"You've been gone over a week. Without a single word."

"Do you know how worried we were?" Mom asked.

"Where have you been?" Dad said. "What happened?"

"Nothing happened, Dad. Mom." Abilene cleared her hair away from her face, her eyes. "Come on," she said, trying a grin. "You guys had all those days on the road, that endless honeymoon. All I've had is this." Her voice tightened just a tiny bit. She pointed at the ground. "This right here."

She looked at Dad, smiling still. "You can't begrudge me a little trip out now and then. My own fabled nights in the glorious boomtowns of West Texas."

Dad watched her a second. "We're not begrudging a thing—"

Abilene cut him off. "I just . . . It . . ." She shook her head. "I just had to get out for a while."

Mom and Dad glanced at each other. "Get out where?" Mom asked.

"No *where*. I just . . . Things got . . . I don't know. I had to run."

I gaped at Abilene's stammer, wishing they would let her go, not make her sound like this, like somebody she'd never really been.

But Dad said, " 'Run'?" as if he'd never heard the word, couldn't understand it in any context.

"There just wasn't enough," Abilene said, beginning to fidget, shifting from foot to foot like a boxer in a corner, impatient for the bell. "You've got to know what I mean. I mean, look around you."

" 'Enough'?" Dad echoed. "Enough what?"

Abilene puffed her cheeks, then let the air leak out. "I don't know, Dad. Okay? The world just gets so small. I had to find a little room to breathe. That's all. Just a little room to breathe."

"'Breathe,'" Dad said.

Abilene looked at him. "Yeah, Dad. Breathe." She inhaled once, noisily, then exhaled.

Dad shook his head, letting her know he didn't understand, that she'd have to do better than that. Then, before giving her the chance, he asked, "What about Gibson's?"

Abilene pursed her lips. "I don't know about that," she said, as if what he'd reminded her of, her job, had totally slipped her mind. "I'll have to call them."

"You just walked away from work too?" he asked, though I knew he'd talked to them, that he already knew the answer.

Abilene couldn't help a little smile. "Well, Dad, it's not exactly a matter fraught with international implications." She flashed her mannequin smile. "'Thank you, that will be a dollar ninety-nine.'" She laughed. "I'm sure they limped along without me. Somehow."

Dad didn't smile.

"Okay, Dad. I'll call them. I promise." Abilene made another move to get around him. "I will, Dad. But I have to get some sleep now."

"Abilene," he said, raising his voice, but letting her slip around him all the same. She edged past the table, then the sink, then Mom.

"Abilene!" Dad called, louder yet.

Abilene hesitated.

Mom said, "Clayton," though she most always called him Clay. Or Dad.

Dad gave her a glance, then looked back to Abilene.

"I'm just tired, Daddy," she said with a smile, maybe letting him hope that though she was twenty now she'd just had some late teenage-type thing to blow out of her system. "That's all."

Mom dropped the frayed terry cloth of her towel and caught Abilene's hand, holding it with both of hers.

Abilene shook her head. "It's nothing, Mom," she whispered. "Nothing." Freeing her hand from Mom's, she stroked the top of Mom's head, smoothing the flyaway curls.

Without another word, Abilene walked off toward the stairs, leaving us alone out there. But Mom scrambled after her, running after that touch. We all stepped that way, pulled along by her wake, winding up in a little clump at the base of the stairs, watching Abilene climb.

"Honey?" Mom asked. "Are you in any kind of trouble?"

Abilene turned and shrugged the question away, shrugged us all away. "I'm not *in* trouble, Mom," she said. "I didn't do anything wrong. I'm fine now."

"But . . ."

Abilene had one foot lifted, the last step before her. "I nearly boiled over," she said, trying a smile on us. "Been simmering twenty years. The kettle finally whistled. That's all."

That wasn't that unusual a way for Abilene to talk, but we all glanced away from each other, each of us wondering on our own what she meant, what exactly had reached the steam point.

Abilene used the second of distraction to slip away to her room.

Mom called out, "We love you, honey."

We were all quiet a minute before Dad turned to me, like he just remembered I was there, that he had a son at all, his souvenir from that romantic night in Austin. "Well?"

I shrugged. "She came back for the norther. We just drove around, waiting to see if it'd rain." I knew I couldn't tell them anything more, though all I could see was Abilene in the outfield when the water came on, rushing past me with her stolen sprinkler heads, needing to breathe.

"Did she say where she'd been?" Dad asked. "What she'd been doing?"

I shook my head. "Nothing. We were just hoping it'd rain."

They both looked at me, wishing there were secrets I could share. I hadn't said a word about the day she left—our big baseball game, my big win. "She got some baseballs for me," I volunteered. "A whole box."

"More baseball," Mom said, shaking her head.

"Can I go back to bed now? We've been up all night."

"We all have, Austin," Dad said, but he stepped away, clearing my path to the stairs.

As I stepped by him, Mom reached out to pet my shoulder. I glanced at her and smiled. "I don't think it's going to rain," I said. "Norther or no."

Six

I crawled up to my room but didn't come close to sleeping. In a while I heard Dad drive away to work, and then at lunchtime Mom came up to check on me. She didn't even mention me skipping school. I sat up, still dressed, and followed her down to the kitchen. We ate quietly, until Mom asked, "Do you know where she went, Austin? What she did?"

I shook my head, filling my mouth with a sandwich.

Mom cleared her plate and we waited for Abilene.

She didn't come down all afternoon. Mom walked around the house, going through the motions, doing all she could to keep herself from going up there, from looking to see if Abilene was okay. Finally, with dinner all ready to put out, Dad home any second, I said, "How about I check on her, Mom? See if she's hungry."

Mom bit her lip, like it was something she had to think over. "Be careful not to wake her," she agreed at last. "If she's asleep."

I slipped up the stairs, then stood outside Abilene's door, trying to hear the slightest trace of her. I tested the knob, and though I'd never known it to be locked, it surprised me that it wasn't now. I eased myself inside, the room gloomy behind the drawn curtains.

"Ab'lene?" I whispered before my eyes could adjust. "Ab'lene?"

There was no answer, but I could hear the soft slips of her breath, in and out. I stepped over scattered clothes, though Mom had straightened up in here. I'd warned her not to, warned that Abilene wouldn't like to see that we'd been in here while she was gone, but Mom had told me not to be silly, that we had no secrets in this house.

I reached Abilene's bed and realized the clothes I'd walked over were what she had peeled off on her way to collapse. She hadn't even pulled up a sheet.

Sprawled on her back, her arm flung up over her eyes, hair tumbled across the pillow like a red storm, Abilene had left on nothing but her underwear, but underwear so completely unlike the sports bras she'd always worn, I could barely breathe. These were black and lacy, tiny on her long body, covering nothing. She was so unlike any Abilene I had ever seen that for a moment I could only stare. I looked again at her face, what I could see of it beneath her arm, just to make sure it wasn't some stranger who had come here, maybe some elaborate trick Abilene had decided to play on us.

Then, unable to stop myself, I glanced at her breasts, the jutting strain of them pushed up high and hard in the feathery lace, her ribs rising quietly with each breath, the long hollow of her belly. Her skin was chickened with tiny goose bumps lifting almost invisible downy hair, and as I stepped away, backward toward the door, my feet tangled up in her clothes. I reached for anything, but went down hard, crashing into the floor, ducking my head against Abilene's embarrassment and rage.

But she didn't even budge. Just lay there breathing so quietly.

I got to my hands and knees and scrambled up, wanting to run, but then just stood there, not knowing what to do. If I was ever out like that, naked and helpless, there was no way Abilene would just leave me.

So, as quiet and slow as if wading through rattlesnakes, I eased the door closed, twisted the lock shut. Then, without looking any more than I had to, I pulled Abilene's sheet over her, thinking of those goose bumps.

Holding my breath, I eased up the window sash and crept onto the porch roof. I scooched across the gravelly shingles and hung from the eaves, dropping down into Mom's flowers. Keeping low, I crept across the driveway and walked off into the desert.

I didn't straighten till I hit our road, long out of sight of our house. I walked faster and faster, until finally I was in a mad dash, holding my arms out like wings, picturing that last bomber out of here the way Abilene had talked about it the day she left; crawling into the sky, heavy with its cargo, so glad to escape this place it couldn't help but shoot up the oil tank, all its guns blazing.

I remembered how I used to run down our road this way to meet Dad on his way home from work. I was tiny then. I didn't stop running until I saw his car, my arms still out like wings.

He slowed, rolled down his window. "What are you flying?"

"B-29," I answered, letting my arms drop.

He nodded. "Well, how about a ride, Tex?"

It's what he'd always said, and I walked around and climbed in.

When I was in, he said, "Did I ever tell you that when I was a kid, the old Rattlesnake base was loaded with those bombers? They mothballed them there. As far as you could see, B-29s, B-17s, B-24s. They stretched out forever."

He'd told me that a hundred times.

Then he said, "How's Abilene?"

Abilene didn't get out of bed for two days. And when she did, she seemed worn near to nothing, just barely dragging around. For the rest of that week she didn't meet me after school, didn't drive out to the base with me, didn't pick up so much as a single baseball the whole time. Saturday I asked if she wanted to pitch a game, but she barely smiled. "I feel like a rosin bag, Austin. All squeezed out and flopped down on the back of the mound."

I walked out to the base myself, hiking for hours to throw baseballs into the desert through the center of the motionless tire. Then I crawled through the dirt and thorns collecting the balls. It was a joke without Abilene.

Every morning I checked the driveway first thing, hoping Abilene's truck would be gone, that she'd snuck away at night, that there'd be some sign she was back in the world, even if it meant she'd left us again. But it was still right there, the windshield glazed with dust, and I'd troop downstairs, Mom and Dad and I somehow picking through breakfast, Abilene up in her room.

Instead of Abilene, Dad took me on the twenty-minute run into Pecos, offering to drop me at the school. But I'd just get out with him at his office, where he worked as a land assessor, keeping his finger on the fading pulse of his country, even Pecos itself dwindling down below ten thousand souls. I'd walk the last blocks, past Gibson's, the hardware and sporting goods store where Abilene used to work, cutting across the cemetery, around those old stones, and under the water tower, the big purple Pecos Eagle screaming down above me.

At first the rides to town were pretty quiet, Dad sometimes asking about the weather—"Think we'll ever see rain again?"—and telling stories about yet another rancher forced out, his starving cattle sold off at staggering losses. Sometimes he'd ask about baseball—"Think you'll actually play this year?"—but as

Abilene's withdrawal grew longer, Dad talked more and more about her.

"Have you and Abilene gotten together lately?" he asked one morning.

I couldn't help but glance over to see if he was somehow kidding.

"Austin, your mom and I, we think Abilene might be sick. We think——"

"I think she's going to be fine."

Dad smiled. "Well, so do we. But we've been talking to a doctor, Austin. In Midland. A psychologist. There are some patterns we've seen. We think she needs some help. We don't think this is something she can get through on her own."

I quit listening. There wasn't a thing Abilene couldn't do on her own. Not a single thing. As Dad went on, I nodded or shook my head, whatever I thought he wanted, the whole time just waiting for the ride to end.

At his office I was halfway out the door when I heard him say, "She'd like to talk to you."

I stopped, ducking down to peer in at him. "The shrink?"

Dad held the steering wheel. "She thinks it will help her with Abilene. To know more about her life. About the two of you."

I closed the door and bent down through the open window. "If the two of you want to waste your time driving a hundred miles just to talk to a stranger, that's your business. But you leave me out of it. Abilene too." I turned then and walked off to the cemetery. He didn't call me back.

After that I stalled around in the mornings until he'd have to leave and I'd have to take the bus.

I didn't like talking behind Abilene's back. Didn't like the feel of plotting some sort of cure for her, when I doubted there was anything wrong beside being stuck here, in the deal of Dad's life; our piece of the nothing costing just about that, back when the oil went bust, the gas prices shooting up to where the cotton farmers couldn't afford to pump their water seven hundred feet up out of the ground anymore. It was another of Dad's favorite stories: him moving in to scoop up the land for a song, settling in with Mom already pregnant with Abilene. "We were newly-weds, you know." Feathering his nest.

After school I'd quick check under the water tower for Abilene, then take the bus back home. I'd sit alone, ignoring the other kids' chatter as I gazed out the window, hoping for a glimpse of a white truck racing a dust devil across a field some-where. Dropped off at the section road, I'd run the last mile of dirt to our house, not wanting to miss a minute if Abilene had come back to life.

But most of the time Abilene would be up in her room— resting, Mom called it—and I'd have to dodge around Mom until Dad came home. Used to be I could enthrall Mom talking about geometry, social studies, whatever I'd done that day, but now talking with her had got to be just like talking to Dad. "Is there anything you've noticed about Abilene, honey?" she asked, her whisper a reminder that we had to be careful, that Abilene was only asleep. "Anything that might help the doctor help her?"

"Can't you just leave her alone?" I snapped when I couldn't stand it anymore, all their prying. "Couldn't you try that? Just once?"

Mom's eyes got wide, and for a second she glanced around the room as if she might have got the wrong house, the wrong son. "Austin, we're trying to help her."

She stood and looked at me, letting that sink in. "Did she ever say anything about college to you? Anything about why she came back?"

"Just that it was only Midland. Nothing that counted."

"But she's brilliant. Look what she did in high school."

Abilene had graduated in three years. Still a record. Valedictorian. For a while, it was all Mom and Dad could talk about. I knew all the teachers wondered what had happened to me. "You don't have to convince me, Mom," I said.

"But the scholarship offers. She could have gone anywhere. *She* chose Midland."

I shrugged. "She just didn't like it."

"We're wondering if that wasn't the first time. An episode we should have seen."

"Episode?" I tried to make it sound as dumb as it sounded to me.

"Come on, Austin. Student president as a sophomore. Straight A's. Honors classes. Playing baseball with the boys. From that to flunking out in one semester at Midland Community College?"

"I just think she can't stand it here anymore. Living out in the middle of nowhere. That's all. I think it's driving her crazy."

Mom stared at me a moment, the only sound the TV's murmuring. She drew a quick breath and said, "Don't ever use that word in this house."

I rolled my eyes and started out of the room.

"The doctor asked if she's ever done anything violent."

I turned back around. "Violent? Abilene?"

"I know, Austin," she said, her air leaking out. "It doesn't make sense to me either. But she's trying to learn who Abilene is. She needs to know as much as she can."

"She throws so hard she can make a baseball bleed. How's that for violent?"

Mom blinked in surprise. Then her lips tightened, the red turning to white. It took a second, but she made her face go slack and rubbed at her forehead with the heel of her hand. "Thanks, Austin. That will help." She straightened up. "That will really help. I'm sure if Abilene only knew, she'd thank you again and again."

"If Abilene knew what *you* were doing, I bet we'd see some violence."

Mom spun back to her stove, her shoulder blades, thin as wings, pointed at me like shields. "Go away," she said, the words hardly squeaking through her clenched teeth. "Just go away."

I steered clear of Mom the rest of that long afternoon until Dad came home. Like every day, he whispered, "Any change?" before he was through the door—as if Mom wouldn't have called him if Abilene had only asked for something unusual for lunch.

We picked at our dinner the same way we scratched around our breakfast. Then I went upstairs, claiming homework, while they settled in front of the TV, though I heard their worried mumbles over the TV for hours afterward.

seven

When Abilene finally started leaving her room again, Mom was right there, gluing herself to her side. And though I could hardly believe it, Abilene seemed to glue right back. Sometimes they'd talk quietly, but often as not they'd just sit in the kitchen over coffee that'd get left on so long the whole room reeked of its scorch, neither one of them speaking for ages. Half the time Abilene would have her eyes closed, or be staring out the window in the door, like she was still thinking of walking out, climbing into her truck, and never seeing this place again. Sometimes Mom would be holding her hand, or just barely touching her, stroking her arm, her quicksilver fireballer's wrist.

At the same time, Dad tried partnering up with me, like *he* could be Abilene. After dinner one night, Mom and Abilene safely off in front of the TV, he came up out of the basement with an old baseball glove, a first baseman's I couldn't remember ever seeing before. "You must be getting rusty," he said. He tossed a ball to me that might have been a hundred years old, the leather so dry and shrunken that the faded red stitching pulled at its holes, stretching each one into a nasty tight grimace.

I held up the ball, pointed at his glove. "Where in the world did you get these?"

"Don't think you're the first ballplayer this family ever produced," he said, smiling.

With all his stories, he'd only ever let loose a few scraps about his playing days, his famous arcing long ball, but I'd never seen a trace of it for real. Until this glove. "Ab'lene's the first," I said.

He thumped his mitt against his chest. "Four years in Lubbock's pinstripes."

I tossed the ball to him. His mitt, clapping around the ball, was just as dry and chapped looking. I still wasn't sure any of those dusty old baseball stories of his were true.

"Really?" I asked.

"What do you mean, 'Really?' " He smiled. "Go on and grab your mitt. I'll catch for you."

"How come?"

Dad let his mitt droop to his side, his smile fading.

"I mean, how come I've never seen that mitt? How come you never played before?"

"You never asked," he said, trying to make it sound like a friendly joke.

"I've been pitching since I was born," I said. "You don't do anything but tell stories. How—"

I was going to go on, but Dad stood there looking like the skeleton of a creosote, ready to break loose and tumble away. "You really don't remember ever playing catch with me?"

"No," I squawked. "You never—"

"Sure I did, Austin. All the time." He made this sort of grin. "By the time you were a year old we had to hide all the baseballs in the house. You were already breaking things with them."

Abilene had told me that.

"I brought friends over just to show them," Dad said.

Friends? I couldn't remember the last time anybody but Abilene's friends had come to this house, back when she was in high school. And they had vanished after her baseball disaster as if they'd never existed. Since then it was like we'd been wiped off the map, no one able to find their way here.

"Maybe you really can't remember," Dad said. "You must have been about four when Abilene took over." He shook his head. "We thought it was cute. She came up to me and said something like, 'I'm going to take care of Austin's training from now on, Dad.'

"I missed playing with you, but she was so adamant." He shrugged. "You know how she is once she sinks her teeth into something."

Dad rolled the baseball through his fingers, trying to remember its touch. "And you seemed to love it, Austin. Playing with her. It was the first time she really paid any attention to you. It was fun watching the two of you always together. Always so serious. Abilene bringing home her rule books. Her training manuals. I remember once, eavesdropping from the kitchen, listening to her say, 'You threw Ripken the same thing the last time he was up and he knocked it out of the century. What makes you think this time will be any different?' You must have been about seven. Mom wanted me to get her to ease up, but I was laughing so hard I almost gave myself away."

I suddenly wondered if I didn't remember Dad out tossing a ball around with us. On the driveway, but without the rocks. "Had you put the rocks down yet? Back when we all played?"

"The rocks? Oh. No." He glanced to the floor. "That was a year or two later. By then Abilene wanted me to build a real baseball diamond. Out here." He waved his arm toward the world around us, showing that even he knew how ridiculous it would have been. "God, how she pestered. She said she needed it for your training. She called it *absolutely essential*. She said, 'Your own son's career hangs by a thread and all you do is look for a scissors.' "

Dad shook his head, hiding the ball back inside his desiccated mitt. "I got a deal on the rock," he admitted. "I thought it might at least knock that idea out of her head."

I watched Dad and remembered Abilene tugging me off into the wash behind the house, scratching a strike zone into the crumbly cut of the dirt. "Is that when we started playing in the desert?"

Dad nodded. "And then when she started driving we thought we might never see you again."

When he didn't go on, I asked, "Was Abilene like me when she was little? Did she start throwing so early?"

Dad shook his head. "Not Abilene. She never even looked at a baseball until you started winging them around." Dad smiled. "Though I tried. Bought her a glove and everything. Mom used to tease me about wishing for a boy. Of course once she started, she took to it like a catapult. I've never seen anyone throw like she did."

"Does," I corrected.

Dad nodded there at the edge of the kitchen, almost out the door, his old ball still clamped inside his dried-out glove. "Believe me, after her high school, I spent some time wondering if I ever should've pushed a baseball at her."

"But you still could have played."

Dad gave me a look. "It wasn't in Abilene's game plans," he said. "We weren't looking for signs in that kind of thing back then."

"But . . . but you could have at least . . . You could have told me about when you used to play. When you——"

Dad waved me off with a tired sweep of his mitt. "That was

all before the two of you came along," he said, like that was somebody else's life. With his free hand he caught the door latch, pushing the door open with his foot, waiting for me to follow.

I ran upstairs to retrieve my mitt, then back down, stepping out onto the porch, holding up my glove.

He threw me a lazy little warm-up toss. "I've missed this, though," he said so quiet I could barely hear. "Don't think I haven't."

I threw the ball back. He caught it flat-footed, a tiny smile breaking his face. "Feels good," he said. "Like looking up an old friend."

The next time I had the ball I ran my fingers around it, amazed at how rough the old leather was, like sandpaper, something you could really put a vicious curve into. Something he'd saved for a long, long time.

Dad held his mitt up for my return throw. "This is how your mother and I met. Baseball." He tossed the ball back to me. "That's really how all this started."

"I thought you met in high school."

"At the baseball field."

We threw the ball back and forth, Dad holding it longer and longer between throws, dropping away into his story, scaling his life back to just the two of them.

"Ruby's girlfriend." He thought a second, then smiled. "Roma Lee Agostinelli." He even laughed. "How's that for a handle?"

I smiled back.

"But let me tell you, there wasn't a boy in that school who didn't want to get his mitts on her handle. Or anywhere else." Dad shook his head in admiration. "A hot ticket.

"She was steady with Vernon Klee, though. A great guy, Vernon. Our star pitcher. Star quarterback. Star everything. Frankly I don't know what he saw in Roma Lee. Other than what anybody could see."

I kept smiling, holding my glove up for the ball.

"One day Roma Lee brought her girlfriend to a game. I'm sure just to keep her company through the whole boring thing. I remember sitting in the dugout, waiting for Vernon to come in off the mound. So I could ask about that girl with Roma Lee."

"Why weren't you playing?" I asked, picturing Dad, the big, slow kid in the dugout, dreaming of being part of the team.

"I was only a sophomore." He grinned. "I could hit a country mile, but I had some work to do on my fielding."

I pictured Mom in the stands, a gangly, frizz-haired, carroty redhead, dreaming of Vernon Klee; Dad in the dugout, pretending Mom was the one he wanted, that the hot ticket Roma Lee was some sort of booby prize.

"So Vernon introduced you? You and Mom?"

Dad nodded, finally throwing the ball back. "She'd been after Roma Lee to take her to the games for weeks. She was so nervous about meeting me she stuttered. All that night."

"You guys go out together? The four of you?" I quick-fired the ball back.

Dad nodded, not really with me at all. "After the game. Cruising the drag in Lubbock." He gave a big fake whistle at what he used to think were hot times.

I thought of Mom, all stuttery so close to Vernon Klee.

"That Vernon," Dad said. "I wonder what ever became of him. He was a great guy. A great guy. A guy just like you."

He reared back and threw a real pitch, hard, slapping into my mitt. "A guy just like you," he said again.

I wondered who he thought a guy just like me would be, but I couldn't shake the picture of the two of them: Mom the scrawny tagalong; Dad the big, slow power hitter. I'd never imagined real lives for them before that night in Abilene.

I threw the ball back fast, both of us starting to heat it up, making each other work, and for a while we just threw, hot and hard, the rhythm of it enough.

Finally I uncorked pure heat, just to see what he'd say.

Peeling the ball out of his mitt, he held it at arm's length, out where he could focus. He wrapped his fingers around the laces, changing the positions, like he knew the different pitches. His trucked-in white rock crunched beneath our feet. "Mistake of my life," he said. "Letting Abilene take this away from us."

"You could have played, too," I said again. "I would have made Abilene let you."

Dad almost laughed. He tossed the ball back to me. "If you'd ever actually joined a team," he said, "played for real, I might have forced it." He shrugged. "As long as it was just the two of you, I thought—"

"What we play *is* real!" I hissed, whipping out a snapping curve, suddenly wanting to hurt him, at least shock him. The old ball broke hard, too fast for Dad, who didn't block it with his body either.

But Dad just gave me a look, one I could see him force his smile through. "Always was more of a hitter than a fielder," he said, then turned and went after the ball.

I watched him trot off into the desert, then spun around and went inside.

But even with that for a start, Dad and I actually got into a routine of playing catch most nights, Mom doing the work of bringing Abilene back into the world. Gibson's wouldn't take her back—Dad had made the call himself, asking—and when he announced the news, Mom only said that Abilene wasn't ready to go anywhere anyway.

Dad kept shaking his head. "What is she going to do, Ruby? How is she going to get along? It's not like they give work away around here."

"She'll be fine, we'll—"

"How?" Dad blurted. "College lasted—what? A semester? Gibson's tried with her, but—"

Mom interrupted this time, saying, "Honestly, Clay, Abilene working there was like Einstein cleaning toilets," which sounded exactly like it came straight out of Abilene's mouth.

And though Dad said, "If it was the only job he could hold on to . . . ," he left it at that, and things started to even out some. Sometimes, while Abilene slept, Mom and Dad and I would even sit around talking about something other than Abilene.

While we played catch, Dad kept asking about the high school team, why I didn't join. When I finally told him about Abilene redshirting me, he checked his arm in midthrow, holding the old ball in his big hand.

Balk, I thought.

Dad stared at me, starting to shake his head. "Are you serious?" he asked, really meaning it, not how most people say that.

I didn't bother answering. For the first time I felt myself blushing about Abilene's plans. They didn't make the sense they did when she was there mapping out every tiny detail.

"Those guys have been playing together their whole lives, Austin," Dad said, finally throwing the ball back. "You've got to break in or it'll be too late. They'll shut you out. Abilene should have shown you at least that much."

And though I could almost hear Abilene's laugh, hear her insist—"The only people getting shut out will be the opposing team"—I only said, "I grew six inches last year. My speed is up. I'll be fine."

"You play with what you've got, Austin. You wait for everything to be perfect, you'll never make the jump."

I threw the ball back hard, at the ankles, but Dad scooped it out. "Like you and your fielding?"

It didn't even touch him. He just smiled and nodded. "Yes, like me and my fielding. If I'd waited until I was a golden glover,

I never would have discovered that perfect, invincible, palm-tingling crack of a home run."

I grinned back, Abilene's grin. "If I'd've been pitching, you never would have." Even Abilene's words.

"Maybe so," Dad answered. "But you don't know that yet, do you?"

eight

Dad talking that way about the team, about its being too late to ever play for real, started me thinking I'd better at least meet the coach, maybe show him what I could do. But Abilene had never told me a thing about how any of that worked. I stood outside the coach's locked door for a few minutes after school one afternoon, as long as I could without missing the bus, then finally scribbled him a note, asking to talk to him sometime, before racing down the emptying hallways to the buses. I didn't write down my last name.

Dropped off at the section road, I dragged the rest of the way home, nothing to run for anymore with Mom and Abilene huddled in each other's shadow. Still wondering about what I'd say to the coach, what kind of tryout he might give me, I climbed the porch steps and reached for the screen door, but stopped dead at what sounded like someone crying. Because it was so hard imagining it coming from our house, I turned back out to the desert, as if I might find that some whimpering coyote had trailed me home.

But then I heard Abilene—sniffling, but still Abilene—say, "What, Mom? What am I going to do? This wasn't supposed to happen to me."

"It's okay, Abilene," I heard, Mom's whispery, soothing best. "It's okay."

"Okay?" Abilene's voice shot off the charts. "Okay? How is this one bit *okay*?"

Mom didn't have an answer for that. Soon she was just saying, "Shhh, shhh, just shush now," and Abilene strangled out more of those horrible cries.

When she quieted some, Mom asked, "Who, Abilene? Maybe we should talk to him. Maybe—"

"For God's sake," Abilene blurted, almost a laugh. "Half the time I didn't know where I was, let alone who I was with. Anybody who could keep up with me. That was my daunting criterion. There wasn't anybody who could do it for long, but I could always find somebody fresh for extra innings."

"Oh," Mom said in a puff of air like she'd been hit.

"Yeah, Mom. I don't know who. Not a name. Not a clue."

Mom gave her own trembly gasp. "Abilene, honey."

"I know," Abilene said, and they were quiet a few seconds.

"I can't have it, Mom," Abilene said then, the crying gone, her voice as taut and hard as when she'd bear down on me for losing my concentration on the mound. "I can't."

Mom didn't say anything.

"My own life is a fucking wreck, Mom. I can't do that to a baby. I mean, look what I've already done to poor Austin!"

I fell off the porch as if I'd been shoved. I took a backward step across Dad's rocky drive. Then another.

"Abilene," I heard Mom say, "we'll get through this too." She went on, but I'd reached Abilene's truck and I couldn't hear anymore. I eased open the door and crawled into my old place in the passenger side, closing the door to cut off Mom's words. I swallowed once, then lay down, curling myself into a ball on the cracked vinyl of the seat. *Poor Austin?*

I was still curled up there when I heard the screen slap shut. My breath caught and I wondered what I'd tell Abilene, how I'd explain lying there, wondering if I'd be able to ask her to take me with her wherever she was running off to, let me take care of her. But instead of Abilene, I heard the door of Mom's car open and shut. I was almost sitting up, ready to dash in and see Abilene finally alone, finally away from Mom, when I heard the other door slam shut too. The car started so gentle and easy, backing smoothly out the drive, that it could only have been Mom driving, taking Abilene away.

After the sound of their car faded into the whispers of the breeze, I sat up. I slipped into the driver's seat and put my hands up on the wheel, like I might give chase, but after a while I only slid out and walked inside. There wasn't a thing started for dinner, and I wondered how long Mom and Abilene had been sitting there, how long that little heart-to-heart must have gone on.

There was a note on the table, a quick scrawl, Mom writing that she and Abilene had gone into Midland, that they wouldn't be back tonight. Maybe not even tomorrow. Using an exclamation point, she called it a girls' weekend out.

"It's Tuesday, Mom," I said out loud, wondering if she'd ever had to lie before, if now, this late, she'd be able to get the hang of it.

I walked around the oddly empty, echoey house, ending up out on the porch again, hoping Dad would come home early for once, wondering what he'd do when he came home to just me. After sitting there waiting for a while, I jumped back up, going inside and retrieving Dad's old baseball glove, my can of neat's-foot oil.

By the time I heard his car crunching down the dirt road, I was almost done oiling his glove. It was too far gone to really restore, but at least this way it had a chance.

Dad parked and got out, smiling a little when he saw me on the porch. He thumped his hand on the roof of his car, looking this way and that, not coming toward me.

I held up the mitt for him to see, and his face cracked into a big smile. Even bigger than the one I'd been imagining. I couldn't help but smile myself.

"Trying to resurrect the dead?"

I shrugged. "You should have seen how it soaked up the oil."

"I bet." Dad still just stood there watching me.

I lowered the mitt, gave it one last rub with the ball of my oil-sheened hand. "Mom and Abilene are gone," I said, making myself look back up to him. "They went to Midland."

He glanced around for a second, then clapped the roof of his car again, rubbing away a circle of road dust. "Well, boys' night out then," he said and I knew she must have called.

I chucked his mitt at him and went inside, hearing the mitt scrape and bounce against the rocks. But he was right behind me, closing in. "Austin. Austin!"

"There's nothing here to eat," I said.

nine

When Mom and Abilene came home, three days later, Abilene seemed to have a little of her old energy back. But from the way Mom looked, her face jittery, wound tight, they might have done a transplant, taking from Mom to give to Abilene. As soon as they were in the door, I asked Abilene if she wanted to pitch. Mom shot me a look, a quick, tight shake of her head, but Abilene shrugged and walked back out of the house. I jumped after her, just hearing Mom hiss, "Austin!" as the screen banged shut behind me. I hesitated, watching Abilene getting into her truck, then leapt off the porch, running after her.

There was nothing off-road about our drive to the base this time. Abilene just eased along the normal route; even the last dodge through the mesquite—Abilene always mixing up the way we went, not leaving a trail anybody might follow—was a slow roll, Abilene winding carefully through the thorns, sparing her tires.

And then, once she parked beside the tank, Abilene just walked away, out toward the runway, leaving me half in the blackness of the tank, twisted around to watch her, not knowing whether to get the balls out or not. "Ab'lene?" I called, but she kept going. I left our stuff in the tank and followed after.

She reached the runway before I fell in step beside her, our feet crunching across all the dust and gravel doing its best to bury the concrete, any trace of all those old bombers, of everything that had ever happened out here.

Without slowing, Abilene asked, "You ever think you'd want a little brother?"

I almost stopped, then stagger-stepped to catch up. "No." I tried a grin. "And have to listen to a whole new installment of How All This Started? 'And then there was the night outside Pecos! We were old, you know, and we're not sure how it happened, but . . .'"

Abilene wasn't smiling.

"Have a little kid running around named Pecos?" I tried.

"Yeah, I suppose," Abilene said. "But this would've been more like How All This *Stopped*."

I didn't say anything else, and neither did Abilene. And I was glad for that. The time she told me about The Facts, though she'd been as clinical as a textbook, she'd pointed at my crotch like an accusation. "And then he sticks it into her." I'd been too young, too amazed, to be that uncomfortable then, but now I could see her sprawled across her bed, hardly held in by that flimsy underwear, and I didn't want to think about what had happened with her, what she'd done with who she didn't even know.

Abilene scraped at the sand with her foot, clearing a tiny spot and sitting down. Then she stretched out completely, on her back, not bothering with clearing away any more of the grit, just lying with her hands behind her head staring up at the vacant blue.

"I still can't believe it."

I didn't say anything.

"That I could have been so stupid."

"You're not stupid." I lay down beside her, hands cocked behind my head, our elbows almost touching.

"Crazy then."

"You're definitely not crazy."

"'Not stupid,' but 'definitely not crazy.' What does that mean? There's a chance I might be stupid?"

"No." The blue was so empty that little tracers and squiggles wormed across my eyes. I shut them.

"One minute you're foolproof, the greatest thing to ever happen, the next you don't even know what you're doing. Or why."

I didn't say anything.

"I have to learn to stop it there, just before the brink."

Again I kept quiet, but Abilene didn't say anything else. It was so quiet for so long, only the hiss of the sand and dust blowing around us, that I thought Abilene might have drifted off. It was something she did now, dropping into some private world of her own. Anywhere, anytime.

"Ab'lene," I whispered. "They're talking to doctors." I could hardly get it out. "Mom and Dad. About you."

"My great new friend, Dr. Nancy Pape."

I tilted my head to look at her, but opening my eyes made the world flash white, dazzling, Abilene only a washed-out blur beside me.

"I had to go see her with Mom," she said.

"What did she say?"

"Lots of questions. Lots and lots of questions."

"And?"

"And? And what? And what's wrong with me?"

I could see now, enough to know that Abilene's eyes were

still shut against the blinding sky. "There's nothing wrong with you."

Abilene sucked in a long breath. "Bipolar disorder," she said, like she'd come out here only to utter those two new words. I watched her eyes, still shut tight. "That's what she called it. Like I'm some kind of magnet, Austin. Like I'd make a compass dance."

"Bipolar?"

"It's doctorese for manic-depressive. Which is nothing but nicey-nice for stark raving."

"They're the crazy ones, Ab'lene. There's nothing wrong with you. Nothing but being stuck here."

"Ah, but you're stuck here too, Austin," she whispered. "And you haven't been caught up in anything like this. Haven't gotten yourself knocked up like some dumb-ass, white-trash whore." I could see the first wetness of tears squeaking out of the corners of her clamped-shut eyes.

I closed my own eyes again and turned away, just in case she looked she wouldn't know I'd seen. And I thought of Mom, taking Abilene away to Midland, just the two of them, so Mom could work on her alone, could trade her baby for a trip to their doctor.

"Are you going to have a baby, Ab'lene?" I asked, hardly louder than the sifting of the sand.

I heard the rustle of her hair against her hands as she shook her head. She whispered, "Not anymore."

And we lay there, inches apart, the sun beating us into the runway until finally I was afraid Abilene had decided to stay there forever, let the sun mummify her in place, the sand creep over us until we were gone.

"Would you coach me again, Ab'lene?" I asked. "Would you pitch?"

She didn't answer.

"Dad's been trying to fill in for you. It's pathetic. Every time he misses a ball, makes a bad throw, he talks about what a big hitter he was. A million years ago in Lubbock."

I turned to look and found Abilene staring off into the sky again.

"They want me to take all these pills, Austin. They say I'm chemically imbalanced. They say I'll be taking them the rest of my life."

"We don't need any pills, Ab'lene. There's nothing wrong with us."

"They want me to be more like them." She was still staring up into the empty sky. "Can you imagine anything worse?"

"Mom and Dad could have done it in Lubbock. That would have been worse. What if that's how all this started? Your name would be Lubbock. Lubby. Lubbs. Or what about Amarillo? Balmorhea?"

She cracked the smallest smile I'd ever seen. "Wacko."

I laughed too loud. "Hey, Waco," I said, saying it right, "please come out and play-o."

Abilene sat up, rubbing at her face. "I wouldn't have even known what to call mine. I didn't know where I was."

It took me a second to follow her, and when I did, I couldn't keep up even the fake laughing.

At last I just stood up. "I need help pitching, Ab'lene. Really. You're the only one who can do it."

She reached out a hand for me to pull her up, and when I did, she just kept coming, the two of us the exact same height, standing inches apart on that endless stretch of deserted, ancient runway. "You're home team this time," she whispered. "Your famous home opener for the soon to be renowned Pecos Eagles."

Breaking apart from me, she started for the tank, showing only her back. "Nobody is going to believe their eyes," she said. "Your first fastball is going to pop them right out of their seats. You are going down in history."

I nodded, bearing down already, almost hearing the flapping

of the purple and gold pennants along the foul-line fences, the honking cheers of the car horns under the mulberries, their flashing headlights, Abilene in the seats, finally seeing for real what she'd been seeing in her head since I could first pick up a baseball.

ten

Through the rest of that fall Abilene slipped back into her old self, waiting for me after school, driving out to the base, putting me through her grueling workouts. Since the day she'd told me about her baby, Abilene seemed to take coaching me even more seriously, never pitching herself. Fine-tuning, she called it, getting me set to be her avenging phenom bursting onto the Pecos Eagles scene. But other than that—all her talk of burning up the record books, hundred-mile-an-hour fastballs, twenty strikeout games—she seemed so normal that we all pretended to forget about her vanishing act; her and Mom's trip to Midland. As the fall wound out into winter, though, the start of the baseball season closing in, I saw Abilene getting antsy, impatient with me, wild about balls I threw that should have been strikes, about how she, a girl, could still throw harder than me.

There were other changes too. Now and then, without warning beforehand, or explanation afterward, Abilene just wouldn't show. I'd be halfway to the water tower before realizing her beat-up white truck wasn't there waiting. I'd have to sprint then to catch the bus before it left.

And usually on those days, after walking down the road and into our kitchen, I'd find myself alone in the house, something it seemed had happened maybe only two or three times before in my life. Abilene's truck would be in the drive, but not Mom's car. They were in Midland, it seemed certain, Abilene somehow trapped into seeing their doctor. But no matter how hard I tried getting Abilene to say where they'd been, she'd shrug me off, sometimes answering with "You tell me," her line from when I was just a kid asking too many questions.

So, in February, on the day the baseball season started, the first practice and tryouts, I had at least a small hope that Abilene wouldn't be waiting for me. But she was in her spot under the tower, pointed at the school, visor down blocking the sun, eyes wide open, just staring at nothing while she waited for me to jump in beside her.

But this time, instead of swinging open the door, I only leaned in the open window. "Hey Ab'lene," I said, wondering what she'd do without me now, feeling guilty I'd hoped Mom had her in Midland squirming under all the doctor's questions.

She turned to look at me.

"Practice starts today. Tryouts." I took a big breath, trying not to smile. "Our big day."

Abilene watched me, her face dead flat. "'Our'?"

I shivered. "Yeah, Ab'lene. What we've been working for. Want to watch?"

"Tryouts? I doubt I'm up for the thrill."

"Okay." We stayed there, looking at each other.

"Well," I said.

"Better get going."

I nodded. "Okay. I'll let you know how it goes."

"Better get ready to start every game." She was smiling, so I stood up straight, backing out of the window of her truck.

I took a step away, bringing my hand up in a wave.

"How are you getting home?"

I shrugged. "Dad, I guess."

She lifted an eyebrow. "You two have fun."

I trotted across the street and waved once more, but Abilene was just a smudge behind the glare of the windshield. I turned and dashed for the field, hoping I wasn't late, that Abilene wasn't watching how fast I ran.

By the time I reached the field, kids were already scattered all across the grass, some tossing balls easily back and forth, some sitting and stretching. I found the coach, a guy I'd never talked to in my life—except for that one note I'd left, which he hadn't bothered answering—standing beside the dugout watching them all. Before I could stop myself, I stepped up beside him and blurted, "You've got yourself a new pitcher, Coach Thurston!" The line I'd rehearsed for weeks.

He glanced away from his players, looking me up and down. "Uh-huh. And who's that?"

"Me," I said, my voice going too high.

His lips parted to grunt out a little laugh, but he waved me toward the guys warming up, and as soon as I found three playing catch, I held up a ball, waiting for one of them to break off and throw with me. I recognized almost everybody, but had hardly said a word to any of them.

When I was loose, I started putting some zing into it. The guy I was throwing with started throwing back hard too. Soon I was only half there, blanking out everything but that high Nolan Ryan/Abilene leg kick, the whip of body around ball. Eventually, Mr. Thurston walked over behind the other kid and watched.

Sending everybody to their drills, Mr. Thurston sidled up to me, keeping me from following the others. "Where have you been hiding?"

I breathed hard, sweating. "I practice at home."

"Well, I'll be glad to see a little more. Who taught you to throw like that?"

I almost said, *My sister,* but realized how that would sound. "Nobody," I said quietly, feeling my cheeks heat up, like somehow Abilene might hear. Wiping her out like that with just one word made me feel like I might be sick. "Just been practicing myself," I said, making it worse.

I could feel the coach looking at me, but I stared out at the field, the green, green grass—Abilene's sprinklers long since replaced—the bare branches of the mulberries against the blue.

"You feel like throwing some of your best?" Mr. Thurston asked. "Just to give me an idea of what exactly you've been practicing?"

I shrugged, suddenly not at all sure I could do this without Abilene. But I nodded and the coach walked toward the mound, waving for a ball.

Trotting to catch up, I said, "There's one thing."

He turned to me, slumping. "Folks won't let you play?"

I shook my head. "I just need a ride is all." There was no way I could ask Abilene to drive me home from this, to sit in her truck alone waiting for me. And riding with Dad asking about each practice, or grilling me again on Abilene, would be even worse. "After practice. I'll miss the bus."

The coach asked where I lived, mumbling through some names before shouting, "Martinez!"

A squat, dark guy jogged over.

"You live way out in the boonies, don't you?"

Martinez only lived a few miles from us. Our closest neighbor. Though I recognized him, he was older than me, a senior, and I had never said a single word to him. I looked down at my shoes. I didn't even own cleats.

"Could you give this kid a lift home after practices?" Then the coach asked me, "What's your name anyway?"

"Austin," I said, dreading saying that much, but hoping it would slip by.

The coach dodged his head back a tiny bit to eye me, surprised, but catching himself. "Well, Austin, this should work. Martinez is even a catcher. You two might end up battery mates."

Martinez looked somewhere over my shoulder. "What about Giles?"

"Let's work out Austin, Martinez. Get your gear on. This kid has what it looks like he has, there'll be plenty of room for him here."

Martinez stood another second, until Coach Thurston pointed him toward his catcher's gear. "Go."

As soon as Martinez trotted off, the coach turned back to me. "Austin Scheer?"

I stepped up onto the mound. I twisted the baseball he'd given me through the different grips.

"Abilene Scheer?"

I looked down toward home, like I did at the base, pretending a signal would come.

"Abilene. Austin. Cute."

Martinez was walking over, his shin guards on. He was fitting his mask up over his helmet.

"Am I right?"

I gave one tense nod, like I would accepting the catcher's signal.

Coach didn't say anything for a second or two. Then he stepped off to my side. "Actually I've kind of been waiting for you." He gave a quiet chuckle. "Hoping for you."

Martinez took a knee behind the plate.

"Abilene teach you any of her stuff? Can you throw anything like that girl could?"

"Can," I said. "Not could. Abilene can still throw better than anybody here."

"And that's where you've come from? You've been working with her? She's your coach."

I nodded again.

"Toss a few easy," he said.

And when I had, he said, "You know I wanted her to play."

I bit my lip shut, but then couldn't help saying, "I thought you were the coach."

"I was. I am. But if she played, no one else would. Good as she was, she wasn't a team by herself."

Not without a chance, I thought, but I kept quiet, staring down toward Martinez.

"You ready to put some zip into it?"

I nodded.

"Fire away."

And I did, seeing nothing more than the base's tire, Martinez not there at all. I threw fire. Coach Thurston didn't have a batter step in against me, just had me throw pitches—a few curves, but mostly he asked for one fastball after another. High and tight, low and away, down and in. "Just groove one," he said. "Fast."

When the ball cracked in Martinez's mitt, Mr. Thurston gave a low whistle. "Tomorrow I'm bringing the gun." The radar gun, to measure my speed. Before practice was even over, he told the manager to get my uniform measurements. Grinning, he said he was glad to have me in the rotation.

"I won't ride the bench," I said. He didn't hear me, and I said it again. "Not the way you made Abilene."

"Not a chance, Austin. I've got to admit, though, it's a relief you were born with balls. If you were her *sister*, I think I'd resign right now." He laughed a little. "But if you're even half as tough as your sister, you might end up being my workhorse."

When Coach whistled the end of practice, he yelled Martinez

over. "Take care of this one. Looks like he may have the real goods."

Martinez gave a sullen nod and told me, "Come on."

As I followed him to his car, Coach called, "Say hello to your sister for me. Tell her I haven't forgotten a day she was here."

Though I knew he meant it, I didn't turn around, just kept following Martinez to his car.

Martinez was still worried about his friend Giles, the weakest pitcher from the year before, and he didn't say a word until we were long out of Pecos. I was working mostly on not smiling, on not repeating "Glad to have you in the rotation" right out loud, when he said, "So that girl's your sister? The one who wanted to play baseball?"

I looked toward him, then away. The bone-dry desert flitted past us. I nodded.

"She nuts, or what?"

"No. She's a pitcher." Then, before he could say anything else, I said, "So, how did you get stuck way out here? Your dad scoop up all the land for free? Does he brag about living here being the deal of his life?"

"Brag?" he asked, finally looking right at me. He pulled over at the end of our road. "About being stuck here?"

I pushed open my door. "My dad does. He's the one who's nuts in our house."

I started running as soon as my feet hit the dirt, yelling, "See you tomorrow," over my shoulder.

I was halfway home when Abilene roared past. Choked by her dust, I staggered to a stop, watching her rocket down the road, no brake lights, not even a glance over her shoulder, like somehow she might not have seen me.

I walked the rest of the way, just so I wouldn't be out of breath when I stepped through the door.

When I came into the kitchen, Abilene was already in her

seat at the table, acting like nothing had happened at all. Mom and Dad babbled all anxious: Where had I been? What happened? Why hadn't I called?

All I could do was look at Abilene, finally blurting, "I made the team!"

Abilene stared straight ahead. "Never a doubt," she said, as Dad said something about congratulations and Mom still talked about having to call if I was going to be late.

"I'm in the rotation, Ab'lene," I said, leaning down to look her eye to eye.

"They don't have a rotation. They just pitch their best as many innings as they're allowed. You know that."

"Well, yeah. I know, but—"

Abilene finally glanced right at me. "Did you really think, Austin, for one instant, that they wouldn't take you?"

eleven

Through the whole dinner Abilene just watched me, peering up from under her eyebrows, half a smile on her face as Dad rattled out questions about the tryouts, about what the coach had said, about how every little thing had gone.

Finally, caught in Abilene's sights, I blurted, "Would you relax, Dad? *I* made the team, not *you*." I tried laughing a little, but Dad sat back in his chair, his next question dying before it could get out.

Abilene chuckled.

I couldn't think of another thing to say, just sat there picking at my food until Mom said, "Austin, we didn't even know you were going to do this."

I pushed a trio of peas around with my fork. "It was a tryout is all," I said, hardly more than mumbling. "Not a game or anything. There wasn't even a batter."

Nobody said anything.

"I still haven't ever pitched against a batter," I said, as if that explained everything.

"That tire and I have given you more problems than any batter ever will," Abilene suddenly said, her first words since I'd sat down to dinner. "Don't you worry about that."

And then Dad, recovered maybe, or maybe only looking for vengeance, said, "I've still got my bat, Austin. If Abilene wants to catch, I'll take a few rips at whatever you can do."

Dad was the size of three high school kids. It'd be like pitching against Mark McGwire. But, remembering his fielding, how he was always anything but quick, I said, "You got it." He'd still be trying to get the bat off his shoulder when the ball whacked Abilene's glove.

"Boys, boys," Abilene said all of a sudden, holding up her hands, stopping us all. "It's not the bat. It's the ball. You still don't see that, do you?" She shook her head.

"Okay," she said, as if this were the last time she'd bother explaining it all, though, really, this was the first time she'd explained this. "Say an average good high school kid can throw, what, sixty-five miles an hour? That gives a batter"—Abilene paused—"about two-thirds of a second to see the pitch and get the bat around.

"Now, Austin, on the other hand, I'm going to have up to a hundred miles an hour soon." She pointed at me, waving her hand as if throwing a ball. "What does that do to your batter? We're under half a second. A hair over four-tenths. You see?" She lifted her eyebrows, hoping she'd made everything clear.

We just sat and watched while she went on, talking fast enough it was hard to follow.

"I don't think that for Austin one-twenty is out of the question." Only Nolan Ryan had ever broken one hundred miles an hour, and he'd never broken one hundred and one. "At that speed we're down to a third of a second. Half the time the average high school pitcher gives a batter. These kids won't even see the ball. Their eyes won't work fast enough, their brains won't. Half the batters in the majors will have the same problem. The other half will only see a blur. Nothing they have the slightest chance of hitting. The biggest challenge of his career is going to be finding someone who can catch him."

"Abilene," Mom said, having to say it twice to interrupt her.

Abilene gave Mom the quickest glance.

"Slow down, honey. You're talking too fast. We can barely understand you."

"That's what I'm saying," Abilene cried, clapping her hands together. "It's speed. Fastballs. Fireballs! There's nothing else on this planet that makes a bit of difference!" She was jubilant.

"If I can only get him to graduate early," she said, flashing me a look like this was something we'd talked about, that I'd long resisted, "he'll have Rookie of the Year the year after next. First rookie ever to win the Cy Young. First thirty-win season in thirty years. First forty-win season in a hundred. There won't be another pitcher winning the Cy Young until Austin decides to hang up the spikes! He'll own it! Hell, by the time he retires they'll have renamed it the Austin Scheer Award. Cy who?"

Dad cleared his throat, then slowly pushed back his chair, not looking at Abilene. "I'll get my bat, Austin."

Abilene laughed. "Have I been talking to myself? Don't you get it yet? This is not about Austin playing high school baseball, firing strikes by pimple-pasted children, hormone-addled little boys. This is not about him embarrassing an old man out on his driveway."

Mom pressed both hands through her frizzy curls, clamping them down against her skull. Still looking at the table, still holding her head, she said, "Clay. Austin. Abilene. This is not about baseball at all. This is——"

But Abilene's chair clattered over backward, stopping everybody. Grinning, every eye on her, Abilene stood in front of the door, hands up at her chest, peering down at me as if waiting for the signal: heat or change-up?

I didn't know what to do.

She dropped her hands, then started them back up, tilting her head and taking a step to her right, setting up against an imaginary pitching rubber. Kicking up her leg, she swung her arms around into the windup. Pausing long enough to peer at me over the straight, horizontal line of her shin, chest high, she whispered, "And here's the pitch to Ventura."

Mom and Dad only gaped, but I launched out of my chair, dropping into a batting stance, smiling at just the idea of our old game. All of us had been watching the game the day Nolan Ryan beaned Robin Ventura. Nolan was practically fifty, twice as old as Ventura, but when Ventura charged, Nolan just wrapped him in a headlock and gave him a noogie, like some kind of kid. But something snapped in Nolan then, and he started pummeling Ventura, his head still trapped under Nolan's arm—wham, wham, wham—like a punching bag.

Abilene had gone over Nolan's move with me the next afternoon, adding the headlock and punches to our workout: "Proficiency in every part of the game, Austin. That's what legends are made of."

Now, while Mom and Dad stared, Abilene finally let her leg fall forward, driving herself off the mound toward me, letting go her pure Nolan Ryan heat.

I staggered back, grabbing my elbow. I took a step toward first, same as Ventura, then charged around the table at Abilene. She whisked me in with that smooth Nolan Ryan move, tucking my head under her arm, giving me the little noogie before suddenly jacking her fist around in those lightning-fast uppercuts.

I heard Mom gasp, heard her call, "Stop it!" heard Dad bellow, "Abilene!" as though they were afraid she would actually hurt me, as though this was her "violent" nature revealed at last. All bent over with my head safe beneath her arm, I watched Abilene's fist clenched white: tight, hard stripes of flesh and bone screaming toward my mouth, my nose, my eyes, always stopping just short. With my cheek pinned against her ribs, her heart hammering in my ear, I hardly even blinked.

Then, letting go as quick as she'd grabbed me, Abilene spun me off toward the door. "All part of the game," she said, breathing hard, smiling at Mom and Dad. "A little rhubarb. A bench-clearing brouhaha."

Dad was on his feet, his arms drooping to his sides. He whispered, "Abilene, are you on drugs? Is that what's really going on here?"

"Clayton!" Mom blurted.

"Well, for Christ's sake, Ruby," Dad started.

But Abilene laughed, stopping both of them. "No, Pops. I'm right as rain." She winked at him. "Right as rain and twice as rare."

Nobody said anything else until I murmured, "He picked off Ventura's runner next play." I looked to Dad. "Remember?"

"Cut down the next thirteen batters in a row." Abilene jerked her thumb up, signaling an out. "'Take your bat and take your seat.'"

"Who?" Mom asked, her voice climbing.

I rolled my eyes. "Nolan Ryan, Mom. The Fireballer."

"Austin's going to be the next," Abilene said. "You just wait and see. He's going to make Ryan look like a little-leaguer."

Dad glanced between Abilene and me. He nodded slowly, the adrenaline of whatever he thought he was going to have to do leaking away. "I'll get my bat."

But Abilene shook her head. "No time for games tonight, Dad. I've got to get Austin out pitching for real."

I reached for the door, but Mom stood up. "It's almost dark, Abilene. It's too late."

"Night games, Mom," Abilene answered. "They've even got them at Wrigley now. Never too late anymore."

"Really, Abilene," Mom started.

"We won't be long," Abilene assured her. "But you heard Austin. His season is upon us already. First one ever. Time to go beyond fine-tuning. Time for the supertune. Austin will spend no time riding a bench, believe you me."

"Why don't I get my mitt?" Dad said. "We could all throw it around."

"On your rocks?" Abilene snapped. But just as fast, she smiled, shaking her head. "We've got a spot. All smoothed out, measured regulation. Sixty feet six. Even built a mound. Consistency, Dad. That's the secret. No time to be bringing somebody new into the mix."

"I am not somebody new," Dad started, but Abilene stopped him with another wink and stepped past me out into the evening. She let the screen slap behind her and I caught it on the bounce, slipping through before Mom or Dad could say another word.

And then we were out. Just like always.

twelve

Abilene drove hard, not crazy, but fast, and with a second to think, I started to wonder where we were really off to. There was no such thing as a night game, no matter what Abilene told Mom, the base at night as black as the inside of the tank.

But the options kept narrowing, Abilene flying toward the base as if pulled by a magnet. The hangar walls, when we could finally see them, stood aglow in the blazing sunset, only minutes of light left. Headlights off, Abilene skidded into the desert, the brush hard to distinguish in the dusky gloom. We crashed straight through one little dead mesquite, the air filling with splintery cracks, the sharp smell of the broken wood, Abilene's laughter. I tried to laugh with her, but by the time I glanced her way, her face was set like it got when she was pitching her flaming hardest.

When Abilene roared down the old runway, sliding to a stop at the tank, she only said, "Okay, time for the supertune. For you to show me this great stuff you got. All those blistering pitches that will wing you straight to the Hall of Fame."

"Abilene, I just want to see if I can pitch against a real batter."

She lined the truck up carefully behind the mound, just off to one side, pointing at the tire. "Nonsense."

"You want me to pitch now? It's practically dark, Ab'lene." I pictured her standing out there swinging the tire, as likely to get cracked by the ball as the tire would be. "I'll kill you."

Abilene laughed. "*You* kill *me*?" She launched herself out of the truck. "I want to watch you pitch, Austin."

"How?"

"Oh, where there's a will . . ." She rummaged in the bed of the truck, retrieving a square blue box from behind the spare.

Yanking open the cardboard, Abilene sprung loose a handheld spotlight, its coiled cord dangling beneath. Leaning into her truck, she flicked on her headlights, the glimmery light glancing off the side of the tank, the oval hatch where the pipe used to go, our entrance, gaping black and empty. A moment later, the spotlight plugged into the cigarette lighter, she flicked it on, a blinding blue-white cone of light knifing out. Pointing at the power pole, the beam turned everything flat and fake, a jumble of snaggly shadows in the stark electric glare, the tire a spooky, silvery ring. Glass knobs glinted on the tilted crossbar, the broken wires dragging away. "This is the big leagues, Austin!" Abilene yelled. "Stadium lights!"

"Where did you get that?" I pointed at the spotlight. "When?"

Instead of answering, she ducked into the tank and came out throwing my mitt to me, lugging our box of balls to the mound.

Abilene opened my door, wedging the spotlight in so it lit the tire. "Get yourself ready."

I walked back to the runway and sat down, stretching. Then

I did my sprints, touching each edge of the runway and reversing quick as I could. Everything Abilene had taught me.

Standing inside the eerie, half-blinding light, we tossed warm-up until Abilene said, "Ready?" Without waiting for an answer she dropped her mitt and stepped to the tire, pulling it back, all set to whip it loose.

I found my place on the mound, setting my foot against the worn plank of the rubber. My shadow, etched hard and black against the rocky ground, stretched almost all the way to Abilene. Drawing myself up, I whispered, "Set."

Abilene swung the tire so hard her toes left the ground.

I didn't mess around with anything but heat. I threw straight blazing fire. No matter how hard Abilene swung the tire, I aced pitch after pitch through the hole. Baseballs scattered through the desert behind the weathered old pole, dim glimmers in the black shadows.

Abilene was breathing and sweating as hard as me, wearing herself out on that tire. But I was throwing like nothing she'd ever seen, and she couldn't do a thing with the tire to touch that.

By the time we had to break to gather the baseballs, the middle of the fifth inning, I caught her looking at them, their hides tattered and gray with all the pitching I'd done. But she just flipped the balls into the box and took her position at the tire, waiting for me to give the okay from the mound, starting another inning. She never said a word.

By the ninth I hadn't given up a run. Nothing more than a single, and only one of them. O and two on the last batter, I reared back and fired one more time. The ball shot through the tire clean, kicking up a bullet spurt as it sliced off into the night. I slapped my mitt against my thigh. A nine-pitch ninth inning! Three batters, three K's! Untouchable! I lifted my cap, wiping sweat away. Maybe 120 miles an hour wasn't impossible!

Abilene stood by the tire, watching me.

I stepped off our gravel mound, the gray and splintery two-by-six pinned down with our giant spikes. I was pitched out, my arm tingling, but she'd seen something to remember.

"Okay," Abilene said at last. "Now, ready to pitch a real game?"

I spun around to her. "What? What do you think that was?"

"Playing with yourself. Anybody can do that."

I stared hard at her, her face flat and vaguely blue in the spotlight's glare.

"Won't get far on varsity playing with yourself," she said, leaving the tire to walk toward me. "Won't get the girls that way."

"What do you want me to do?"

"I want you to pitch against someone who knows what they're doing."

"You?"

"Know anybody else?" She tossed a punch into my left shoulder and slipped behind me to her truck, invisible against the lights when I turned to watch her.

I worked my shoulder up and down, rubbing it with my glove hand. "I just pitched a whole game, Ab'lene."

"With yourself."

I squinted into the glare, but couldn't see her. "Okay," I said at last.

The tailgate crashed down the instant I said "Okay." A moment later Abilene was back beside me, dropping a box of brand-new baseballs onto the mound. It kicked up a cloud of dust that hung sparkling in the lights. "Varsity time."

I poked at the box with my toe. "Where did these come from?"

"There are five more boxes in the truck. It's all Gibson's had."

Instead of imagining her stewing out in her truck all through my tryout, I now pictured her racing around town gathering supplies for this night game—these balls, that light.

"You really think you're ready to pitch against me?" she asked, smiling. "Ready for the humiliation?"

"I've beaten you before," I said without thinking.

Abilene glanced across the mound at me. "That's right. So your record's one and five hundred? One and one thousand?"

I tapped my mitt against my leg. "I've been pitching, Ab'lene. You saw that. You've only been coaching."

"*Only?*" Abilene ripped open the new box, picking out a fresh white ball.

"Not *only*, but . . ."

She tossed the ball up and down, winding her long fingers around the red laces like a pro: four-seam, two-seam, change-up, curve. "You think I haven't been pitching?"

"I know you haven't, Ab'lene."

"You don't know how much you don't know." She kept smiling, tossing the ball from hand to hand, finally flicking it toward me.

We tossed the ball back and forth again, gradually working farther apart, putting more behind the throws. My arm stung, but I'd work it down to a rag to pitch with Abilene again.

"Where've you been practicing?" I said, grunting a little as I heated one up, hoping she'd say something about my speed.

The ball smacked into her glove. "Around. Had to keep busy while you gathered lint at school."

"Around where?"

"Here, there. You know." She lifted her leg high and grooved one at me that made me wish I had a pad in my mitt. She grinned. "You going to be home team or visiting?"

"You pick," I said automatically, but before she could answer I said, "No. I'll be home."

Abilene stepped to the tire without taking her eyes off me.

She pulled it up as far as she could, but before letting fly she said, "Don't forget whose home this was first, Austin. Don't forget who showed you this place, who hung the tire, who taught you to pitch. Who taught you everything."

"I'm not forgetting a thing."

"We'll see about that." Then she called, "Batter up!" giving the tire a vicious swing. I wound up and fired, sending my first pitch off the outside edge of the tire. A double.

Abilene nodded, like it was just what she'd expected.

It went downhill from there. My arm hurt more than I guessed it would, pitched out before the game started, but I couldn't believe how having Abilene pitching against me made me go all to pieces.

It took me days to get out of the inning. By the time Abilene got on the mound I was already down four runs.

When Abilene called, "Batter up," I flung the tire as hard as I could, harder even than she had. I looked up to watch her, but found I was blinded by the spotlight, the headlights. That whole almost perfect game I'd pitched, that last terrible first inning, Abilene hadn't seen a trace of me, just stood out here by herself, lit up like a Christmas tree, surrounded by nothing but the blinding night.

So I watched the tire, and as soon as Abilene's first pitch streaked through, I knew the game was over. It pierced the tire clean. Until I heard the hiss of her ball slicing the air, I'd been able to convince myself my pitches had grown to sound as dangerous. I cradled my throbbing pitching arm and watched the quick white flashes of her strikes.

She threw one bad pitch, missing the tire completely, a gopher ball she didn't say a word about. Then she K'ed the last batter of the inning.

"I gave you one," she said as we traded places.

"I gave you four."

After five innings I was down sixteen to one. My arm was thrown to mush, a solid stretch of pain. But the last thing I could ever do was complain to Abilene, make an excuse for anything. The rule was, once a game started, nothing stopped it, nothing but rain. Just like the pros.

Rain. Out here.

Instead of taking the ball from her at the top of the sixth, I only held out my mitt. She dropped the ball in. Up fifteen runs and her game face was still clenched tight.

I stood on the mound sweating, my right arm feeling six inches longer than my left, waiting for her to see what she was doing to me. But even if she'd wanted to see, against all that light I was invisible. Abilene swung the tire again, her feet still leaving the ground when she let go.

I lost track of the score, surprised when Abilene came to the mound. I didn't know the inning was over.

Even in the cool of the night my shirt was soaked through, clinging tight. "I might have to check for a spitter," Abilene said.

"Go ahead." I shuffled to the tire, giving it as much of a push as I could with one arm. In the full harsh glare of the spotlight I saw black speckles of blood on the thigh of my jeans, neat, regular stripes of tiny dots. My pitching fingers had blistered and burst.

The last innings hazed over. I chewed my lip, tasting blood, doing anything I could to keep from crying. I threw wobbling, crippled ducks, wondering if Abilene would let me pitch left-handed. Some of the throws didn't even reach the tire.

By the ninth the tire was a blur. I couldn't tell if it was swinging or not. I stood straight as I could, trying to lift my mitt and pitching hand to my waist, working from the stretch, when Abilene touched my shoulder. I staggered sideways off the mound, the ball rolling out of my mitt.

"You can't do that!" I cried. "You can't push me! Who do you think you are? Since when can you shove the pitcher?" Tears started down my face. I couldn't help it. "Who do you think you are?"

"You got the last guy."

I sat down where I was, my legs giving out. "I knew I would. It was the curve, wasn't it?"

"It wasn't much of anything."

I slumped forward, resting my head against the hard, rough dirt, each tiny rock bright, casting its own shadow, until my shadow eclipsed everything. Abilene finished the bottom of the ninth, throwing straight through the motionless tire while I lay off to the side. She walked to the tank and sat down at the edge of the light, leaning back against the steel.

I think she just watched me for a while. Or I passed out or something. Her voice came from a million miles away when she said, "For crying out loud, Austin. Game's over. Get off the field."

I cracked open an eye, saw her waving me over. I rolled onto my back, the dust and dirt loud against my ear. Above me the stars scattered across the sky, bright in the blackness, the Milky Way like a stain.

"Austin," she called again.

I pushed myself to my feet, tottering to the side, but catching myself and shuffling over to the tank, collapsing again beside Abilene. "What was the score?"

"Forty-three to one."

"I wasn't at my best."

"I guess not."

"You settled down," I said, trying to think of her old announcer talk. "Made that one mistake in the first, but then got right down to business."

Abilene touched my face, turning it toward her. "Austin?"

"I haven't been pitching both ends of that many doubleheaders."

Abilene shook her head. "Forty-three to one against a pitcher," she said, sounding confused. "Red-hot playing with yourself. How do you figure that?"

I closed my eyes, the screaming hot throb of my arm something it seemed I could hear, an insistent thumping.

"How do you figure that?" she said again.

"What do you mean?"

"You tell me."

The first game, I knew now, didn't make any difference. She'd walked out of her truck and thrown a one-run game, hadn't practiced in months, though now I was beginning to believe she might have somewhere else, might have sneaked in practice just to come out here and demolish me.

"I don't know, Ab'lene." I let my shoulders slide down the tank till I was flat on the ground.

"Don't know what?"

"Don't know how to figure that," I whispered, biting my lip.

"Forty-three to one. Do you think that'll impress them at that high school of yours? Do you think your cheerleaders will be peeling out of their sweaters for you after that?"

"Why are you doing this, Ab'lene?" I interrupted, my voice just a croak.

Abilene brushed off the thighs of her jeans. "And you think you got what it takes to star in the majors," she said, shaking her head.

"Ab'lene, this is a tire in the desert."

"Do you think you got what it takes to play even high school ball?" she said, louder.

"You said I did. You said there wasn't a doubt. You said—"

"Never mind that. What I want to know is what *you* think. I want to know if you think you can just run off to your high school and your cheerleaders and forget who started it all for you. I am *everything* you'll ever be."

I lifted my mitt off the ground, letting it fall with a slap. "That's not—"

"Forty-three to one. You really think you're ready to run off all on your own?"

"I don't know, Ab'lene," I shouted, pushing myself to my feet, walking away from her. "That's not even what this is about. I'm not—"

She stared and stared at me. "You *have* to know, Austin."

I reached out my mitt hand, holding the edge of the tank doorway with it, steadying myself. "It's not leaving you behind, Ab'lene. This is what we always planned. Don't you remember? We're fireballers. We both are."

"We both are? Forty-three to one and we both are?"

I stepped into the tank, saying, "I don't know, Ab'lene. I don't know anything anymore."

The inside of the tank was as black as ever, nothing but the dim constellations of the bullet holes. Holding myself against the door, I suddenly wondered if this was what Abilene's world was like: her head filled with her very own stars; captivating at first, but finally terrifying when she realized that everything else that was light had gone dark.

Thinking of Abilene trapped in a place like that staggered me, and I took a few weak steps forward and lay on the floor of the tank, my heart oil-canning.

It took a moment before I realized the weak glow of the headlights wasn't pouring through the door anymore. Abilene was standing there, blocking it off. "Ab'lene? Days I come home and you and Mom are gone, are you at that doctor's?"

"I humor them."

"Do they still talk about the pills? Do you take those?"

Abilene laughed. She thumped her fist against her chest. "This is my temple, Austin."

I shut my eyes.

"Come on," she said. "It's getting late. Doubleheader and all. And you still have the balls to pick up."

"You go ahead. I'll walk." I opened my eyes, looked at her stars.

Abilene was still in the door, though I wasn't sure if she could see me in the dark. The light fell back in when she stepped away. A moment later I heard her truck just barely start, the battery drained from lighting the game. It idled a long time before I picked myself up. I wondered if she'd boxed the balls herself and I smiled, thinking of her doing that for me, returning the favor. But when I crept out, the balls were still scattered all over, looking like toadstools in the headlight beams. It was her rule.

Rigging a sling out of my shirt for my arm, I kicked around the new box, dropping balls in one at a time, feeling Abilene watching. When it was full, I dragged the box into the tank, using my knees to help push it to the top of the foundation wall.

Outside I stopped and squinted against the glare of the headlights. Abilene gunned the engine a couple of times, and instead of walking away down the runway, I edged around the truck and slid into my old seat. Abilene pushed it into gear and we started off, leaving the base behind.

Hitting the highway, Abilene pulled a shoe box from beneath her seat and slapped it down between us. "Here."

I looked at the box and she told me to open it.

I pushed the lid aside: a pair of baseball shoes, black and new, their metal spikes glinting dully in the dashboard light.

"You'll be needing those."

I rubbed my thumb along the filed edge of a spike. "What for?"

Abilene stared at me.

"You can't use metal in high school, Ab'lene. You know that."

"High school!" she snorted, like it had always been this huge joke between us.

thirteen

After stopping in front of our house, Abilene just sat behind the wheel. I threw open my door, but didn't move from my seat. "Are you coming in?"

She ran her hands across the top of the steering wheel, as if winding through huge looping turns. "I'll be back. Just right now I've got something to do."

"It's the middle of the night, Ab'lene."

"Days aren't long enough. Ever notice that? I've quit sleeping. It wastes so much time."

"What do you have to do?"

"So much," she answered, kind of singsongy. "So, so very much."

"Are you coming back, Ab'lene? Are you going to take off?"

"And miss your whole career? Not a chance, Austin. Not the slightest chance in the world."

I held my pitching hand in my lap, curled in on itself like a claw. *My whole career?* "It'll be a while before I can pitch again I think."

"Cut some of Mom's aloe. Rub the juice on the blisters. Be gone before you know it. Won't even remember them."

I waited a minute before saying, "I don't think I'm going to forget this."

"A shellacking like that is hard to put behind you. But you have to, Austin. If you're going to get anyplace in this world, you have to."

I wanted to yell, *Whose world? What crazy world are you in?* but I picked up my arm and scooched my legs out the open door, ready to jump to the ground. "So, I'll see you tomorrow?"

"Soon. You'll see me soon."

My feet hit the driveway. "Be careful, Ab'lene."

She laughed, gunning the engine. "Give my best to Mom and Dad," she called. "Those little lovebirds. I bet they still talk about them in Abilene and Austin."

I didn't bother watching her drive off, only trudged into the house, past Mom and Dad in the living room.

Dad followed me upstairs, but I slid into bed before he got there, all my clothes on, shoes still on, my back to the door.

He stood there a long time before saying, "You're by yourself."

"I know."

He waited.

"She had something she had to do," I murmured.

"At this hour? What?"

"I don't know."

Dad waited again, then asked, "What did you two do?"

"Pitched," I answered, short and sharp. I tried softening it. "I pitched too hard. My arm's trashed."

"And Abilene?" he asked—all he really cared about.

"I don't know, Dad. Okay? She said she wasn't taking off, that she'd be back, that I'd see her soon, that she just had stuff to do."

There was no answer, and I blurted, "Okay?"

"Okay," Dad whispered after a few seconds. "Okay. You take care of that arm. . . . Good night." He closed my door only halfway, like they'd always done, like I might be afraid of the dark. After giving him time to get away, I got up and shut it tight.

I lay in bed then, my arm throbbing, my throat tight and dry. Nolan Ryan stared down at me from my poster, his eyes hard, peering over his shin just like Abilene, the word *Fireballer* blazed above him.

Balling is what guys called it at school, and I couldn't stop myself from picturing Abilene out there without me, Abilene pregnant, Abilene home, stretched across her bed in that underwear, worse than naked. Throwing my good arm up over my eyes, grinding it hard against those pictures, I wondered if that was what Abilene was out after right now, if there weren't some guys somewhere who called her Fireballer for a totally different reason, without knowing a thing about what it really meant.

fourteen

The following morning, before Mom and Dad were awake, I crept downstairs, and after coating my fingers with the slick sap of Mom's aloe, I slipped out into the pale yellow dawn. Each shuffling step kicked up tiny clouds of dust that drifted after me. At the end of our road I sat in the gravel and took out the supplies I'd stolen from the medicine cabinet, wrapping each weepy fingertip tight in gauze and tape. Then, starting to think, I dodged back farther into the mesquite and waited for Dad's car to pass on its lonely trip into Pecos. The bus wasn't much behind him, and I dropped into my seat, pressing my head against the rattling window, hoping for just one glimpse of Abilene.

When Coach Thurston saw the bandages, he had me unwrap one, then held my hand up in the air, like it was something new to him, a hand. He shook his head and stared at me, finally saying, "What in the world, kid?"

"I went too hard."

"Is this how you've been practicing all along? Until you bleed?"

"Sometimes. Sometimes I concentrate too hard. Forget what else is happening."

"Well, you can forget pitching too. With those fingers."

"They'll get better fast."

"How's your arm then?"

My arm felt like the muscle had been pulled from the bone, left dangling loose inside the skin. "It's fine. Just a blister is all."

"Bli*sters*."

"They'll heal."

"I was already thinking of you for the opener. We'll push that back."

"I can throw already, Coach. With them wrapped this way."

"Uh-huh." He finally gave me back my hand. He told me to go with the other pitchers, but as I turned to leave, he asked, "Is this stunt the sort of thing I should get used to, something that will keep popping up?"

"No. I just got too excited."

He shook his head again, but couldn't keep back a smile. "'Too excited.' I wonder what we got with you."

As I trotted away he yelled, "Just watch! Don't even think about touching a ball!"

And that's what I was doing when I noticed a few guys stop playing, then a few more. They were looking past me, behind me, and I turned to see what had happened.

Halfway across the outfield already, I saw Abilene marching toward me, her truck parked out by the gap in the outfield fence, same place we'd parked the night of the sprinklers. Even at that distance Abilene looked different, her hair freed of its constant braid, out and blowing, a red electrical storm, Saint Elmo's fire. The lean stretch of her too seemed caught in the wind, curved and swaying. Glancing back at the team, I saw that most everyone had stopped whatever they'd been doing. Gaping at Abilene, they all looked like little kids. Children.

Abilene walked right up to me, smiling. She was wearing a pair of jeans I'd never seen before, tight and black. She still had her jean jacket, faded and worn, but only the bottom button was closed now, the rest staying shut as best it could, but open plenty wide to see she wore nothing but that black bra beneath it, the tiny lacy one leaving nothing to wonder over.

She nodded at everyone. "Hello, kids."

Coach Thurston came over from the dugout. "Hello, Abilene." It sounded more like a warning than a greeting.

Abilene fixed him with a glance, then slowly smiled. "Hi, Coach. Still out here guarding the old status quo?"

But before he had a chance to answer, Abilene asked, "So what do you think of my big project?" She waved toward me.

Coach nodded. "Pretty impressive." Then he pointed at my bandages. "That your doing?"

"Not my fingers, are they?"

"No, I don't suppose they are."

They just looked at each other then, until Abilene asked, "Are you planning on benching him too, Coach? Have another star ride the pine?"

"No, Abilene. Not after those fingers heal."

"Those fingers. That reminds me." Abilene dug into her coat pocket, making the opening gape. "I've got something for you. Just a little something for my doll baby."

That was what Dad always used to say, never returning from an out-of-town assessing trip without some kind of present for each of us. But it sounded dried up and played out coming from Abilene's mouth; not something you'd ever want to hear, though we used to look forward to Dad's presents way back then.

Abilene tossed me a baseball. "Sorry it took so long, but Alvin's a long haul."

I caught the ball and held it against my hip.

"How are those fingers?" she asked.

"Getting better."

"Just like I told you." She glanced around at all the guys. "Well, I know you boys are busy. Playing and all." She shifted from one hip to the other, making her jacket hang open, then lifted her eyebrows at some of their looks. "You better get after it, Coach. I'm expecting great things from this team."

I looked away from them all, down at the ball. It was signed by Nolan Ryan. "For Austin," it said. "My partner on the Express." That's what they called his fastball, the Ryan Express. The word *Fireballer* was inked in above that, just like on my poster. Alvin was where Nolan Ryan lived, clear across the state.

I glanced back up at Abilene and she grinned. "Take care of that." She turned and started away, calling, "See you, Austin."

Somebody next to me, his voice hushed with awe, whispered, "That's your sister, isn't it?" Other murmurs broke out. A "Holy shit!" A long, low whistle.

I looked down at the ball. "She's my sister."

Coach Thurston clapped his hands. "All right! Let's get back to work." As the kids started to move, make the first throws, Coach asked, "What did she leave for you?"

I held up the ball, my hand covering most of the signature. "A baseball."

"She sign it herself?"

I shook my head. "Nolan Ryan."

Coach watched Abilene slip through the fence back into her truck. "Is that who you're supposed to be?" he asked, waving down at the ball. "The next Nolan Ryan?"

I shrugged.

"Is that what she says?"

I shrugged again.

"You just make sure to give yourself time, Austin. Even Nolan Ryan wasn't Nolan Ryan his whole life."

I glanced up to see if Coach was smiling. I spun the ball through my bandaged fingers; four-seam, two-seam, split-finger, curve.

I watched Abilene's truck flicker white between the silver-gray trunks of the mulberries, then disappear down toward the interstate. She must have driven straight through, all the way across Texas and back. Just to apologize.

Picturing that thousand-mile mad dash, I shuddered, hoping she'd still been wearing her shirt when she knocked on Nolan Ryan's door.

That evening, before I even had a chance to pull my chair back to sit down for dinner, Dad asked, "What happened last night?"

I looked up, my left hand on my chair back, my ruined right hand in my pocket. "Nothing. We pitched."

"Abilene hasn't come home," Mom said.

I sat down and nodded. "She showed up at practice today."

They stopped even breathing, and into the quiet I said, "She got Nolan Ryan to sign a ball for me."

They both asked, "What?" at the same time, then, "How?"

Dad asked, "Where is she now, Austin?"

I shrugged. "I don't know. She just said, 'See you,' and drove off."

"Why didn't you stop her?" Dad blurted.

"And what, Dad? Chase her truck through Pecos in my cleats?"

"Austin," Mom said quietly.

"What do you want me to do?" I said, my voice getting too loud. I pulled the ball from my pocket, waved it at them. "She drove across all of Texas to get this for me. Walked right up to Nolan Ryan and had him sign it. For me!" I glared at them. "What am I supposed to do after that? Jump on her? Hold her down till you can drag her off to your doctor?"

The room was silent, only my breathing, rough and raw. Dad cleared his throat. "What happened to your fingers?"

I'd hid them till then. Now I looked at the bandages I'd forgotten to unwind in the bus while I'd sat staring at Abilene's ball.

"Blisters. I told you I threw too hard."

"Must make pitching tough."

"They're all right."

Dad lined his fork up on one side of his plate, his knife on the other. "All she said is 'See you'?"

"That's all."

"Not when?"

"No."

"Then I guess we'll wait."

"I guess so."

We all looked away from each other. I said, "She said she wouldn't miss my career. She said she'd never do that. I think I might start the first home game. Next Thursday."

Mom glanced at me.

"Maybe she hasn't gone anywhere," I said. "Maybe she was just gone to get this ball signed for me. Maybe she'll be back tonight."

"Maybe you're right, Austin," Mom said. "She'll want to help you. She's always wanted that."

Dad said, "I could throw with you. Keep you sharp until she comes home." He seemed to think a second before remembering Abilene's term. "Do some fine-tuning."

I looked down at my fingers, Abilene's supertune. "Coach told me not to touch a ball."

"So," Dad said, blowing out a big, long breath. "We just sit and wait for Abilene."

"She said she'd be back," I offered.

But Dad just stood up, carrying his plate to the sink. "Of course she did."

———

As soon as I cleared my plate, I slipped out and started for the base. I ran a way, then walked, then ran, making the most of what was left of the sunlight. By the time I reached the tank, the sun was almost on the horizon, a huge, blinding ball, still hot-looking though the night's chill would drop down soon. The whole way out I'd held the Nolan Ryan ball in both hands, not risking a single toss, where a mishandle could mean dropping it into the rocks and the spines.

I'd even started imagining, or hoping maybe, that I'd find Abilene's truck beside the tank, find her maybe pitching a few easy ones through the tire, or just sitting alongside the tank, like she'd been doing nothing but waiting for me her whole life.

But, of course, she wasn't there. It was just me alone. I stooped down and crossed into the tank's blackness, too excited with the ball to even remember to check for rattlers.

Twisting the Nolan Ryan ball through the different grips, not needing to see a thing, I remembered the first time Abilene had held my hand in hers, showing me how to fit my fingers around the ball. My fingers were too small to make any of the grips, and in frustration Abilene decided we'd skip all that finesse and just grab the ball and let it fly; that we'd be fireballers.

Sitting on the tank's foundation wall, I lifted the ball to the pencil of light poking through one of the bullet holes. Turning it slowly, I read the inscription in that one tiny shaft of brightness. *Nolan Ryan. Fireballer. My partner.* I smiled. Abilene had never once in her life apologized to me for anything.

Finally, setting the ball safely along the foundation opposite the door, as far as possible from getting mixed up with the box of practice balls, I ducked out of the tank again, the sky edged purple, the sun just a slice on the flat line of the horizon. I jogged straight for the jaggy, dark lumps of the Davis Mountains way out there, knowing I could make the road before it was too dark, that once there I could make it home.

When I walked through the kitchen door long after dark, Abilene was still gone, and Mom and Dad were frantic about me disappearing. I couldn't stand it, and I waved my hands like a trooper at a wreck—slow down. "I was just out looking for her," I lied, anything to get them to ease up. "I checked a place we go. To pitch. I thought maybe she'd be there."

"Where?" Dad asked. "The bomb shelter?" The kids at school went there sometimes. To drink, mostly.

I shook my head. "The old bomber base." Though Abilene had said it was our secret, I figured that wasn't when she was making the most sense in the world. "We've got a mound out there."

"That's quite a walk," Dad said, eyeing me, probably wondering whether he'd have to begin doubting me too.

"I know. About got eaten by the mesquite."

Dad smiled a little, but Mom said, "Not at night, Austin. You can't see what might happen."

"I know. I kept waiting for some snake to drill me, or—"

"That's enough!" Mom blurted. She forced a smile weaker even than Dad's. "I don't want to hear it, Austin."

We were all quiet then, until Dad touched Mom's shoulder and whispered, "He's fine, Ruby. He's fine."

fifteen

Abilene didn't come home that night. Or the next. Or
the one after that. I traveled with the team to the first game,
spending the game riding the bench in my ridiculously clean
uniform, sneaking peeks at the scattering of fans in the stands,
wondering how Abilene could have spent a whole season like
this, no one ever saying a word to her. Big Spring, the favorite
for the championship, gave us a nine-to-two drubbing, and
though I couldn't help looking for her, I was almost glad there
was no trace of Abilene.

At practice the next week, still no sign of Abilene, Coach had
me throw batting practice, my first time against batters, though
I was supposed to let them hit it. After they'd slapped the ball
all over the place, Coach let me know I'd start the home opener
against Fort Stockton. Martinez, who'd almost started speaking
to me, clammed up all over again after hearing the news, but
after he dropped me off, I practically floated down the dirt road,

playing the little kid's game—if this, then that—figuring Abilene would have to be home now, since my career was finally starting for real.

But the driveway was as empty as our old runway, and when I told Mom and Dad about starting, though they were excited and happy, without Abilene it was like a consolation prize.

The day of my start I was near sick with butterflies. I didn't hear a single word in any class, just sat like a corpse in my uniform shirt, rubbing at the sleeves, staring at the bright pink skin of my healed blisters, thinking about Abilene hanging that tire at the base, about how many games she and I'd played alone out there, about real batters suddenly swinging real bats at all my pitches.

Instead of going home for dinner with Mom and Dad, I slunk out to the dugout after school, hanging out alone on the empty bench. I was too sick to eat anyway. The purple and gold game-day flags hung limp in the dead, hot air, kids wandering here and there, laughing, girls bent down to lean into the windows of the low-riders, the throaty rumble of those engines. After forever the team began trickling in, Coach on me like stink, keeping me talking while the teams warmed up, going through every play: covering first on a grounder to that side, home on a bunt with a runner on third—just keeping my mind busy, keeping me from throwing up the butterflies.

At the last second I told him I had to pee and I ran to the pay phone in front of the school. When Mom answered, I blurted, "Is Abilene there?"

There was a long pause. "No, Austin. We still haven't seen her."

"Oh."

After another pause, Mom said, "Dad and I were just getting ready to leave. To come watch you play."

"Oh, yeah. That." Suddenly I couldn't stand the idea of anyone watching me. This was our private game, Abilene's and mine. Without her I could hardly remember why I was here at all, all her old speeches and all my nerve disappearing along with her. Like our whole life together, all those thousands of hours by ourselves out at the bomber base, had vanished just like everything else in this place: the cotton, the cattle, the oil, the rain.

"Mom, that's why I called. Coach switched me to next week's tournament. I'm not playing at all tonight."

She murmured something about its being a shame, but I could barely listen. "I have to go." I said, hanging up while she was still talking.

I got back to the field just as our team was running out to their positions. I jogged out to the mound and threw my warm-up pitches to Martinez, the umpire all in black off to the side, bored looking. I tried to get into the consistency of it, every movement the same, my right foot planted against the rubber, my left foot falling into the exact same spot in the dirt, each cleat dropping into the same neat hole as the time before.

When the umpire called last pitch, and I stepped aside for Martinez's throw through to second, I caught a glimpse of Abilene in the stands. I was not looking on purpose, not wanting to see anybody, trying to pretend this was just another game at the bomber base, but somehow she stood out, all alone on the bleacher seats, a few people walking past her, finding their own spots. I looked away quick as I could, but then knew she'd seen me see her.

Glancing back, I flashed a quick thumbs-up, but Abilene didn't smile or do anything else, like she didn't see me or didn't know who I was anymore. Like we were strangers now. Me and Abilene.

I stood and stared at her, waiting for some sign of recognition, until at last her eyes met mine and she lifted her arm and pointed. She was only showing me the batter, that he was up and waiting, that I'd been standing daydreaming, a complete failure of concentration. As I climbed back onto the mound, I saw her shaking her head.

Spooked, I walked the first real batter I ever faced in my life. On four pitches. Then I walked the second. Coach came out, telling me I had nothing to be afraid of, that if I just grooved it down the pipe, no hitter from Fort Stockton could get his bat around in time. I believed him. They were the worst in the division. I hit the next batter on the hip.

Watching him squirm on the ground, I hoped he'd get up and charge. I took a step back, waiting to take him in that Abilene/Nolan Ryan sweep, ready to wing punch after punch into him. Maybe I'd get thrown out of the game.

But the batter didn't get up and charge. Pretty soon they had a doctor out and they messed with him awhile before finally helping him stagger off, somebody under each arm. Another kid trotted out to first to run for him, and both coaches and the umpire came out to the mound, the umpire telling me the next batter would be my last if he thought I was so out of control as to be dangerous.

While they walked back to their spots, I glanced to the stands, half expecting to see Abilene up there waving a big sign, "43 to 1!" painted all over it. But she wasn't. Everybody around her sat in their seats, talking, ignoring the game, like they'd seen too many wild pitchers already, but Abilene stood straight up, staring at me.

I held her stare, everything else in the world falling away until the next batter stepped in. Then, turning from Abilene, I worked from the stretch, grooving a strike down the pipe. Did the same thing with the next pitch, knowing this guy would wait for a walk. He was probably too afraid to get close, thinking I might kill him. All I saw was Abilene, heaving the tire so hard her toes left the ground, daring me to bear down.

The batter swung at the third pitch, which was about at his

shoelaces. The dugout cheered, and though I still had the bases loaded, I had an out now, on three strikes. When I K'ed the next two batters, on only eight pitches, it hardly seemed like it was me up there at all, more like I was watching Abilene lash pitch after pitch through the whipping tire. Each time the ball smacked into Martinez's glove, I could hear the hissing whistle Abilene's pitches made cutting the air.

I stayed in that trance, mowing down batter after batter, though I walked a few getting tricky with the strike zone. After the fourth inning our third baseman came up to me in the dugout and slapped me on the shoulder: "Hey, Ace, what say you slow one down enough they can hit it? Give the rest of us out there something to do."

I was picturing the next inning, so I stared at him a second before I could smile and stutter, "Yeah, we'll see."

But Coach Thurston was on top of us like lightning, shoving our third baseman away. "All you guys leave him alone. Can't you see he's concentrating? Maybe some of you could take a lesson from that." Coach glared at the bench, every player.

But the game really wasn't much to pay attention to. We were up seven–zip, and we added two more in our half. I was working on concentrating, but I didn't much appreciate the coach setting me out like that, making me even more separate from the team.

High school games are only seven innings, and it wasn't until the fifth, when I still hadn't given up a hit, that people really started paying attention. The crowd leaned forward in their seats with every batter now, not just when one of their friends or kids came to the plate.

I got the last guy of the sixth with a called strike and trotted back to the dugout, pulling my hat down extra low. Watching Nolan Ryan, Abilene had taught me everything about no-hitter jinxes. I was sure she wasn't looking at me. She was probably even talking to the strangers beside her, doing her best to pretend that nothing in particular was going on, nothing we could put the hex on by hoping for.

When I hit the bench, the cars outside the fence were still flashing their headlights and honking in applause. The sky had gone rosy, the field lights on and bright. Nighthawks flitted over the field. I put my arm through the sleeve of my warm-up and wiped the sweat from my face. Coach Thurston plopped down next to me, as nonchalant as can be. "How are you?"

I nodded. "Okay."

"You're starting to get it up. Your fastball's rising."

I nodded again. In the middle of the inning my shoulder had begun a strange slipping click, something I remembered from the end of the doubleheader Abilene had put me through. Something deeper than blisters. It scared me more than it hurt, but it made me pull back, rolling my shoulder away from the follow-through, making my pitches sail.

"You're feeling all right?" Coach asked, leaning closer, almost whispering.

"Sure."

"Your arm's okay? Your shoulder?"

"Sure."

He watched me while I pretended to watch the game. The third baseman stroked a single. Coach Thurston didn't even blink at the crack of the bat. "It's a long season," he said as our right fielder stepped to the on-deck circle.

I didn't say anything.

"You could be pitching a long, long time."

I still didn't say anything.

"You're going to have plenty of shots at no-hitters. Plenty a lot more important than this."

I blushed when he said "no-hitter"—the worst jinx of all— but I nodded, wishing Martinez would ground into a double play, let me get back on the mound.

"You throw your arm out this young, you might be done

before you get started. Your bones, your cartilage—little things like your rotator cuff—they aren't hard enough yet to take the way you throw. Not for long. Not unless you're careful."

"I'm okay," I whispered.

He kept looking at me. I could feel it. "Nothing hurts?" he asked at last.

I shook my head.

"All right." He adjusted his ball cap. "Go out there and relax. Don't go so hard you hurt yourself."

I nodded again, leaping out of my seat as soon as the right fielder made the last out, before he'd even stopped his hopeless run to first. But Coach Thurston snagged my mitt hand, stopping me at the end of the dugout. "Austin, nobody could be happier about how you're pitching than I am." I thought of Abilene, but Coach shook my mitt, making me listen. "Great as it is, this no-hitter stuff doesn't mean a thing. If you're hurting, you're through. I'll pull you as soon as I see it. No maybes about it."

I nodded once more, starting for the mound. He called after me, "I won't let you hurt yourself."

My shoulder clicked with each warm-up pitch. I could hear it; a raspy, grating kind of noise up close to my ear. But I struck out the first batter, their number-nine hitter. He swung blind at everything, no matter where it was. I wouldn't bet he had his eyes open. Only two more outs and I'd have a no-hitter in my first game. Even Nolan Ryan didn't have that.

But I'd walked their number one hitter twice already, and I walked him again. He just sat back and watched my fast ball whip past, chin high.

First pitch on the next guy I tried a curve. It stunned him, dropping in for a strike, but it made my shoulder scream. I decided to stick with the fastball, aiming at the front edge of the plate, thinking the rise would bring it in knee-high.

But it didn't do that. Instead it stayed low, right where I aimed. Bounced off the front edge of the plate, ricocheting over

Martinez's head. The guy on first took second standing up. Wild pitch.

The crowd groaned, and I thought it was just because they were with me. Only two more outs. The game was over anyway—we were up nine–zip. The guy on second didn't mean squat.

But the crowd wasn't groaning at my wild pitch. I took the rubber and stared down at Martinez, but he dropped to his knees and pointed toward our dugout, Coach trotting out to me. Martinez started toward us, but Coach waved him back.

"Shoulder, right?" First thing Coach said.

"What?"

"It's your shoulder. Feels like you got a load of gravel in it. Am I right?"

"I'm okay," I insisted, my voice rising wild on the *kay.*

"You're fifteen years old. You don't know okay from DOA."

"I'm okay, Coach."

He snapped his hand out, catching my shoulder in a quick squeezing pinch.

I tried not to wince, but even my knees started to go. Coach turned and waved toward Giles, warming up behind the dugout. The crowd booed a little.

"I'm sorry, Austin. But I can't let you destroy yourself over something as dumb as a high school no-hitter."

"It's not the no-hitter, Coach."

"You're shredding your rotator cuff for fun?"

"It's Abilene."

He stared at me, waiting for me to go on. "Abilene?" he asked then. "I wish we could bring her in in relief."

"She wouldn't pitch relief. Whole show's got to be hers."

The booing died out, and Giles stopped at the edge of the mound. I still held the ball and he didn't know what to do.

"Even Abilene can't save your arm if you wipe it out now," Coach started.

"No, it's not like that. You can't pull me out. She won't take it. It's against her rules."

Coach reached into my mitt, pulling the ball out though I squeezed hard. "Austin, you've just pulled off the best start I've ever seen at this high school, at any high school." He leaned in close, whispering low so Giles couldn't hear. "Don't let your sister ruin this for you."

"But Coach, Ab'lene . . ."

He gave me a swat on the rear, pushing me off the mound toward the dugout.

The crowd gave me an standing O as I ran for the dugout. I couldn't help glimpsing up, but Abilene wasn't in her seat. She was at the fence beside the dugout, her fingers clawed through the wire, her face crimson. She shouted, "Turn around, Austin! Get out there and finish it!"

Some men, fathers of my teammates probably, were rising up from their seats in back of Abilene, whispering to each other. Abilene pushed her face against the wire mesh. "Two more outs!" she screamed. "You finish it!"

I stood at the side of the dugout, bracing against the warm, purple cinder block. "I can't, Ab'lene," I said, every eye on me. "I'm done. I'm out of the game."

"You're not done till I say you're done!"

"Ab'lene," I whispered. "It's the rules."

"Not *our* rules!"

"Ab'lene, I'm on this team. It's not *our* game anymore."

"You finish every game!"

"That's only at the base, Ab'lene."

"*Only?*" she shrieked, shoving even farther forward, the wire pressing diamonds into her skin as she tried to push me back toward the mound with just her eyes. But she caught Coach Thurston coming in, and her lips curled into a half sneer, half snarl.

"You needle-dicked cocksucker!" she shouted. "You weren't fit to hand *me* a baseball, let alone take one away from *him*!"

Coach stood beside me, barely glancing at Abilene. "Come on, Austin. Let's get some ice on that shoulder." He put a hand on my back, saying, "Come on, Austin," again.

"Touch him and I'll kill you!" Abilene screamed, the men behind her moving in.

Coach kept his hand on my good shoulder, guiding me into the dugout, and Abilene sprang up the fence. She would've made it clean over if it weren't for the men grabbing her. I heard one say, "It's only a game," before Abilene whirled around, swinging punches.

Coach Thurston kept pushing me into the dugout, but I saw the man's nose blossom, the bright, bright blood. He staggered back, hiding his face in his hands. The other men smothered over Abilene.

"Ab'lene!" I shouted, but as soon as I tried backing out, Coach only shoved harder.

I fell into the dugout, dodging around the bat rack and scrambling to the far end and out the gate there. Outside the fence I tore into the group of men around Abilene, not swinging or hitting, just pawing them away so I could get to her.

Abilene stood alone in the center of their ring, blood smeared on her pitching hand, though I didn't know if it was hers or the man's she'd hit. Another man held his forearm, saying, "The crazy bitch bit me!"

Abilene's hair flew staticky, like some supercharged lethal voltage. Her shirt hung wide open, and I could picture the popping flight of buttons as she'd wrenched out of their grasp. Her bra, red this time, was twisted around, Abilene nearly popping out one side of it. But even so, all I could see was the huge red and blue stain across the white, freckled skin of her chest.

The word *Fireballer* blazed out, falling out of her bra on one side, the pulled-down feathery edge hiding the *F,* then rising up the swell of her breast on the other, nearly nipple to nipple. Underlining it was a streak of comet, the red laces of a baseball barely visible in the fiery head. Fireballer.

I think that freakish tattoo, more than the biting or hitting, is what made the men step away from her. Abilene didn't make the slightest move to close her shirt, and I looked a second more at that word before stepping up and pulling her shirt closed. "Ab'lene," I whispered.

"The crazy bitch bit me," the man said again.

Peeking around Abilene's shoulder, I whispered, "Say that again and *I'll* bite you."

Abilene was still windmilling her head, trying to see where the next threat might come from. She had her fists up, like this was something she was used to.

"Ab'lene?" I said, keeping her shirt pinched shut and touching her shoulder, trying to get her to recognize that it was me, that it was over, that it was time to go.

She looked at me almost as if she knew me, and I said, "Ab'lene," again, and took a step forward. She followed.

Seeing her maybe under control, the men opened a gap for us. But one of them said, "Now wait just a minute."

From the dugout, Coach said, "Let them go," then, "Austin, you ice that shoulder. Come see me tomorrow."

I walked Abilene down the aisle behind our third-base dugout, behind home, and out the first-base side, heading toward where I knew her truck would be parked by the foul pole. All I could hear the whole way was her breathing, raspy and hoarse, and the skittery, hard scrape of my cleats against the concrete. I wished Giles would let loose a pitch, distract some attention.

The crowd parted for us like some Texan Red Sea, and just before we left the seats, somebody whispered, "Helluva game, kid."

Without looking up, Abilene said, "You don't know the first thing about what he can do."

I nodded a thanks at the man, though mostly I was thinking about Mom asking whether Abilene was violent. It wasn't till we reached Abilene's truck that I noticed it was nearly dark, dusk wrapping warm and close around us.

sixteen

I opened the door of Abilene's truck and she climbed into the passenger seat without saying a word about me driving. I wondered if I could somehow take her away long enough for this to blow over. But it sounded as safe and nice as one of Dad's old bedtime stories. Just as possible.

Leaving the baseball field behind, I flashed past the cemetery, getting out of town as fast as I could. My cleats kept slipping off the gas pedal, and I glanced down at my shoe, almost surprised to find myself in my uniform. Across the cab Abilene sat like part of the truck, pinched against the door and twisted toward the window. Her fists were still clenched tight, and now and then she'd pound one against her thigh. "Son of a bitch!" she blurted once. "A no-hitter. This close!" She smacked both fists against her thighs. "This close!"

At the salt flats I turned off the road, and for a long time I just blew along, going anywhere, chewing my lip as the rough patches of the flats tore at my shoulder. We drove that way for most of an hour, me just circling the flats, giving myself time to think, Abilene time to cool.

Finally Abilene shouted, "Ha!" slapping both hands against the dash. She flipped the radio on, dashing up the volume so loud it hurt. Though the game was long over, she spun the dial to KIUN, and it was only a minute before they went through the scores. We'd won nine to two. Abilene snapped the radio back off as soon as she heard.

"You're one and o," she blurted. "Undefeated!"

I glanced at her, but she was gazing straight ahead, her lips moving as she figured. "ERA one point four two."

I got a shiver, feeling maybe she'd just compiled my lifetime stats. "Undefeated," I whispered.

"Forget wherever you think you're going here, Austin. Let's head home. Share the news with Mom and Dad. They are going to be so proud." She was all out of place on that side of the cab. "And can't forget Coach's orders. We have to get that shoulder iced."

"I'm okay," I told her, but she waved her hands forward, saying, "Go, go," and I circled away from the long string of lights that was Pecos, and when we reached the road, I turned for home.

The house was dark when we pulled in, and even before we'd quite stopped, Abilene snorted, "Unbelievable. Your first start and they don't even wait up for you, let alone come to the game."

I was surprised too, and though, with Abilene the way she was, the dark house was a relief, it was disappointing, until I remembered I'd lied to Mom, told her I wouldn't play.

Abilene shoved open her door, flooding us with the cab light. Before she could hop down, I whispered, "Ab'lene?" and pointed at her shirt, her bare chest, that tattoo.

She hesitated, and I hunched over, pulling up the knees of

my uniform pants and slipping out the safety pins holding up my socks. "They kept falling down," I explained, holding the pins out to her.

But Abilene didn't take them. Glancing down at her chest, she just smiled. "Fireballers." Then, still not moving, she said, "You mowed them down, didn't you. The poor little bastards."

I shrugged. "I wanted to see if I could do it against a batter."

"They're not batters till they hit the ball, Austin. Those kids were nothing but victims."

"Your tire made it seem pretty simple."

Abilene kept smiling. "I knew it would." Then she stepped out, starting for the house.

I scrambled after her, my cleats twisting on Dad's white rock, my socks drooping around my ankles. Above us the stars scalded the sky, stars everywhere, drowning even the constellations.

"What's your ERA?" she asked as we reached the porch, my cleats scraping the wood.

"One point four two. Unless my runner got picked off or something. Then it'd be zero."

Abilene laughed. "That's right!" she said, clapping me on the shoulder, nearly dropping me in my tracks. "You're undefeated. Retiring at the peak of your powers, like only the very best of them. A class act. Not fading away, but out in a blaze of glory."

Then she flung open the door, my career wrapped up tight.

Before I was even inside, Abilene had the freezer wide open, hauling out ice trays, making way too much noise. She pulled the towel from the door handle and cracked the cubes into it, folding the cloth up around the ice. "We'll have you right as rain in no time." She spun a chair out from under the table and waved me into it. Tying the ice to my shoulder with another towel she yanked from the stove door, she said, "We'll get you back out to the base, into rehab. No more new coaches for you, ruining your arm, pulling you out of no-hitters."

She never quit talking, and the whole time, with her hands

busy, her shirt flopped open. The scratchy lace of her bra brushed against my cheek once as she worked, before I could turn my face away.

"Just act one. When we come back, they won't believe their eyes. You are going to blow them away. You'll have hitless *seasons*! They'll never see joy in Mudville again!"

She went on and on. I rattled my cleats against the floor, the ice already soaking through my uniform. I couldn't listen to her anymore.

It was a moment before I realized she'd stopped talking. I glanced up, Abilene standing only a foot or so away, right in front of me, staring down at me.

She blew out a big breath, like she was barely holding off laughing. "Hey, Austin, did you really see this?"

She knelt down so we were eye to eye and held her shirt open wide to her sides, like wings.

She giggled. "You've got to check it out!"

Abilene tossed her head back to get her hair out of her way while she worked at some kind of clasp hidden in the middle of her bra.

"Ab'lene," I whispered, wanting to look away, wondering if something in her had snapped deeper than ever. "Don't."

In the bright kitchen light the red and blue letters staining her skin were brilliant, almost glowing, the skin still red and puffy around them. But the startling rise of her breasts, barely held into the lacy bra, then suddenly tumbled free as Abilene opened the clasp, made it impossible for me to read anything.

Abilene was still laughing that way, hardly making a sound. Her fingers trembled. "Can you believe it?"

She cupped her breasts in her hands, pulling them to the sides, just something to get out of her way. "Can you believe it?" she said again, breathless.

Bared now of even the slimmest band of lace, the word blazed from her chest. Dropping her right breast, she reached out and shook my iced shoulder. "Can you?"

I looked up, the light glinting in her wide, wild eyes, her smile sparkling twice as bright. "I saw it in the truck, Ab'lene," I whispered. "At the game."

Her eyes squinted a second, puzzled, then her smile flashed back. "Fireballer!" she said, almost a shout.

"Fireballer," I repeated.

"You got that! You and me!"

"Is it real, Ab'lene?" I asked with a faint flare of hope.

Abilene blurted out a laugh. "Of course it's real, Austin! It's you and me! The Fireballers!"

"Where'd you get it? What happened?"

"I did it for your start, Austin! To commemorate the day!" She tagged my good shoulder with a punch and hooked her bra back together, laughing. "It's great, isn't it?"

"Ab'lene, you—"

"Tell me it's great, Austin," she said, her voice suddenly less charged, more demanding.

"It is, Ab'lene, but—"

"The greatest," she ordered.

I sat in my soggy uniform and raised my hands off my knees, then let them fall back down. "It's the greatest, Ab'lene."

Her grin split her face again. "The greatest!" she shouted.

"Shh, Ab'lene. You're going to wake up Mom and Dad."

"Mom and Dad," she said, snapping her fingers. "That's right. We haven't told them yet."

Abilene jumped up, tugging me out of my chair. She pulled on my good arm, getting me in front of her, pushing me toward the stairs.

"No, Ab'lene. We can't wake them up."

I slowed, but Abilene only pushed harder. "We shouldn't even *have* to wake them up. They never should have gone to bed. I'm going to have to give them a little talking to just about that. Your first start."

I grabbed the banister with my good arm. "Don't, Ab'lene."

"Go, go," she said, prying at my fingers, pushing at my back.

"I told them I wasn't playing, Ab'lene. That's why—"

"No time to be modest, Austin." She got my hand off the railing and pinned it to my side. She ran me up the stairs. "You're going to be the greatest that ever lived. You can't keep that under a bushel forever."

We didn't make it to Mom and Dad's room. By the time we reached the top of the stairs, they were standing there, both frowzy with sleep, blinking in the light. Dad had a white crust of dried toothpaste at the corner of his mouth. "What is it?" Mom asked.

"Your son!" Abilene cried. "He pitched like lightning. Not a single hit!"

I stood in front of Abilene, trying to block their view of her.

"And you two sleep through it all. You're going to have to wake up before your whole life ends up with you still in the rack."

"I thought you weren't playing," Dad said.

"Can't believe everything shy boy says." Abilene tossed an arm around my neck, giving me a shake.

They could see her now, her shirt hanging open, her tattoo.

"Abilene," Mom gasped. "What have you done to yourself?"

"It's game day, Mom! Somebody had to do *something*. The two of you slept through his whole high school career. How are you going to forgive yourselves that?" Abilene laughed. "Or weren't you sleeping? Did we interrupt something? The two of you reliving those nights on the road?"

Her arm still around my neck, Abilene twisted me away from Mom and Dad, making a show of tiptoeing back down the stairs. "Don't mind us," she whispered loudly. "You two just go back to what it was that you were doing."

"Abilene," Dad shouted.

"We weren't even here," Abilene said, stifling a giggle. "Never saw a thing."

She was laughing out loud by the time we reached the bottom of the steps. She let me go and clapped me on the back. "Good one, Austin. Good one."

Mom and Dad were coming down the stairs behind us, but before they got to the bottom Abilene was gone. We heard the slap of the screen and the roar of her truck.

I turned to Mom and Dad, the three of us standing close at the base of the stairs.

"What on earth?" Dad said.

I shook my head. "She came to the game."

I looked down the hallway, toward the glow of the kitchen light and felt Mom's hand touch my back, but it was Dad who asked, "What happened to your shoulder?"

"I'm undefeated."

seventeen

I made it through almost the whole next day at school before Coach Thurston hijacked me, signaling without a word for me to follow him to his office. As soon as he closed the door, before he could launch into whatever speech he'd prepared, I blurted, "You were right, Coach. I thrashed my shoulder. For a stupid no-hitter I didn't get anyway. Just like you said."

He blinked, the office quiet around us. Then, as if I hadn't said a word, he sat down on the corner of his desk and started in on how we'd take care of my arm, what different exercises we'd try, and how careful we'd watch it in the future.

I nodded, but when he stopped, I whispered, "I'm going to work on it at home."

He looked at me, watched me watching the floor, holding my right arm up with my left. "You want to do this on your own?"

I shrugged, studying the tile squares, the almost matched intersections of the corners.

"Is your sister going to help?"

"No. She's pretty much through with baseball, I'd guess."

"You too?"

I shook my head. "I'll be back." I said, hoping it was true. "When I get my arm feeling right."

"And you won't let me help with it?"

"I have to do this myself."

"You're still part of the team though. I can use you at practice with some of the other pitchers. If you could teach them half what——"

I shook my head, remembering Abilene wrapping up my high school career. "I don't think I can."

He looked at me. "I'll expect you at the games. At least."

I shook my head again. "I don't know. We'll see."

I thought he'd keep working on me, but instead he asked, "Does Abilene still live with your family?"

"Of course," I answered, caught off guard. "She is my family."

"Just you and her? The only kids?"

"Just me and her."

"How old is she now?"

"How old?" He kept looking at me until I said, "I don't know. Twenty, I guess. Twenty-one."

"And she still lives with you? Still helps with your pitching?"

He said it like it was something hard to believe, and I couldn't help staring back at him. "So?"

He shrugged, and I said, "Ab'lene's not like other people. You don't know a thing about her."

He held up his hands. "I don't know much about anything. But there aren't a lot of teachers here who have forgotten Abilene.

"That year she decided she was going to play ball, she stormed in here shouting, 'Here's your ticket to another championship!' I remember leaning to look around her, to see who she had with her. I'd have been plenty happy to have another championship.

"I still remember how she looked at me then. Her excitement faded away as if she'd just found herself standing in front of the most disappointing turd humanity ever let fall."

Coach wiped the edge of his desk carefully, pinching the edge between his thumb and forefinger. "Most everybody's got something, Austin—one thing they've blown royally. That they'd give anything to redo. But this place just wasn't ready for her yet. Hell, it still isn't. And though I would love another championship, I'd trade it in a second for another chance with Abilene. I'd play her no matter what anybody said."

He looked at me. "You know, every practice she'd stand behind the dugout and pitch into the net. All by herself. Full speed every pitch. Nobody saying a word to her, nobody even acknowledging that she was there. I sat in the dugout watching the other kids, listening to her grunt with each delivery."

I looked at the floor.

"At the end of the last game that year, she tossed me the ball she always held in the dugout and told me, 'This is the season you'll remember. When you're plugged into your respirator, your kids huddled around you, waiting, this is what you'll be thinking about. Me.' "

Coach shrugged. "I've still got that ball." He pulled open a drawer and showed me a dirty old baseball. "That kind of determination, I thought she'd be something big by now. I thought we'd be reading about her in the papers."

I kept looking at the floor.

"Well, never mind. The only thing I know for certain now, Austin, is that you came out of the blue pitching like no sophomore I've ever seen."

"Ab'lene can still pitch rings around me. The last time we played she beat me forty-three to one." Before I could stop myself, I blurted one of her best old lines: "Nolan Ryan retired just so he wouldn't have to face her!"

Coach shifted on the edge of his desk. "Yeah, I think I read about that. In *Sports Illustrated* maybe."

I turned away fast, looking around his office, which suddenly seemed nothing more than a locker room, sweaty and socky. "I got to go."

"Austin!" Then he said it again, quieter, so I turned to look at him. He eased off his desk, still smiling. "I'm just trying to understand. The sister who went to school here, the sister teaching you to pitch, the sister at the game—they're all the same person?"

I shook my head, swallowing, wondering if my voice would work when I tried to talk. "You want to know about Ab'lene? About me and Ab'lene?" I waved my arms around his office the way Dad used to in our living room. "You want to know how all this started?" I waved my arms wider, even my hurt one. My voice cracked so high I had to swallow again, and when I saw how Coach looked at me, I squeaked out, "Well, I can't tell you. I don't have one single idea."

I was out the door, dashing down the hallway, before he had a chance to laugh or call me back, whichever he would have done.

Without practice holding me late, I ran straight for the bus, but the line took forever to straighten itself and file on board, and I fidgeted at the back, timing my breathing to the tiny heartbeat pulsing in my shoulder. I was in my seat, leaning my head against the window, the bus grinding up to speed, before I realized we were driving right past where Abilene's truck would have been parked.

I was positive we wouldn't see her for weeks, months, and I wished I could make her appear right now, catch a glimpse of her holding the steering wheel as if she were driving someplace important, when she wasn't doing a thing but waiting for me.

A ball of paper shot by my head, aimed at someone else. Everyone was talking, shouting. Stupid stuff.

I remembered her whooshing past me the day I made the team, like she'd watched my every move, but then suddenly didn't want to see me anymore. Maybe she'd waited under the water tower for me every day of practice, even when we thought she was gone, waiting in case something happened, in case it didn't work out, in case I needed her for a ride, for anything.

But suddenly a whole new picture of Abilene's world took shape, and the roar of the bus faded the way the crowd noise had when I pitched. I lowered my head into my hand, scratching beneath the sweatband of my ball cap. Instead of waiting because I might need her, maybe Abilene parked there day after day just because she needed me, as alone as I'd been when she was off at college. Maybe without me she didn't have anything left; nothing but hanging around the house with Mom; driving out to the bomber base and back; driving out to that bridge and dangling over the edge, thinking of flying.

I held my head in both hands, my cap pushed up so high it fell off as soon as the bus bumped onto the gravel road. I shut my eyes, keeping my head so low I got that dizzy bridge feeling. This new world of Abilene's seemed so empty and dull without me, I couldn't help smiling.

eighteen

At the end of the long walk home from the bus drop, I found a new car in the drive where Abilene's truck should have been. It was low and sleek, its hard-waxed finish slipcovered with road dust. At first all I could think was that Abilene had returned with a wild upgrade, and I couldn't help wondering who she'd be now. It was kind of a shock too realizing how much I'd miss her truck. But as I climbed the porch, I began to suspect who might have been called out here.

I stepped into the kitchen, into the wisps of a stranger's perfume, just barely there, but hugely out of place. Mom, I remembered, used to wear a perfume like that, years and years ago. I touched the edge of the kitchen table, listening to a clinking from the living room, ice against glass.

The couch springs creaked and I knew they'd heard me, that Dad was twisting to catch me if I tried slipping by. "Here's Austin now," he said before I'd taken a step from the kitchen.

I shuffled to the living room and peered around the entrance. Dad was barely perched on the front edge of the couch, flattening it down, Mom beside him, smiling nervously.

The stranger, across the room, was nice enough looking really, neat and trim in khakis, a loose, silky shirt that looked cool in the spring heat. Holding her iced tea with both long-fingered hands, she smiled at me almost shyly.

"Well," Dad said, smoothing his pants over his thighs, then giving Mom's hand a pat. "Austin, this is—"

"Dr. Pape," I interrupted.

She nodded. "Nancy."

A silence stretched long enough it seemed you could see the shift in the perfumed air as we faced each other. "The famous Dr. Pape," I said.

"Austin," Mom started, "Nancy has—"

"You think you can cure us?" I asked, staring at the doctor. "You think you can go back in time? Change how all this started?"

"Austin," Mom warned.

"I'd just like to talk to you, Austin," the doctor said. "Just talk."

I glanced at Mom and Dad. "This was your idea? This total stranger? You think Ab'lene would talk to her? About things she won't talk about even to me?"

Dad stopped smoothing his pants. His hands just hung useless by his knees.

"Coming here was my idea," Dr. Pape said. "Ordinarily I would never come to a patient's home, but I think that now, for Abilene, we have to do extraordinary things."

"Nancy's already helped a great deal," Mom said. "They've made great progress."

I thought of Abilene like a magnet, the wild dancing of all our compasses. "Brilliant."

"*Does* she talk to you, Austin?" the doctor asked.

"She doesn't talk to anybody. Ever."

"What about when you pitch?"

"We throw fire. Faster than Nolan Ryan. Faster than words."

The doctor watched me a moment. "I'm not the enemy, Austin. There isn't an enemy. Abilene has a disease. It's called manic-depressive illness. Bipolar disorder."

"Ab'lene told me all about your diagnosis."

"So she has talked to you. Was it between innings?"

I stared at her.

"It's a disease, Austin. Like diabetes. Only, instead of blood sugar, this disease affects behavior, the mind. It's nothing to hide from or be embarrassed about. It's not something Abilene chose. It's not something any of you *caused*. It's not anybody's *fault*. It's a disease."

"There's nothing wrong with Ab'lene."

"No, not wrong, Austin," the doctor said, her voice soft. "But there is a chemical imbalance. Abilene needs medication, lithium. She needs therapy." Dr. Pape glanced around the room at Mom and Dad and me. "She needs all of you."

"She needs you to leave her alone," I said.

I could see the doctor take a breath. "If she had diabetes, you'd want her to get insulin, wouldn't you?"

"There's nothing wrong with her!" I insisted. Starting to shake, I took a step backward. "I mean, just look at this place."

"What do you mean?"

"I mean just look at this place. A patch of cat's-claw and creosote, some trucked-in rock. Our closest neighbor is an abandoned bomber base! Who wouldn't go nuts here?"

"Abilene is sick, honey," Mom said.

I shot her a glance. "I wish I was that sick."

"No, you don't," Dad said, lifting his head to look at me. He pushed himself up and walked to the window, turning his back on us. Clearing his throat, he added, "That's not true."

I watched him peer out at the desert surrounding our house, as if Abilene were simply late, would reappear at any moment to make his world whole again. And watching him gaze out at all that blank emptiness, I thought for a second, without wanting to, how much easier things might be if she didn't come back at all; how we wouldn't have doctors deciding they had to join us out here, how I wouldn't have had to sit in Coach's office telling him I couldn't be on his team anymore.

"I know you're trying to help," Dad said without turning back to any of us. "Don't think we haven't recognized that. But—"

"I haven't been *trying* anything," I blurted. "Me and Abilene just do what we do."

Dad stepped around toward me. "—But we're trying to help too."

"You know what you could start with?" I said, my voice a raspy croak.

Dad looked up, hopeful.

"Don't ever tell that story again. About the names. How All This Started."

Actually, Dad hadn't told that story in a long, long time, and he looked startled.

"What do you mean, Austin?" the doctor asked.

I couldn't keep from shaking my head, rolling my eyes the way Abilene would have. I pictured Dad waving his arms at his whole life since that night in Abilene, waving away everything before that, like we'd made it less than nothing. But I remembered how they both used to smile at that story, still amazed at their wild luck, their great good life together, and finally I saw that that's really what the story was about—their lives *before* all this started—*when we were young, newlyweds.* I wished I'd never heard a word about it; that I didn't have any way to guess how happy they'd been before me and Abilene.

"Go ahead, Dad. I can't believe you haven't enlightened her already."

"What, Austin?" Dr. Pape asked. "Why don't you want him to tell that story anymore?"

"If you knew what it was about, you wouldn't—"

"I do know. Your father told me. I think it's beautiful."

I gaped. "Beautiful? *Beautiful?* It's pathetic! Don't you get even that much? With all the talking you and Abilene have done? You and Mom and Dad?"

"Why pathetic?" Dr. Pape said quietly.

"Why?" I blurted. "Take a look around! How *what* all started? This is it. The two of them and their happy, little lives shriveled up and vanished for a goddamned patch of empty desert! A lunatic daughter! Me!"

Then, before Mom or Dad could fight back, before I could go on, Dr. Pape said, "I heard about your game yesterday, Austin."

I stepped back. "How?"

She shrugged slightly. "And Abilene's gone now?"

I couldn't help nodding.

"This isn't just her problem, Austin. It's yours too. You see that, don't you? It's all of yours."

"But it's not yours," I stammered, still stepping away.

"Listen," she said, firm now. "What you saw at the ball game was Abilene in her manic phase. She needs lithium to control that. And the manic phase is followed by the depressive. Always. She's in real danger, Austin. We need to find her, we need to get her on medication. We need—"

"You need to leave her alone!" I shouted.

Everyone stopped, their eyes on me.

"That's not right, Austin," the doctor continued, her soft voice relentless. "She needs medication."

I shook my head.

"Think, Austin. Think about all she's done. How she's acted. Do you think, if she had a choice, that that's how she would want to be? That she'd want to treat you that way?"

"'That way'?" I shouted. "Ab'lene's spent her whole life with me. Training me." I pointed a shaking finger at Mom and Dad, pinning them to the couch. "Ask them what they've done."

The doctor just looked at me.

"Go ahead," I shouted, still pointing at Dad. "Ask him. You know when we played our first game of *catch?* Last fall, that's when."

Dad looked at me as if I'd put a knife into him, and I backed away until I bumped into the banister. "Ab'lene and I take care of each other. Leave us alone and we'll be fine."

I spun around the banister, leaping up the stairs and slamming into Abilene's room. I threw myself onto her bed, unable to shake that one second I'd thought how much easier it would be without her: how my arm wouldn't have failed, how I wouldn't have had to walk her out of the crowd that way, how I'd be starting another game next week, and the week after, and the week after. How I wouldn't have had to show Dad what an empty failure his whole dream life had ended up as.

I ground my knuckles against my forehead, swearing I didn't mean it. "Nothing without you," I whispered. "None of it."

nineteen

Almost an hour later Mom and Dad finally walked the doctor out to her car, thanking her. I sat up and looked out Abilene's window, the two of them standing so close they almost touched as the doctor drove away.

The dust trail behind the doctor's car was still hanging in the air when Mom and Dad came up the stairs. They paused at the top, and I heard them talking quietly. Then, when they must have turned for my room, seen my open door, Mom cried, "He's gone!" I couldn't help smiling.

But Dad answered, "I doubt that," and I heard him take the one quick step to Abilene's door. "Austin?" he said, loud enough to make sure I heard, but not shouting, not mad. He tapped lightly on the wood.

"I'm in here."

I heard Mom's tiny step, her whispered, "Austin?"

"I'm here."

"Is the door locked?" Dad didn't try the knob.

"There's nothing wrong."

They stood there awhile, nobody saying anything. I looked out the window.

"Unlock the door, Austin," Dad said at last.

The desert was empty; the dust settled back down. No sign anyone had ever come here at all. "What, Dad?" I said to the window. "Why?"

"Open the door," he said again, still quiet, not demanding, but asking.

I put my hands on the window, ready to push it up, to crawl over the roof and drop down into the desert.

But suddenly I was just too tired and I turned and walked to the door. I gave the knob a twist, letting the door swing open a crack. I stepped back. "It wasn't locked."

Dad eased the door open the rest of the way. "Well." He glanced around Abilene's room as if it were someplace new to him. "Austin."

He stepped through the doorway and stopped, Mom moving in beside him.

I couldn't even look at them. "I think that went pretty well," I said without knowing why. My voice shook, and I didn't want to be this way, but I kept on. "I think she liked me."

Mom sighed. "Don't."

"Well, it must have been a relief for her, seeing there's nothing unique about Ab'lene."

"Austin," Dad said. "We came up here to let you know how wrong you are."

"That's great. Thanks. Always good to hear."

"Would you just listen?" Mom asked.

I looked away from both of them, toward the window it was now too late to use. "All ears."

"This life of ours is not something we are trapped into," Dad said. "You should never think that."

"Well, you trapped *us* into it."

Mom looked right at me. "The way you made yourself and Abilene sound like the biggest regrets of our lives." She shook her head. "Austin, nothing could be further from the truth."

"I can't even imagine how you got thinking that way," Dad started.

"Okay, listen. Here's how it goes. You two get born. You survive somehow until Roma Lee Agostinelli comes along. You get married. The big honeymoon, all those places you stopped for the night. Then you find the deal of your life here, this house in the middle of nowhere, where just the two of you can cozy up forever. So you settle in and spend the rest of your life watching everything fall apart." I glanced at both of them. "You're telling me that was the *plan?*"

"Nothing has fallen apart, Austin," Dad said.

"Don't you use mirrors?" I shouted. "Would you for once look at yourselves? You don't even have lives!"

Mom stared at me, her lips pressed white over whatever she wanted to answer. But she only said, "I can't do this, Clay. Not when he's like this." She turned to go.

"'Like this'? This is me, Mom. All part of the package deal. I'm not some broken piece you can just take back."

Mom spun around. "No, you are not! But I will not try to talk with you when you act this way. Abilene needs more help than we know how to give, and all you do is make everything worse. I am sick to death of your selfish, stubborn silliness. Playing *baseball*. The day you show me you know the first thing about helping, about giving and taking, is the day I will sit down and let you tell your father and me about our lives together."

Dad said, "Ruby," and Mom flashed toward him, as if he were next. But she only looked at him a second before turning and leaving the two of us alone.

Dad and I didn't look at each other. So softly it was hard to hear, he said, "This is the life we have, Austin. It's the life we wanted. It's the life we want. No one ever expects there won't be times that are harder than others."

"And that's what this is? Just a time harder than others? Abilene gone. Shrinks to the house. Me yelling at you. Mom yelling at me."

Dad nodded. "I wouldn't say it's the smoothest stretch."

"No, not exactly. I guess I wouldn't say that either."

Dad looked at me a long time. Finally he turned for the door, but he said, "Come here. I want to show you something."

"Where?"

"Downstairs. In the basement."

"Why?"

He stopped in the doorway. "As a favor to me. Your poor, failed old man. Would you do that much for me?"

"What is it?" I asked, but I took a step to follow.

He closed Abilene's door behind us. "Just some stuff. Just a few things I want to look at."

I followed him downstairs, through the kitchen, and then down into the basement, a place full of dusty, old junk. When we were little, it'd been our haunted house, but Abilene and I hadn't found a reason to come down here since.

Somehow Dad found the light's pull cord in the dark, and we stood a second blinking in the glare of the naked bulb. It dangled from its wire, throwing shadows.

"What?"

When he didn't answer, I asked, "You still keep your old mitt down here?" It was the only thing I could think to say.

"It's safe here. Out of the way."

"And your bat? You still have the famous big stick?"

"I've got all my things stored away down here."

"Is that what you wanted me to see?"

"I suppose so. May help give you a better idea of who the old man used to be."

I didn't say anything.

"Of who I still am."

He stepped to the unused tool bench and reached around its corner, picking his bat from against the wall. It was an old-fashioned Louisville slugger, the handle thin, the taper gradual the length of the bat, not all fat-barreled the way they make them now. The grip was heavily taped, more pine tar staining the shaft than I would have guessed, unless he just sat on the bench, working the pine-tar rag while the game went on without him.

With a little smile, he showed off his stance, waggling the bat tip, menacing looking even though he had to crouch below the pipes and joists. In his dead-eye squint you could just make out a trace of Abilene's game face. He looked, I'll admit, like he could give a bad pitch a long ride.

Suddenly he tossed the bat to me, handle first. I caught it, but set it aside without another glance.

"Right," Dad said. "You're a pitcher."

He turned back to the bench then, digging beneath it. He rolled out his old baseball, or another just like it, dried up beyond repair. Then some wood scraps clattered to the floor. It was a perfect place to get a black-widow bite.

Whatever he was looking for, though, wasn't under the bench, and he got up to dig through some drawers, then the cabinets above the old slop sink.

There he found a tin box, thick with dust even inside the cabinet. It was as if he thought somebody might someday search for traces of him, and maybe he'd just as soon keep it all secret. Setting the box on the tool bench, he swiped the dust away with his sleeve and pulled the lid open.

The box was full of old report cards, Abilene's and mine on top, then down deeper, his own, which surprised me—that he'd ever let his two lives mix. He flipped through them without letting me get more than a glance, finally finding what he really wanted me to see. He pulled out a stack of faded snapshots: a big kid in a clean baseball uniform, a skinny redheaded girl beside him, standing close, but not quite touching. We didn't have any pictures upstairs. Just a couple of me and Abilene when we were small.

"You and Mom," I said.

He nodded, flipping to the next picture. Him and Mom each with an arm around the other, standing beside an old-fashioned car, nothing but desert in the background. He looked at this one so long I finally asked, "Got any of Roma Lee?"

He laughed all of a sudden. "Roma Lee is probably sagging past her knees by now." He laughed again. "Don't you dare repeat that to your mother."

Even I laughed a little.

In another box he found a big blue knit letter *L,* a tiny silver baseball pin at its heart. He waved it at me once, saying, "And you never believed me," then dropped it back into the box, like there was something important he was really looking for.

What he didn't see, though, was that this was exactly what I meant, his whole life boxed up and shut away in a basement. "Okay, Dad. Thanks for showing me the pictures. I'm going to go now."

But Dad just searched faster, saying, "Wait a minute, there's a lot more." He scuttled around the basement, digging behind piles of old scrap wood, old buckets and rolls of carpet, anything that could hide something, anywhere something could have been dropped the day they moved in and not looked for or thought of since.

Some things surprised him, that he seemed to have forgotten all about for good. Finding another box, he just handed it back to me, not saying a word, not even facing me, but still digging through his past. I took it, the bottom half of a shoe box, and saw it was full of tarnished old shell casings, the big fifty-caliber machine-gun rounds you used to be able to find out by Pyote, fallen from target practice in the sky. I rattled the brassy pile, glancing back to him, but he was already into the root cellar, a room I barely remembered hiding in as a kid, then falling asleep inside, scaring everyone to death. The canning jars of the previous owners were still in there, empty except for the twenty-year-old layers of dust.

He groped over the top shelf, above eye level, though what he hoped to find up there beyond a scorpion sting I didn't know, until his hand bumped over something and his eyebrows scrunched together, wondering.

He stood on tiptoes, then lifted, bringing down a long, brown canvas case, the dust so thick on it his fingers left trails.

"I had completely forgot I had this." He tugged the zipper open, then slipped a gun halfway out. "My shotgun. I haven't shot this since I started dating your mother. She hated hunting."

"You used to hunt?"

"For a little while. In high school. We all did."

"What?"

"Doves mostly. Some rabbits."

He pulled the shotgun all the way out of the case, working its pump and looking down the barrel. "Well, good for me. It's not loaded." It was sticky with old grease, the room suddenly thick with its sharp metal tang.

"If we could sneak it past your mother, maybe the two of us could go out and see if it still works. Pot a few jackrabbits."

I took a step out of the root cellar. Dad glanced back for me, then hurried the gun back into its case, leaning it up against the wall outside the cellar.

"Completely forgot about that. I saved up for that gun for two years." He shook his head, glancing around the dingy basement. "Well, what else? Where to next?"

I hung on to the railing, my foot on the bottom step. I couldn't stand seeing one more thing he used to be. "I'm going, Dad." I was about to say *I'm sorry*, sorry for telling the truth about their lives, but I just looked at him looking at me.

He picked his bat up, but only dangled it from the tips of his fingers. "I don't even know what it was I was trying to make you see. Just that . . ." He set the bat tip on his shoe and shook his head. "I don't know. That we're happy here, Austin. That we always have been. We have everything we want."

But you don't have anything! I wanted to yell, but I'd done enough harm already. Instead I said, "Okay," and climbed away up the stairs.

twenty

The next morning I slipped out of the house before
Mom and Dad began to stir. Glad to be away from them, I just
wandered around, watching the world waver in its weak gray
light before the school bus, the blinding scorch of the day. When
I got back after school, Dad was already home, or still home. I
didn't know which.

He was on the phone when I walked in, saying, "Yes, she's
an adult. But she lives with us." Then, "No, we wouldn't be
bothering you otherwise." He couldn't help lowering his voice
when he said, "There's some history of instability. That's why
we're worried." He paused again, then asked, "Could I have her
doctor call you? Would that help?"

Dad hung up and looked to Mom. He shook his head. "Ap-
parently adults don't go missing. And not so soon either. But he
promised he'd do what he could. We'll call again. Tomorrow."

"Was it Tomlin?" Mom was leaning against the counter,

pulling open and pushing shut the hot-pad drawer behind her. "The same one I talked to?"

Dad nodded.

I just stood there by the door, learning what it felt like to be invisible. "You think anybody could actually find her? If she doesn't want to be found?"

They turned to me. They really hadn't known I was home.

"We're doing what we can," Dad said.

"Siccing the police on her?"

"Don't start, Austin." But then Mom shook her head. "They won't help us anyway."

"Say she robbed you," I said. "Say she stole something. Make her a criminal. They'll listen then."

"Honestly," Mom sighed.

"It'd work," I said, sliding by them and up the stairs.

Neither Mom or Dad mentioned my skipping out early that morning, so the next morning, when from the top of the stairs I heard them in the kitchen, Mom's voice going shrill, shouting, "We can't just do nothing!" and Dad answering, "But where would we look? Where would we go?" I turned around and slid out Abilene's window, easing into the desert again. I did the same thing the morning after that, and every morning from then on. Sometimes I'd go straight to the bus drop, hiding in the creosote until Dad drove past on his way to work. They thought I still stayed late after school for baseball practice, so I'd do the same thing then, keeping company with the lizards and snakes, the occasional jackrabbit, only darkness driving me home. Anything was better than getting trapped in the house with them, going through the numbers for the police, the sheriff, the doctor, watching Mom get more and more frantic, Dad more and more soothing. Mom even called all Abilene's old high school friends, sitting with the phone book, circling names she struggled to recall. None of them, of course, had seen Abilene in years.

After a couple of weeks, when it finally got through to Mom that we really couldn't do anything except wait, being home with her was worse. She'd jump every time Dad or I came in, running to see if we might be Abilene.

That's when I finally walked all the way out to the base, wound through the last of the mesquite hiding the sun-faded runway and the bullet-riddled tank. They looked exactly the same as ever. I didn't know what I expected to be different, but it seemed like something should have changed.

Then, just before stepping into the black insides of the tank, I noticed that something was different. I peered past the side of the tank, the rough steel, then glanced around the desert, as if I could have forgotten exactly where it had been, but it was no use. Our pitching mound was gone.

Not that there'd ever been much to it. Just that scraped together pile of gravel and dirt, the spiked-down plank. But it was all gone. The mound, I thought, walking toward its spot, could have washed away, but it had never rained. And the plank? The spikes? I knelt down and saw the scrapes left by the shovel point.

Squatted over that tiny spot of empty desert, I lifted my head, glancing out at the dusty mesquite and creosote, as if Abilene might be spying on me at this very moment. But nothing was out there but the heat waves shimmering up from the ground, the sky's endless blue, a dust haze feathering the horizons the color of bone.

I stood stiffly, starting for the tiny gully behind the power pole where we'd ditched the broken shovel we'd found to build the mound in the first place. I looked around for the plank too, all around as far as Abilene could have heaved it.

But the plank was lying in the gully next to the shovel. The shovel's old dirt was scraped clean in a few places, the edge of the blade shining. The mound must've grown pretty tough after being trampled down so long and hard.

I carried them both back to where the mound belonged and started to rebuild. Sweat poured out of me as I worked, drying to crusty white salts. When I finally had enough of the hardscrabble and caliche scraped together, I beat it down with the back of the shovel, taking swings that would've launched home run after home run, the cracked handle ringing in my hands.

Next I circled through the scrub for the spikes, the same way Abilene and I used to look for the bombers' fifty-caliber shell casings. The way I guess Dad had too. And then I had a quick flash of memory: being out here as a tiny kid, with Abilene *and* Dad. Hunting through the dirt, racing to find the next shell, racing to bring it back to Dad, his laughing, "That a boy!" It was so real and sudden that I stopped and looked around, expecting to see him standing there waiting. I could even picture the windbreaker he wore, a flimsy, tan cloth, with big pockets he slid the dirty casings into. Though I'd hardly been bigger than the creosote bushes, it had been a race, I think, between me and Abilene, to bring each shell to Dad.

And then, just as fast, it was gone. I didn't know if it was real or only something I cooked up after seeing Dad's box of shell casings. I stood a moment, trying to bring it back, but there was nothing left.

It took a lot longer to find the railroad spikes in the empty, pale dirt than I would've guessed. As far away as they'd been thrown, I figured Abilene had worked herself into some sort of a rage even before she'd attacked the mound. The spikes would've been the first things to go.

After nailing the plank down, beating on the heads of the spikes with the flat of the shovel, I stood in my spot, staring down the graying tire's strike zone. Then I realized that before

I'd done all this work I should have gone into the tank and checked for the baseballs. It wouldn't be like Abilene to leave a job half-finished, even if the job was tearing out the best part of my life.

So I shuffled off the mound, already feeling the defeat of the missing baseballs, but when I stepped into the darkness of the tank, I found the boxes even before my eyes had adjusted. Daring any scorpion, I slipped my hand beneath the cardboard lip of the first box and felt the cool, hard leather, the bump of the laces. Picking up the first ball, I curled my fingers around the seams.

I crossed the darkness of the tank, reaching down for my Nolan Ryan ball, finding it on my first try. Holding it up to the weak little ray of light streaming through a bullet hole, sparkly with dust, I read the inscription once for luck, for strength. "My partner on the Express." Then I lugged the box of baseballs out to the mound, squinting against the glare, searching the horizon a last time for Abilene.

I hadn't thrown a baseball in two weeks, since the last time we saw Abilene, the night of my game. Already wincing against the pain I was afraid might come, I took a breath and let loose my first ragged pitch.

I was out of practice, but my shoulder held up. I threw another ball, a total cream puff, but I couldn't help smiling.

I kept that up, tiny little throws, until only a single ball was left. With all the other balls scattered through the desert behind the tire, I went into a full windup and really threw the last one. Almost a fastball. It squeaked through the tire without touching rubber, and I gave a little jump on the mound, like I'd just made some critical strikeout.

Pounding my glove, I scurried through the dirt behind the old power pole, tossing the balls back toward the mound. The last one was the farthest, and as I stooped for it, I found Abilene's mitt.

As soon as I saw it in the rock and the baked, bleached dirt, I glanced back to the tank, to the mound. It was hard to believe anyone could throw a mitt that far.

I stooped down and picked it up, wondering what gave Abilene the power to do things like this. The leather was so dry it was almost white, and I carried it back to the tank as if it might crumble into dust and blow away.

Setting her mitt down beside the Nolan Ryan ball, I decided to come here every day. I'd take it slow, baby my arm. There was no rush, I told myself. Maybe I'd even talk to Coach about it, get some pointers. See if we could work something out for next season, letting me pitch now and then, but not practice every day, splitting my time with Abilene. Maybe that'd keep us both all right. It felt so good to pitch again, I almost let myself believe it could work out that way.

At school, Coach Thurston bumped into me now and then, always accidentally, though we'd never bumped into each other before. He'd ask how my arm was and I'd lie, telling him that things were moving along, that it was feeling better, just not quite up to speed yet. At the base I was throwing bullets.

Toward the end of the season, after the usual question about the arm, he asked, "Everything's fine at home?"

"Sure."

"How's Abilene?"

"Fine."

He looked at me. "Why don't you come to practice this afternoon?" he said at last. "At least make the game this Friday. Last home game."

I looked down the hallway. It was almost empty, the next class starting. "I got to go, Coach."

He reached out and held my arm. "Why the vanishing act, Austin? You think you're the first kid I've had who's hurt his arm?"

"I just can't, Coach. All right?"

He didn't let go of my arm. "Abilene?"

The hallway was completely empty, quiet and waxy smelling. I nodded. "I can't let her see me there, Coach. Not now."

"Why? Is she working with you on your arm? Does she think I'd hurt it? Hurt you?"

I chewed my lip. "Coach, I'm late. I got to go."

"Come to practice. Stay a part of this team. Hell, tell Abilene she's welcome too."

I couldn't keep in a snort. "That'd be a first wouldn't it, Coach?"

He let go of my arm and looked at me. "Abilene stayed on that team the whole season. She didn't quit."

"I'm not quitting, Coach. You just don't know what you're talking about."

"Well, explain it to me. That's why I'm here."

"Ab'lene's gone!" I blurted. "All right? We haven't seen her since the night I played. We don't have any idea where she is, but she could be anywhere." I shifted my books and started down the hallway away from him, walking backward, not hiding. "She could be watching that field just to see if I'm playing, if I've forgotten her already just so I could play high school baseball, chase a few cheerleaders."

That Friday Dad was waiting in front of the school, standing around by the bus lines. He couldn't have looked more out of place if he was naked. I glanced around, walking up to him. "What are you doing here?"

He nodded toward his car, parked out by the left-field fence, and I followed him that way.

"Want to get some dinner?" he asked.

"It's three-thirty."

He shrugged and slipped into his car. I stood by the other door. He waved me in.

"Mr. Thurston called me," he said when I got in. "He said you hadn't been to a practice in two months. That you'd quit the team." Dad looked straight ahead, out at the ball field.

"I didn't quit. Just on the disabled list."

"He said tonight's the last game."

"So I've heard."

"I'd like to go. I haven't seen a game in a long time."

"Enjoy yourself."

"Well, let's get something to eat then. We've got some time to kill."

He put the car into gear and drove across the street to the DQ. "What do you want?" he asked.

While we waited for our burgers, Dad asked, "So, where have you been keeping yourself? If you haven't been practicing with the team?"

I shrugged. "I'm doing my own rehab on my arm."

"Where?"

I shrugged again. "Does it make any difference?"

He turned in his seat to look at me. "I just found out that you've been lying to us for two months. Yes, it makes a difference."

"I never said I was at practice. When would I have said it? When was the last time you said anything to me that wasn't about Abilene?"

The girl came to Dad's window with our order. He pinched the bags in his hand and told her to take the tray. Then he handed it all to me and backed out of our slot, driving across the street again, swinging in behind the seats at the field.

Taking the bags back from me, he opened his door and got out. He walked up into the stands, right behind home plate, right in front of the announcer's booth. He spread a napkin on the bleacher in front of him and laid out his burger, his fries, his shake. He did the same for mine.

I sat down next to him.

"Did I ever tell you how many times your mother and I did just this kind of thing?" He took a big bite of his burger and chewed, looking out at the empty field.

"Many times."

"I tried to get her to come tonight. But she doesn't like to be away from the house. In case she comes back. Or calls."

"I know."

We sat like that the rest of the afternoon. The teams filed in around six. Coach Thurston gave us a wave Dad returned. The game started at seven.

Dad asked about a few of our players. What they were like, what were their strengths, their weaknesses. I just answered, "I don't know."

"Come on, Austin, you must know something. They're your teammates."

"I played one game, Dad. *Part* of one game."

We didn't say much after that. We lost five to four.

At the last out, Dad clapped his hand down on my thigh as he stood up. "Thanks."

We trickled out with the rest of the crowd. Made the long drive home.

Mom had been waiting for us in the kitchen, just sitting at the empty table, doing nothing, but now she jumped up, ready for something. I don't know what. Maybe more of the family fun Dad and I had had. She smiled at me and, her voice just barely quaking, she asked, "How was the game?"

"We lost," I said, and stepping around her, I headed upstairs.

Even after school ended that spring, I kept going out to the base, pitching every morning, then, often as not, staying out at the tank all day, pitching again in the evening. Working just a little harder every day, even taking a rest day now and then, I began pitching whole games, calling strikes and hits the way Abilene would have. Bearing down. I never felt that rolling twinge in my shoulder again, and by midsummer I was once again the strikeout king of Pyote's Rattlesnake Bomber Base.

But that whole time we never heard a word from Abilene, and sometimes, walking out across the first little strip of desert beside our house, the air not burning yet, the horizon only paled by the coming sun, I'd go almost hollow, my legs weak and jittery, thinking that this was all that was left, Abilene gone for good.

At home we all went through the motions, Dad leaving for work every morning, coming back every evening, Mom cooking dinner, waiting for him. I'd slip in at dark, pulling out whatever Mom had left over for me in the refrigerator, eating in my room, until the night Dad pulled me aside, my plate in my hand, and steered me back to the kitchen. He pointed to a chair and said, "Sit. Sit and eat."

He watched me sit down. I put my fork and knife beside my plate.

"Dinner," he said. "We'd like you to come home for dinner. We'd like to see you again."

"I'm pitching, Dad. Every evening. It's not quite so hot then."

He shook his head. "You'll be here for dinner. From now on." He looked at me. "Don't you think this is hard enough on her already? Without you disappearing too?"

So we had dinner together again, a quiet half hour of clinking silverware and shifting chairs. I didn't know if they even talked to each other anymore. Some nights, up in my room, I'd listen for them, but all I could hear was the shushing babble of the TV. Then, later, I'd hear their slow steps coming upstairs, the usual settling-for-the-night sounds. Then nothing.

twenty-one

It was in the middle of yet another of those silent dinners, four months now since Abilene had left, that the phone rang. Its sudden jangle was huge in the quiet, stopping the scrape of our forks. It wasn't a complete rarity, usually somebody selling something, but we all froze, Dad with his water glass halfway to his mouth. Not even Mom made a move until the second ring. Then she pushed back her chair, though it used to be Dad who dealt with the dinnertime telemarketers, giving them the chance to identify themselves before wordlessly hanging up.

Mom said, "Yes?" not hello. Like she already knew.

She said, "Yes," again. Then again. "Yes, she is."

She waved to Dad for paper, but I jumped first, finding an opened envelope and a tiny stub of pencil in the junk drawer.

Mom sat again, pinning the phone to her shoulder while she jotted down notes. Her hand shook, her writing like an old woman's. She asked, "What?" then, "What procedure?"

Finally, twining her fingers through her hair, biting at her lip, she whispered, "But she's all right?"

"'Stabilized,'" she repeated, like it was something so completely out of reach it wasn't even meant to be believed. "Do you know about her illness?"

There was a long pause.

"Yes. Manic depression." Mom whispered so softly I could barely hear, standing right beside her. "No. She never would take it. Lithium." She gave them Dr. Pape's name.

Mom ended by saying "Thank you" a couple of times, then lowering the phone to her lap.

"She's in a hospital." Mom lifted her face to us. "In Oklahoma." She glanced back down at the phone in her lap. "Chickasha, Oklahoma," she said, as if it was only the place that was remarkable or sad.

"She tried to kill herself," Mom said, thumping the phone against her legs. "Abilene tried to kill herself."

Dad slipped out of his chair, kneeling beside Mom. He held down the phone, keeping her from hitting herself.

"Our Abilene," she said again. "She tried—"

The phone started its off-the-hook wail and I slammed at the hook, then just stood there, hanging on.

Dad worked the phone out of Mom's hand and eased it onto the floor. I reeled it in by the stretch-damaged cord.

"What happened, Ruby?" Dad asked at last.

Mom shook her head, kept shaking it. "She went to the hospital for a procedure. They wouldn't tell me what. She came back with an infection. They checked her in, and that night . . . Her . . . She . . ." Mom sawed weakly at the inside of her wrist with the edge of her hand. "Her wrists," she whispered.

"In the hospital?" Dad asked.

Mom whipped toward him, face-to-face. "Don't you dare say she wasn't serious," she hissed. "That it was only a call for help. Don't you dare!"

Dad didn't even blink. Just wrapped his arms around Mom, chair and all. He lowered his forehead to her shoulder.

"It'll be all right, Ruby," he whispered. "It'll be all right. We'll go get her now. We'll bring her back. We'll take care of her."

I slid out of the room. It didn't seem like something I should see. It wasn't something I ever wanted to see.

"And leave Austin?" I heard Mom, her voice like a slap. "Leave him here alone?"

"He can——"

"*I'm* going to get Abilene." I heard the scrape of Mom's chair, Dad's quick steps to get up, get out of her way. "*I'll* bring her back. *I'll* take care of her."

"Ruby . . ."

"What do you want?" she yelled. "To get her her job back at Gibson's?"

Dad went quiet. The screen banged.

"Do you even know where Chickasha is?" Dad called.

"We spent a night there!" Mom shrieked from the driveway. "When we were young! Newlyweds!"

I was only halfway up the stairs, but I leapt up the last steps, not wanting to see Dad's face after Mom had thrown that broken scrap of How All This Started into it.

twenty-two

Dad came for me as soon as Mom was gone, catching me at the top of the stairs, not knowing where I should go, what I should be doing.

"Austin?" he whispered.

I looked over my shoulder. "Hey, Dad."

He nodded his head, as if we were nothing but old friends who hadn't bumped into each other in a while. "Mom's gone to help Abilene."

"I know. I heard." Then, because he looked so stranded there on the steps below me, I said, "You only forgot because there wasn't a kid that time."

He stared. "What?"

"Chickasha. Your night there. You'd have remembered if you'd had a kid. One named Chickasha."

He smiled a little.

"Chickasha. Would that be a boy or a girl?"

Dad let his shoulders sag. "No telling. You can't know a thing until they're born."

"I suppose."

Dad reached up with one of his giant hands, rubbing it back and forth over his entire face. "I wonder if you'd like to play some catch? If you'd like to work on your pitching?"

"Now?" I asked, staring. "Now?"

Dad shrugged. "Yes."

I glanced down the hallway to her door. "She couldn't have really tried, Dad."

"What?"

"Ab'lene. If she had, there'd be nothing that could've stopped her." I thought of her flying off her overpass. "If she'd really tried, there'd be nothing left."

Dad shrugged, nodding at the same time. "Grab your mitt," he said, turning and starting down the stairs.

But when we reached the kitchen, something seemed to leak away from Dad. He stopped, setting his hands flat on the table, holding himself up. He didn't say a word or move.

I watched for a minute. Then another. "You want me to go down and get your mitt?" I asked at last.

Dad straightened. "Wherever we were, your mother and I used to try to take in a game." He took a breath. "Majors. Minors. High school. Even softball. It didn't matter to us.

"We saw them all. All over. Wichita Wranglers. San Antonio Missions. El Paso. Abilene. Austin." He paused a moment before adding, "The Chickasha Fighting Chicks."

He looked back up at me. "You know all that already, though, don't you?"

"I know." When he still just stood there, I asked, "You want me to get your mitt? It'll be dark soon. Too dark to see."

Dad gave one small nod and I raced down to the basement. The ball was tucked into the pocket of his mitt, that ready to go. I leapt back up, but Dad was still just standing at the table.

"Dad?"

He was looking out the window, probably seeing Abilene bloodied in some hospital, Mom screeching alone down the highways to her rescue, while we got ready to play a game of catch.

"Dad, it's almost too late. If we don't go now, it'll be bedtime."

Still gazing out the window, Dad smiled a little. "Do you know I used to carry you up to bed at night? When you were babies. Your mother and I used to fight over whose turn it was. Rock you and sing you songs. Do you remember 'We Went to the Animal Fair'?"

I shook my head.

"'The birds and the beasts were there.'" Dad smiled. "Of course not. That was forever ago."

"Dad . . ."

"I used to do the same for Abilene too. Get up with her if she was sick. Or just scared. Bad dreams. Rock her and hold her. She never was the sleeper you were." He cradled his arms together and turned away from me. "I used to sing her 'Take Me Out to the Ball Game.' I didn't know any kids' songs yet."

His voice got tighter as he went on, and still with his mitt and ball clapped under my arm, I stepped quietly out of the kitchen toward the stairs.

"Well, good night, Dad."

"Night. We can finish up down here tomorrow."

"All right," I whispered, and when I climbed the stairs, he stayed down there alone.

I don't know if Dad went to bed that night at all. I was asleep, I think, when the phone rang at three-thirty in the morning. Dad caught it on the first ring, and listening to the low rumble of his voice, I knew he was in the kitchen, not upstairs in his room. It made me feel bad for sleeping, and I crept out onto the stairs, where I could hear him talking to Mom, mostly just trying to calm her down, mostly just saying, "I'm glad she's all right, Ruby." "You do whatever we have to." "Don't worry about money." "I'll check the insurance." "Don't you worry about anything."

He ended with, "Just say the word, Ruby, and I'll be there beside you. Me and Austin." Then, "We love you."

Hearing the click of the phone hanging up, I slunk back to my room.

Dad didn't go into work the next day, and when we went out to play catch, he left the door open and stuck close to the porch, where he could hear if the phone rang.

But the phone calls always seemed to come in the middle of the night. Maybe that was Mom's lowest point, the dark blankness bringing the fear too close, and she'd need to hear Dad's voice. The ring would wake me, startled and small as a kid in the blackness of my room. Then I'd turn on my baseball-player lamp and lie still, straining to make words out of Dad's low murmurs, sometimes from his room, sometimes from downstairs, even at one or two in the morning.

He didn't go to work the next day either. Instead, over a breakfast he cooked himself, for the two of us, he told me about the night's call. About Dr. Pape going to Chickasha. About their decision to involuntarily commit Abilene to the hospital there. She was so low, he said, they couldn't yet risk moving her somewhere bigger, somewhere closer, even slammed down with all the antidepressants.

The drugs, though, Dad said, should even her out, give the lithium a chance to build up in her blood. It shouldn't be too long, he kept saying. "Not too long at all."

Dad stood suddenly and set his plate in the sink, still full of his scrambled eggs, his bacon and toast. "Mom is going to stay there with her. She's going to stay until she can bring her home."

"How long will that be?" I asked, my eggs like so much sawdust in my mouth.

"Not too long. Only a few weeks, we hope."

I set down my fork. I pictured Abilene strapped to a bed somewhere, every muscle in her body taut and straining as she whipped her head back and forth screaming to me for help. I wondered how long not too long could be.

"Finished?" Dad asked.

I nodded and he picked up my plate.

"Austin, I'm not going to be able to stay here with you. This whole thing is going to cost a fortune. I've got to go back to work."

"Okay."

"What will you do all day by yourself?"

"Pitch. Same as ever. It'll be no change for me." I stood up, dumping my silverware in the sink beside our plates. "I'm already late." I snagged my ball cap from its peg, the big gold *P* for Pecos on the front, the little eagle on the back.

"I was so proud," Dad said as I swung open the door. "When I heard you were actually playing. And your coach—"

I turned back. "Dad, if you got all that stuff down in the basement, the pictures, why don't we have any up here on the walls? Of you and Mom? Before us? Why didn't you ever bring some of it up here into the light of day?"

Dad fumbled to pick up a dishrag. He shrugged. "I don't know. None of it seemed very important. We had so much to look forward to with the two of you, I guess we didn't need any reminders helping us look back."

I couldn't help but notice how he said, "We *had* so much to look forward to." Not anymore.

I eased the screen shut between us and said, "Well, we'll see you."

He lifted his dishrag in a wave.

twenty-three

Dad worked every day that week, staying longer and longer every day. The next week, he only took Sunday off completely. And then he just spent the morning going through the finances, muttering about the thousand-dollar days in Chickasha. Finally slamming all the forms and papers back into their tin box, Dad pushed himself away from the table. "You'd think at that rate they'd at least be able to straighten her out enough to send her home!"

He ran his fingers through his thinning hair. "But that would be killing the golden goose, wouldn't it?"

Turning suddenly to me, he said, "Let's go out and throw some heat."

That, no matter how much he worked, how much sleep he missed talking to Mom, was the one thing he wouldn't allow us to skip. Every night, sometimes with dusk making it dangerous, we'd go out and throw to each other.

But now it was the middle of the day, probably 110 out there, the light so bright it hurt. Even so, the quick hurl and catch, hurl and catch, the blazing heat and our boiling sweat, was something we both fell into with relief.

We'd only just begun to really bear down when I heard something and stopped in midwindup.

Dad eased out of his crouch. "What?"

I held up a hand for silence, craning my head toward the desert. The sound disappeared for a second, then came back, a little louder, and I pictured Abilene's truck sinking into a dip, then surging back out, coming on, coming stronger.

"Dad," I said, but by then he'd heard it too.

We turned toward the road, the two of us standing sixty feet apart, watching and waiting.

Then I saw the car crawl the last leg of the road toward us, as if dreading the reunion. "It's Mom."

Dad blurted, "She never said a thing," like he had to let me know this wasn't something he was in on. He gave a small chuckle. "She must have saved it for a surprise."

Squinting against the flash of windshield, I said, "She's alone."
"What?"

"Abilene's not with her."

I stepped out of the way and Mom inched up the driveway and stopped. It took Dad a second before he could walk around to her door, open it for her, help her out, and wrap her in his arms.

Neither of them said a word, and I watched Mom caught in his big arms, her own arms limp at her sides, holding nothing. I wondered if they'd ever been apart this long—two full weeks—since that spring night Roma Lee had brought Mom out to the Lubbock ball field.

"We couldn't hold her any longer," Mom said, her voice flat, like a recording, like she'd been saying the same thing over and over, the whole long ride back from Oklahoma. "Legally we couldn't hold her. And Abilene wouldn't stay. And she wouldn't come back with me. She just walked out."

"Where to?" Dad said, patting Mom's head into his chest, stroking her hair.

Mom shrugged. "I have no idea. I chased her as long as I could, but she ran. She ran away from me."

Dad hugged Mom tighter. "We'll find her," he whispered.

Mom straightened in his arms. "Like last time? Your great plan? Wait until some hospital calls?"

Dad kept on holding her.

"Do you know why she was in the hospital, Clay?" Mom asked, her voice all spooky flat again. "The first time? Before she tried to kill herself? The procedure? What the infection was from?

"She'd had her tubes tied. She had herself sterilized, Clay. Abilene did that. She only just told me today. She said she searched through half the country before finding someone who would do it."

"But she's only twenty-one!" Dad said. "Who on earth would let her do that? Who would do that to her?"

"She's an adult," Mom said, like a recording, only repeating what some doctor had told her. "It was her choice."

Dad's jaw worked before he could gasp out, "But, why?"

"She said she had to be sure . . . ," Mom began, but her voice gave out and she had to start over. "She said she had to be sure she would never do to another human being what we'd done to her. What we'd *done* to her."

Dad's hands still petted Mom's back, but automatically now, not pressing near so tight. "What have we done to her?" he asked at last.

"Everything," Mom cried. "That's what she meant. Everything. Her whole life."

They stood together then, each holding the other up. Mom cried for a while, strangling, gulping noises, and Dad lowered his head to hers. I couldn't tell if he was crying, if some of those awful noises were his, and I was glad I couldn't see his face. I stood out on the white rocks alone, my baseball mitt hanging from the ends of my fingers.

"That's why she tried to kill herself, Clay. Even after being sterilized, she realized *she* was still there." Mom sucked in a breath and held it until the sobs quit. "She had them cut into her, Clay! She'll never have a baby. Never. Never a family."

"Ruby," Dad whispered into her hair, so soft I almost didn't hear. "Ruby, Austin's here."

And as soon as he said my name that way, like a caution, Mom jerked her head back. "Do you think he shouldn't hear?" she blurted. "Do you think he shouldn't know?"

"Ruby," Dad said.

She forced her way out of his grasp. "He keeps pretending there's nothing wrong!" Mom spun toward me. "Tell me," she shouted, "do you think *this* is all perfectly normal? Can you still pretend that now? She had herself mutilated, Austin! And then, when she decided that wasn't enough, she tore a Coke can in half and tried to hack open her wrists with the jagged edges. She said her blood was a poison that had to be let out."

"Ruby," Dad said.

"So what, Austin? What now? *Extra innings?*"

"Ruby!"

She spun back around to Dad. I moved my baseball mitt behind my back.

"This is not Austin's fault," he said.

Mom stared up at him, searching his face, but then her legs went, too fast for Dad to catch her, and she sat down right there in the middle of the driveway. "I know," she whispered, her voice cracked and failing. "But whose? What did we do so wrong?"

Dad was beside her in an instant, but she had her arms folded tight around herself and all he could do was put his hands on her shoulders. "Ruby?" he whispered.

Letting Dad rock her forward against his chest, she said, "You worked so hard, just so I could stay home and watch the children go insane."

I stood looking at Dad, looking for some sign from him, but he never took his eyes away from Mom. Pretty soon he was murmuring things to her, and that's how I left them, the two of them down on the driveway while I slipped away into the desert, on the long haul out to the base.

twenty-four

Wrapped in the darkness inside the tank, I couldn't think of any reason to go home. Reaching up, I caught a bullet hole's bright ray of light in my palm. I waved my hand, making the dust motes swirl. If Abilene was ever going to come home, I thought, it would be to here, the only place we'd ever had of our own.

But it wasn't really a plan, sleeping out there. At first I just watched the dot of light on my palm grow fainter and fainter. Finally, looking out, finding that I could hardly see the opening of the door against the darkness outside, I realized it would be impossible to find my way back home.

So I curled up on the floor of the tank, knowing I'd get cold, worrying about it, but then not waking until morning, when I heard the crunch of rock and dirt beneath tires, the uncertain approach through the desert so unlike Abilene's.

It was Dad, his little car, headlights still on, easing to a stop at the takeoff end of the runway. I stood beside the tank and lifted my hand when he turned my way, his window rolled down, as if he'd been searching, calling my name out into all that empty.

He turned off the car and into the calm dawn quiet said, "Good morning."

I couldn't quite stop a smile. Good morning?

"Some spot you've got here."

"How's Mom?"

Dad swung his door open, eased himself out onto the runway, slowing stretching up straight. "She's asleep. I got her inside and she calmed down enough to take a sleeping pill. I left a message for Dr. Pape."

I glanced away from him, out toward the shadow of the mountains on the horizon, then back. "Is she . . ."

"Just frightened. Just scared to death. For all of us."

Dad walked over to me, then ducked his head into the old pipe connection, peering into the tank. "This is your secret spot?"

I knew he couldn't see a thing inside there. I didn't bother answering.

"Well," he said, pulling his head out and then just standing beside me. Eventually he lifted his hand, halfheartedly pointing toward the mound I'd rebuilt, then toward the tire. "So this is Abilene's training center."

"Mine now."

Dad nodded. He started back to his car and I fell in step beside him.

"Mom didn't mean any of that yesterday," he said, studying his shoes as we walked. "About you and Abilene. About all this out here. She's just scared."

"I know," I whispered.

He stopped beside the car, but didn't get in. He thumped the metal of the roof. I looked down the runway with him, empty now for fifty years.

"I couldn't face losing Ruby. Losing any one of you. Abilene, or you, or Ruby." He looked across the roof at me. "You know that. Don't you?"

I nodded and he dropped down behind the wheel. I climbed in after him, watched him staring straight ahead.

"I've been thinking about when you asked why we don't have any photos on the walls," he said, reaching for the key. "The answer is, I don't need them. All I want is right in front of me. Every day. That's as far as I ever have to look."

Dad turned the key, drove us around in a big half-circle so we pointed toward the hangars, the broken walls black against the brightening sky. But then he stopped, just pointing that way.

"Dad? When I was little, did you come out here with me? With me and Ab'lene?"

He looked over at me. "Sure."

"Did we look for the old bullet casings? Did we race to see who could bring them to you the fastest? Me and Ab'lene? Is that what that box in the basement is from?"

Dad smiled. "You remember that?"

I shook my head. "No. Not at all."

"When I was a kid, my dad took me here once. We were coming back from my grandmother's funeral in El Paso. There were bombers here then. They sat parked wingtip to wingtip in every direction as far as you could see. These huge old planes nobody was ever going to use again, stretching out into the desert forever."

Dad took his foot off the brake and we crept forward. He drove gently down the cracked, old pavement and said, "Let's get you back to see Mom. You not turning up last night was pretty tough for her."

"She didn't seem much interested in seeing me."

Dad rubbed his hand around the top of the steering wheel. "She's just so afraid, Austin. That's all. There's some genetics to this disease of Abilene's. Ruby sees you torching along in Abilene's footsteps . . . sees herself flying off at you that way. . . . She's afraid—"

"Mom's never been like that."

Dad shook his head, agreeing. He drove up to the hangars, past the faded painting of that poor dead soldier and just kept going, out past the cracked foundation slabs of the old quarters, then bumped through the desert, over what was once road, then through the arched steel pipes, what used to be the entrance, where the letters used to spell out Rattlesnake Bomber Base but was now just blank space. He inched back up onto the pavement of the frontage road and turned toward home.

twenty-five

Mom was awake by the time we got home, standing out on the porch in her nightgown. As she watched us drive up, I wondered how long she'd been waiting there for us.

I eased out of the car. "Hi, Mom."

She smiled. "Hi, Austin." She looked thinner than ever, her gown dangling on her. And her hair too, hung all sleep-frizzed and matted, the red highlights gone brown and dull. Her eyes were dark wells, which, I realized, Dad's were too. I turned as he stood up on his side of the car, realizing he looked a lot like Mom, worn near away though he'd been with me every day, the changes right before my eyes.

"I'm so sorry, Austin." Mom held an arm out for me. She looked like the wooden woman on the front of a ghost ship.

I stepped up onto the porch and let her put her arms around me. "I know none of this is your fault," she whispered. "None of it."

I stood in her hug the way she had in Dad's. "I know. I didn't mean to scare you."

Soon enough the three of us went inside, resuming the wait for Abilene.

Though things in the house were different now, different from the way they'd been when we'd waited before Abilene had tried what she'd tried, Mom and Dad and I not quite so scared to talk to each other, there still wasn't much we had to say, Abilene being the only thing, and none of us knowing what to say about her, or not wanting to say what there was.

With that brittle quiet suffocating the house, I wound up going back out to the base after our dinners, sleeping out there most nights. I took out a blanket, and a jacket, which I'd scrunch into a pillow when I had to.

And though I figured she'd come back to the base if she came back at all, I kept telling myself I wasn't waiting for Abilene, that this was just the best place for me now.

After my second night at the base Dad stopped by again, on his way to work. I stepped out of the tank when I heard his car and he just looked at me a couple of seconds, then lifted his hand in a wave and drove back down the runway toward Pecos.

My next night out he didn't bother checking. I smiled, looking around at the nothing before sunrise, then pitched a full game before the heat got smothering.

That got to be the routine. Dawn games. And I blazed. Absolutely mowed them down. Left batter after batter standing there wringing their useless sticks in their hands.

I'd been doing that about a week when I lobbed out a warm-up pitch, not paying any attention, and it caught the edge of the tire, rebounding almost all the way back to me. I made a reflex stab at it, but it was just too far away to catch, just too close to a one-hop. What Abilene used to call a handcuffer, something she'd throw at me as her most severe punishment. I flubbed it. Grinning, I climbed back up on the mound and picked another ball out of the box, bouncing it back the same way.

I even got to laughing a little, bouncing the balls back at myself, working on my fielding instead of having to bear down with every pitch.

But when I let the next ball go, I was shocked down to my knees by a shattering blast. I dove into a crouch on the mound without knowing I'd moved, but I still saw my pitch jar sideways, the tire twisting at the end of its wire even without the ball making it all the way there.

Then, from just behind me, came Abilene's voice: "It's a whole new ball game!"

I spun crablike on the mound and saw her standing there, a shotgun cradled in her arms, a big grin across her face. I sat down and wiped at my face with my pitching hand. I had to think about taking each breath. "Hey, Ab'lene," I gasped.

"Hey, yourself. Come on, get up. What do you think? I'm going to shoot you?"

I stood slowly and took off my mitt, wiping the sweat from my hand onto my jeans. Her shotgun was like Dad's but brand-new, a price tag hanging from the trigger guard by a little piece of twisted white string. Her face was puffy, almost fat, and her shirt pulled at its buttons, something I could hardly believe. Only her hair looked the same, clamped tight in its braid, not wild and loose.

"What are you doing, Ab'lene?"

She worked the pump, a vicious noise, racking a new shell into her gun. "Just a little hunting, Austin."

"Hunting? That's where you've been all this time?"

Abilene didn't answer.

"Hunting for what?"

"Whatever."

"Jackrabbits? Doves? Like Dad used to?"

"No. Definitely not like Dad." She smiled. "Why, I just bagged my first baseball."

Dropping my mitt on the wooden pitching rubber, I walked away from her, kicking the closest balls back to the mound so I wouldn't have to look at her. She stayed where she was, watching me awhile before climbing to the top of the rebuilt mound. "I see you've been busy. While the cat's away . . ."

I didn't answer, just kept kicking and throwing the balls back toward the mound while she watched. With the last ball in my hand, I stood beneath the old power pole, looking at the balls scattered around the mound instead of up at Abilene.

"Are you all right, Ab'lene?" I asked at last.

She flipped her braid from one shoulder to the other. "Right as rain."

"And twice as rare."

She smiled and tapped her nose with the tip of her finger.

I held the last ball out flat on my hand, studying the freckles left by Abilene's shot. "You blasted it."

"Let's see."

Looking at it once more, I tossed the ball to Abilene. Just a tiny underhand flip.

Abilene grinned, counting the holes.

"Ab'lene?"

She looked up.

"Would you do me a favor?"

"What?"

Not, *Sure,* but *What?* "Would you throw it? Pure heat?"

"This shot-up old ball?"

"Yes."

"I'm not warmed up, Austin. I haven't done any of this in a long, long time."

"Just one pitch, Ab'lene. A fireball."

Abilene shrugged, then smiled. "Okay, Austin. Just for old times' sake?"

She took the ball into her hand, her fingers crossing the seams. "Okay," she said again, holding her gun out for me to hold. She was already starting to concentrate, bringing up her game face for just this one throw, and though I didn't want to, I took the gun.

Then, fast enough I almost missed it, Abilene kicked her leg as high as ever, whipping around the ball and letting it fly. She yelled, hopping out of her follow-through, grabbing her shoulder. The ball sailed a yard or so over the tire, another yard off to the right.

She rubbed her shoulder and laughed. "Looks like you're it on the diamond now. All that's left for me is to wait for the call from the Hall of Fame. Me and Nolan."

I looked at her shoulder. "Are you all right?"

"Of course. Just threw my arm out."

"Good. I mean, that that's all." I held her gun back out for her to take.

When she did, I stepped into the tank, the darkness. I crossed over to the Nolan Ryan ball. I held it in both hands and sat down on the foundation wall. I only had to wait a second before Abilene stuck her head inside the tank.

"Are you home now for good, Ab'lene?"

She pulled her head back long enough to rest her gun against the outside wall of the tank, then stepped inside. I watched her first halting steps in the darkness.

She moved hesitantly, blind until she reached the wall beside me. She sat down inches away. I felt her breathe. "I'm home now. I've already been to the house. But I knew I'd find you out here."

I pressed the Nolan Ryan tight in my hands. Then, reaching out, I touched her, surprised by her flinch. I found her arm, then her hand. I set the ball in her palm.

"What's this?"

I told her.

Abilene gave a chuckle. "You still have this?"

"No matter what, Ab'lene, don't shoot this one. Okay?"

"Shoot your Nolan Ryan?" She laughed like she was truly surprised. She stood up, taking a few steps away from me, her eyes adjusted now to the gloom.

Against the light of the door I saw her lift her arm. "Catch," she said.

I jerked my hands forward but couldn't help closing my eyes, turning my head away. The ball smacked down straight in my palms.

"Look what I found," Abilene said. It was what she used to say when she'd throw me a handcuffer, when I'd dodge away but still snag it. I stared at her in the darkness, the brightness of the door behind her, a few bullet holes glittering above her head.

She windmilled her sore arm. "Come on, Austin. I've got something to show you."

twenty-six

Abilene walked across the runway with her new gun, back out into the desert on the other side, dropping into the little wash there. Her truck was completely hidden in the bottom, and I slid down the gravelly cut after her, the sand and stone hissing loose behind me.

"I snuck into the house," Abilene said, hard to make out as she dug behind the truck seat. "My night vision is incredible."

I looked at the gun she'd lain across the hood.

"Soon as I found your room empty, I knew you were out here." She poked her head up long enough to look at me. "You had to be." Then she was back into the truck, raising her voice, shouting, "Snagged this for you on the way out."

She jumped up, flourishing the long canvas case as if she'd said *Voilà!* She drew the shotgun out like a sword.

I looked at her and the gun. "That's Dad's."

"Was," she said. "Yours now."

I shook my head. "He showed it to me. While you . . ." I looked all around her and her guns. "While you were gone. But he didn't give it to me."

"But, Austin, that's what fathers do. They pass things on to their sons and then get out of their way." She shrugged. "That's what they're supposed to do anyway. Real fathers."

"What are *we* supposed to do? What are we supposed to do with those?"

She poked the shotgun back into its case and threw it into the truck again. She pulled hers from the hood and nosed it down in the cab, the stock sticking up between us. "Come on. I'll show you."

She was already starting the truck and I jumped to keep from getting left behind, to keep her from slipping away again.

Not far from the bomber base there's a stock tank left over from somebody's dead ranch, an old windmill cranking away, still dredging up a trickle of water from who knows where, dampening a cracked concrete trough. Abilene raced straight toward it, swerving only around the mesquite. As she drove, she babbled about doves, how they'd come winging in to that water like rockets. "Gourmet fare!" she called them. "No more of Mom's gruel for us! No more of that poison they dished out at the hospital."

I waited for her to say anything else about the hospital, but she just went on about the doves. "They only move to water at dawn and dusk." She glanced out at the pale blue sky. "I hope we're not too late for the dawn flights."

Flights? A couple of tired, thirsty birds, I figured. At most. And it was already pushing ten. There wasn't a thing moving out here. Just us.

Abilene parked the truck a ways back from the windmill, and we walked the last little bit, Abilene kind of crouching, her gun at the ready, like anything might happen at any second. She nestled us carefully into the mesquite and we waited, a hot breeze rattling the dried bean pods that still clung to the branches. The mesquite here at the water were huge, towering trees, old cattle tracks pressed deep into the iron-hard ground around them, leftovers from some prehistoric time of mud.

Abilene fanned out a pattern of red shotgun shells on the ground in front of her. "Saves time for reloading," she said, catching me watching her. "When things really start hopping."

I couldn't stop a glance up, the thin, dusty leaves of the mesquite the only thing that kept the sky from being the emptiest thing in the world.

Abilene reached into her pockets, chucking handfuls of shells toward me. "Line them up so we'll be ready."

"Ready for what? There's nothing here."

She gave me a sorry smile.

"I've never even shot a gun, Ab'lene."

Suddenly Abilene threw her gun up to her shoulder and fired. Dirt flew at the base of the old trough, a cloud of it hanging in the air. Chips of flaking concrete fell away.

"Tight to your shoulder. Cheek to the stock. Pull the trigger. Couldn't be simpler."

"It's not even loaded."

"Sure it is."

And when she showed me how to open it, I found out she was right. "You gave this to me and didn't even tell me it was loaded?"

"Not much more worthless than an empty gun. Now shoot it. Same place I did."

I didn't make a move.

"Like falling off a log, Austin. Nothing easier."

I glanced down at my gun, and Abilene muttered something and jumped over to me. She leaned her gun against a mesquite and pulled mine out of my lap. "Okay look. This is the safety. Red means fire, black means safe. Mine's always at red. I'm always ready."

She worked the pump. A shell flew out, landing beside me. "Pick that up.

"Now, that's how you load it," she went on, racking the pump forward. "You're ready to fire. Every time you shoot, you rack it again, keep it ready." She flipped the gun over. "When you get a chance, slide a new shell in this way." She snatched a shell from the ground and stuffed it into the magazine tube. She was talking so fast I could barely follow her. "Even if you only shoot once, if you get a second, slide the next one in. Shoot twice, slide in two. Three, three. That way you'll always have a maximum load. These will hold five. Four in the tube, one in the chamber."

She pushed the gun to my shoulder, saying, "Take it, take it."

When I held it up, she pushed my head down to the stock, grabbing my shoulder to keep me from tilting my whole body, smashing me into the gun. "Keep both eyes open. You see more that way. Look down the barrel at the sight. Hold it high and put your eye low so you don't see the barrel at all, just the sight at the end. Point that at whatever you're trying to hit. If it's moving, your target, swing along with it, swing through the target and pull the trigger. It couldn't be any simpler. You won't be able to miss without putting your mind to it."

"Sure."

"You won't." She moved behind me, reaching both arms around me and grabbing my elbows, pushing the left out in front of me, tucking my right down almost against my side. "Left foot out forward. Point it at your target. Right back." She was hugging me, in a way, and I couldn't listen to what she was saying. I could still hardly believe she was back. She kicked at my right shin, making me move my leg back. Her braid swung against my neck.

She swiveled me around to face the trough, kicking at my legs again, hugging me tighter, steadying my arms. She pressed against my back. "Okay. Look. All sight, no barrel."

She slid her hand down my arm, up over the back of my hand, slipping my finger inside the trigger guard. "Finger on the trigger." She started squeezing. "Nice and easy," she whispered. "Breathe in, breathe out. Shoot."

Together we pulled the trigger.

But the gun struck back like a fist. It hit my face and my shoulder, making my eyes water. My head knocked back into Abilene's face and she swore, letting go of me so fast it was like she was throwing me away.

"Tight," she hissed. "Hold it tight. Do I even have to do that for you?"

I wiped my eyes and looked down at the gun in my hands.

Abilene jerked her gun up from the mesquite she'd leaned it against. "Put in a new shell. We've got to be ready."

And ready we were. All day long, baking in the thin shade of the mesquite. And though the sky stayed completely empty, now and then Abilene would say something like, "They're awful fast, Austin. Faster than they look. Lead them a good ways."

"Faster than a baseball?" I asked. But she just kept scanning the skies, searching for any living thing.

It was afternoon before I worked up the nerve to ask, "Where have you been, Ab'lene? Since the hospital?"

"Here. There." She didn't lower her eyes.

"What have you been doing?" I whispered.

"Do you know there are six ball fields in Chickasha? Six. In Chickasha alone."

I followed her flickering gaze into the powder blue of the dry sky. "No," I said. "I didn't know that."

She nodded. "In Chickasha alone."

———

Not until dusk, without a trace of warning, did the whistle of dove wings fill the air. For all her waiting, they caught even Abilene by surprise, and it was a second before she leapt out. Then, though it seemed nothing could escape the barrage she put up, the birds wheeled and disappeared.

Before I had a chance to say a word we heard another group coming in and Abilene hissed, "Down!" I was still sitting under my mesquite. I hadn't budged.

She leapt up again, firing like before, quick and hard. When they were gone, she glared at me. "You fire, too."

So I fired a couple times after the next bunch, leaving us both with empty shells scattered at our feet. Squeezing the gun against me, firing at something so fast, I didn't even notice when the gun went off.

Another handful came in right behind the others, before we'd had a chance to squat back down. I stood there with Abilene shooting into the dusk, watching all these birds flying away, more birds than I'd guessed there were in all of Texas. I watched them all wheel and disappear.

When they were gone, the sky empty again, I said, "Think there's another place out here with water?"

Abilene hunched over her gun, thumbing in new shells. She handed some to me. "There's no place else."

"But how will they drink then? If we don't let them here?"

"Pick up your empties," she said, short and fast. "There'll be more before you know it."

I pictured the birds out there, dying of thirst. "But why keep coming here? Why do they—"

"Pick up your empties!" Abilene shouted.

I stooped down, picking the hollow shells out of the scratchy dirt, the baked and rattly old bean pods.

"Maybe it's just something they have to do, Austin," Abilene whispered, turning away so it was hard for me to hear. "Even if they know it'll kill them, maybe it's just something they can't help."

When the next wave of birds came in, Abilene dropped one with her first shot. From where I stood beside her I saw it skitter to the side and crash into the mesquite. She kept shooting, and I didn't know if the hit was an accident or not. I didn't even know if she knew.

Then the doves were gone, as quick as they came. Abilene lowered her gun, wiping at the sweat above her eyes.

"Ab'lene? Did you see?"

"About time." A tiny smile cracked across her face.

"Finally threw them the dark one," I said, her old announcer talk for the pitch that finishes off a batter.

Her smile grew bigger. "The dark one. Lights out. Doesn't get any darker than that, does it?"

I put Dad's gun down in the brush, opening the chamber so it couldn't go off. I dodged over to where I'd seen the bird fall, a cat's-claw snagging me so I had to back up and start over.

The dove wasn't hard to find. Whether it had been alive enough to try to land, I don't know, but it had made it to a clear spot big enough for me to stand in. Though I thought the shot would have shredded it, it looked clean and whole, just stopped somehow. A bright drop of blood clung to the tiny hook at the end of its dark bill, its black eyes open and gleaming.

I picked the warm bird from the dust. With the tip of my finger I tried to shut its eyelid, but the eyeball rolled under my finger, the lid sliding open again as soon as I took it away.

I half-turned to show Abilene, but she was back where I'd left her, just watching me.

"Find it?"

I grinned, holding up the bird. "You tell me."

"Now we have to get you one."

"Next time."

Abilene nodded. The birds were long gone for today.

I couldn't have cared less. Most of the time I'd aimed, but those birds were so quick, and they bounced around in the air so much, I never expected to hit one. Mostly it was just fun being with Abilene, shooting Dad's gun, getting rocked by it when it didn't hurt.

When I reached Abilene, I held out the bird. She dropped it into her inside coat pocket and started for the truck.

"You should look at it," I said. "Your first one."

She kept walking away, the rustle of the mesquite leaves, the crush of their bean pods, drowning out any talk. I broke into a run until I fell into step beside her.

"You should look at it, Ab'lene. It's completely different than they are in the air."

I glanced at the bulge in the waist of her jacket. The drop at the end of its bill had bled through, leaving a tiny, round, dark stain on the faded denim.

"It's bleeding."

"Feel sorry for it?" Abilene snapped.

I missed a step.

"Things bleed, Austin. It's what they do."

It took a second, but I got back into sync, our legs swinging together. I looked away from her stiff face. "Not baseballs," I said.

"Shows how worthless they are."

I glanced quick at her face, but it was half-hidden now by the dusk, the hair fallen from her braid. As I looked, she brushed it back, trying to tuck it behind her ear. It fell forward again as soon as she moved her hand away.

It was nearly dark when we reached the truck, the sky all purply, the first stars leaking through. Instead of jumping behind the wheel, Abilene dropped the tailgate and sat there, gazing out at the last of the light.

I sat next to her. After a while I said, "Don't you have to gut it or something? Pluck it?"

"I suppose." She finally picked the bird from her pocket. She set it on her thigh, giving a weak try at brushing the feathers smooth. "Do you ever listen to these things, Austin?"

"The doves?" I could almost hear the cry now, the three mournful, trailing coos.

"Sound miserable, don't they?"

"Uh-huh."

"I figure it's practically a mercy killing, dropping one of these things."

I nodded, looking at the rumpled dead bird on Abilene's leg. "They probably see it a little different."

Abilene gave a weak smile and dug a pocketknife out of her jeans. "You want to cook this?"

I stared at the bird, not knowing what to say.

"We can build a fire, Austin. Cook it right over the flames. They're best that way."

"How do you know?" I asked, watching Abilene pull at the feathers below the breast, then make a little cut across the naked skin.

Abilene stopped, her index finger poked up inside the dove. She stared at me and said, "Get some wood. Stay away from the creosote."

"That'd be tasty."

"Get it, Austin." Hooking her finger, she pulled the insides out of the bird. Mostly they were just a shiny, moist gob, but perched at the very tip of Abilene's finger was the heart, maybe pinched there by the edge of her nail. It was tiny and dark, glistening and alive looking. Abilene stared at it.

I'd started to slide off the tailgate but stopped, teetering on the edge.

"Mom told you everything, I suppose. About the hospital."

I nodded, still looking at her hand, that tiny heart.

"No more mistakes for me. No more babies." Straightening up, she flicked the heart away with all the rest of it, out into the desert. "I've closed that door myself. But you. Those cheerleaders of yours. You have to be careful. Don't let them trap you into anything."

I slid my feet to the ground, my face away from hers. "There aren't any cheerleaders, Ab'lene," I murmured. "You know that."

"I know what there is and what there isn't," she snapped.

"How could I have a girlfriend?" I blurted. "How could anyone even squeeze between the cracks when I've spent my whole life with you?"

"There've been some big cracks lately."

"I've just been out here, Ab'lene. Pitching. Waiting."

"Saving yourself for me? That is so touching."

I stared at her and she stared right back. I turned and walked into the darkness, looking for the dead, dust-dry branches of mesquite.

Abilene didn't say another word, just got the fire going fast, its light good to stand around even with the heat, the mesquite burning hot and quick, leaving glowing coals powdered with ash. Skewering the dove carcass on a stick, holding it over the coals, she said, "Mesquite's famous for cooking."

Without its feathers, the bird wasn't more than a couple of mouthfuls. We burned it on the outside, the inside still raw. After crunching through the burnt meat, the raw was slippery in my mouth. I swallowed as quick as I could. I was glad the fire had burned to nothing so fast, so we couldn't see what we were biting into.

After we finished eating, Abilene threw the last of my sticks onto the coals. They flared, crackling and popping, and I glanced across at Abilene, her loose, messed-up hair glowing even redder in the flames. She was staring into the fire like I wasn't there, like maybe I'd never even been born. I tried doing the same, tried looking into the flames and picturing the world without Abilene, but it was impossible. I looked at Abilene instead.

Her eyes were bright, the flames shining in them. She held her chin in her hand, which pulled her wrist out of her shirt-sleeve. It was a second before I realized what I was seeing: the shiny skin of the scars, seven cuts as evenly spaced as the lines on a sheet of paper, like she'd been carefully laying out her most serious project.

I stared until I felt the shift in Abilene. I glanced up, caught her catching me.

She looked like she hadn't focused yet, like she was still seeing only flame. "What?" Then her eyes bore down on me. "What are you staring at?"

"Nothing. You."

"Look at the fire. It'll last longer."

The fire was already out of places to go, the last of the wood down to coals. Even with the heat I shivered. "Ab'lene?"

She hummed something.

"How come you came back?"

"Not happy to see me?"

"No, it's just . . . I . . . I don't know anything, Ab'lene. I don't know why you left. I don't know why you came back. I don't know how long you'll be here anymore."

Abilene stood up from the fire. "I came back for you."

"But why'd you leave Mom, then come back anyway, why—"

"For you, Austin." She kicked at the coals, spraying bits of them all around, covering me with sparks. I jumped up, batting at the bright spots sticking to my clothes.

She whipped open her truck door and I jumped to catch up, but she only pulled out her gun again, pushing Dad's to me.

"What now?" I asked. "Bats?"

Abilene lifted her gun high and fired, tongues of flame lash-ing out the barrel toward the stars. She fired until her gun was empty, and when she stopped to reload, she said, "Fire at will."

"At what?"

"At anything. At the night."

"I don't want to shoot the night."

I felt her watching me. "Okay, Austin," she said at last. "Just watch the flame."

As she fired her next five shots, I remembered the baseballs back at the base, scattered around the mound, uncollected. When she stopped again, I said, "Ab'lene, we have to go back to the base. We left the balls out."

Abilene kept looking up at the sky. She shook her head. "Too late." She threw her gun back into the truck, mine too, still in its case.

I climbed in after her, and she stomped on the gas, chattering through a U-turn that threw me over against her. My head hit her arm, knocking it from the wheel, my face crushing into her thigh. Before scrambling back up, I smelled her, her own regular smell mixed now with the sharp smoke of mesquite and the blood of that tiny dove.

I scrambled back upright and crunched tight against my door. "Sorry."

Abilene let out a breath. "This is our secret, Austin. I know I don't have to tell you that."

twenty-seven

As late as we were getting home that night, Mom and Dad were still up when we got there. When I cracked the door and peeked inside, they were sitting at the table, my place set between them, empty and clean, the silverware ranked around it. I wondered if this was what they'd done every night before Dad had ordered me to come home for dinners—the two of them just waiting and waiting. They smiled at me, looking surprised and glad.

But their hello died on their lips when Abilene nudged me into the room and slipped in after me. Their faces sagged gray and Mom's hand went up to her mouth. "Oh," was all she managed to say.

Dad, even with all his size, had the same nervous, fragile look as Mom. "Hello, Abilene," he said, pushing back his chair, but then sitting still. "Hello, Austin."

Mom glanced to him, then me. She dropped her hand back

down to the table, catching it with her other hand, joining them almost as if in prayer.

Abilene walked in. She sat down in my place, next to Mom. She reached out her hand, covering Mom's with her own. "It's all right, Mom," she whispered. "I'm all right. I'm back."

Mom nodded, looking down at Abilene's hand. I wondered if she saw straight through her wrist, to the scars so shiny on the other side. "I am so glad you're home," Mom breathed.

"Where have you been?" Dad asked, more to me, it seemed, than Abilene.

But Abilene answered, "I found Austin out wandering the desert and we took a drive. Getting to know each other again. It was pretty. The sunset."

I stared at her.

"Your medications," Mom said, her voice barely a croak. "Abilene are you—"

"Every last capsule, Mom. Like a machine." Abilene waved her hand down her front, over the bulging shirt buttons. "Can't you tell, Mom? My sexy lithium look?"

Mom tried harder to smile. "You look fine, Abilene. You look fine."

"Are you home now?" Dad asked. "Can you stay with us?"

Still holding Mom's hands, Abilene nodded. "I'm home now. No doubt about it."

I watched Abilene closely. The whole way home I'd tortured myself over what to say about the guns, if I had to tell them anything, if we had to get them away from her. But now I watched Mom slide one of her hands out from under Abilene's, holding Abilene's hand between her own, and all I said was, "She found me out at the base. One minute I'm pitching alone, the next minute, Abilene is standing right there. Just like always."

———

I slipped down as early as usual the next morning, not intending to sneak off to the base, but only to keep Abilene from being alone if she woke early. Dad was already in the kitchen though, the coffee all made. He was wearing the same shirt he'd worn yesterday, the same pants, and I wondered if he'd stayed up all night long, if he and Mom would split the days into watches now.

"Morning," I said.

"It's something, isn't it? Having her back?"

"Did you sleep?"

Dad laughed. "A little. As much as I could."

"Call the doctor?"

He nodded, not dodging his eyes away from mine. "Of course."

"Is she going to come out?"

"We'll see. We'll probably go in. Whenever Abilene says she's ready."

If I was going to say a thing about the guns, now was the time, with Mom and Abilene both still asleep. What I said was, "She seemed pretty good yesterday. Pretty much her old self."

"Did she really?" Mom said, surprising me, sneaking into the kitchen in her robe.

I looked at the clock and laughed. It was quarter to five. "We just couldn't stand not waiting for her anymore, could we?" I said. "We had to all get up early just to do it one more time."

They both smiled, and Dad got up to pour Mom a cup of coffee. "Let's hope it's the last time," he said.

Dad didn't even mention going into work that morning, just sat and waited for Abilene with me and Mom.

When Abilene finally strolled into the kitchen, it was almost ten. I'd been about to sneak up to her room, find out if she'd slipped out during the night. Abilene was not a sleep-in kind of person.

But then, suddenly, she was there, Mom and Dad both jumping to get her a cup of coffee.

Abilene smiled, but waved them off. She held out her hand, a couple yellow and gray capsules in her palm. "This stuff makes me half-sick as it is. I don't think coffee guts would help at all." She went straight to the sink, pouring out a glass of water and tossing down the pills. "Mmm, delicious. And good for me too."

Then she turned to us, leaning back against the sink. "Ask Austin about my pitching performance yesterday." She glanced at me, making me remember her one pitch, as wild a miss as I'd ever seen her throw. "Another lithium trick. Besides the poundage. I couldn't hit you from here with a basketball, Dad. My coordination is shot."

"Dr. Pape says there are cases where it works wonders," Mom started.

"True enough," Abilene said, still smiling. "I could well be a wonder worker nonetheless."

"It will take time," Mom said, "to work out the right dosage. Dr. Pape said—"

Abilene tapped the side of her head. "It's all up here, Mom. In the steel trap. I know. I know."

We sat there looking at her.

She looked back at each one of us in turn, then suddenly burst out laughing. "Well, I can see I haven't been missing a lot here. Do you people have someone come in and turn you now and then? Check for sores?"

We all smiled, and I stood up and moved away from the table.

Abilene waved her hand, trooperlike. "Come on now. Move along. Show's over. She's taken her pills. There's nothing more to see here."

Mom and Dad got up then too, and we smiled a lot, not quite looking at each other. But we couldn't leave the room, couldn't make ourselves get too far from Abilene. She gave us a few minutes while she ate a piece of plain toast, "for my stomach."

Then she said, "Well, I think I'm going to take a shower."

She glanced around at each of us again. "I don't see how we'll all fit. Someone might have to stay outside the tub. Or, you could draw straws, split up your time with me, take turns."

We laughed with her, and Dad said, "You can't have any idea what it's like having you back. What it means to us."

"I think, however, that I do." Abilene answered. "I've traveled farther than any of you."

That night when we sat down to dinner, we were all still just smiling a lot, wondering what we could talk about, what we could say and what we couldn't. Dad waited until Mom put down our plates—her crusty fried chicken, once Abilene's favorite—before he dove in headfirst. "We'd like to know, Abilene. Whatever you can tell us, we'd like to know."

Abilene smiled down at her plate. "Thanks, Mom. This smells great." She picked up a leg. "Looks great." She nipped off one tiny bit of the breading and closed her eyes. "Still the best."

Then she opened her eyes again. "Remember the food at the hospital, Mom? In Chickasha?"

Mom paled slightly, but nodded.

"I don't know what kind of sad, sour little man they employed, but he had career potential as a mass murderer. He was a genius, wasn't he, Mom? There wasn't a thing he ever touched that turned out to be even a distant relative to palatable."

Mom smiled a little. "The food wasn't very good."

" 'Not very good'?" Abilene laughed. "It was atrocious. Remember that nurse, Mom? The night shift? Sherry?"

Mom nodded. "Of course—"

Abilene cut her off. "You do? Wow. I thought she breathed forgettability." Abilene glanced at me and Dad, including us. "She was built like a mouse, only smaller. Tiny, skinny little shoulders. Mousy brown hair about this long." Abilene flashed up her fingers, a half inch apart. "Skittered around all nerves, just waiting for the cat. I'd named her Minnie a week before she built up the nerve to introduce herself.

"She had the biggest crush on me." Abilene shook her head. "Poor kid. This when I'm in the hospital. Not exactly at my best. But poor Sherry was just smitten."

Abilene tilted her head toward me and whispered loudly, "A switch hitter, Austin. Swung from the other side of the plate."

Abilene shook her head. "I wasn't very good to her. I mean, she was in a state, but finally, the food was so bad, I had be nice to her. I knew if I could leave just the trace of a candle burning for her at the end of the tunnel, Sherry would bring me some real food."

Abilene turned to Mom. "Remember the night you came in and I was eating ribs? You kept asking where I got them. It must have been two in the morning."

Mom nodded, really smiling now, just listening to Abilene talk. "You wouldn't say a word to me. You just kept eating." Mom paused. "I was so afraid you'd sneaked out. But then I knew you wouldn't have come back."

"Ribs in bed. What was I thinking? The sheets were like the world's biggest bib. The mess! I was still licking my fingers and Sherry's stripping the bed, whisking on new sheets. Scolding me like we'd been married for years."

Abilene grinned. "No reflection on the two of you."

I watched Mom and Dad watch her, both of them smiling. I wondered if they were picturing her in high school, when her friends used to come over. The way they used to hang on her stories this same way. They all had crushes on her then. We all did. I was eight or nine years old and I'd hide behind the couch just to listen, to catch what peeks I could.

At the start of her sophomore year she broke her ankle—an accident that was never fully explained to me, Abilene for some reason stepping out of a moving car while she was out with a bunch of her friends. But the trooping of those friends to our house to see her was so constant, Dad set up a chaise longue in our living room, so she would stay put and still be able to entertain the entire Pecos High student body.

Abilene went on and on, all of us laughing, and I wondered if I was the only one who noticed that she hadn't really told us anything.

The next morning, after a whispered conversation with Mom, a quick hug by the kitchen door, Dad went back into Pecos for work. He went the next morning too, then for the rest of the week. The week after.

Abilene hung with Mom again, but as if the roles had been reversed, Abilene caring for Mom now, returning the favor. Once they disappeared together for a whole day, and I thought they'd gone to Dr. Pape, but when they got home that evening, Abilene spread bags of clothes on the table: stiff new jeans, baggy shirts. "Mom took me shopping." Abilene blew out her cheeks, as fat as she could make them. "A whole new lithium wardrobe."

But, as much as she made fun of the pills, she made a show of taking them every morning, every evening, lining them up on the counter, sweeping them up in her fist, clapping her hand to her mouth with a quick "Down the hatch." Then the swallow of water.

Mom would hover around her whenever pill-time loomed close. And with each big production you could see Mom ease up, pull at her fingers less, leave her hair alone; even on the days Abilene would then go sit in her truck "to let the chemicals hit." She didn't drive anywhere, just slammed her meds and sat alone in her truck, staring at our house.

And every day that Abilene stayed without talking about the guns, without barreling off into the desert to search for prey, I let myself think keeping quiet was the right thing to do.

twenty-eight

Like Mom, I hung as tight as I could to Abilene those weeks she seemed so much just a calmer version of her old self. She still slept in every day, Dad and I squeezing in our game of catch each dawn, before he'd dash in and shower and tear off for work. And Mom and Abilene would go into Midland pretty regularly as Dr. Pape monitored Abilene's lithium levels, but otherwise we had a lot of time together. She wouldn't go out to the base with me though, wouldn't touch a baseball. She couldn't stand how the drug made it impossible for her to pitch. "Once you've hurled with the gods, Austin, it's no fun lobbing taters in the Old-Timers games."

But we did all right, just hanging out, taking a drive now and then, killing the rest of the summer. By the end of August, Dr. Pape was satisfied with Abilene's lithium dosage and didn't need her to go into Midland near as much. Just for the therapy sessions. When school started, Abilene began asking if I was going to stack on the credits the way she had, get out of there as fast as I could, but I managed not to answer. Neither of us said a thing about me playing baseball next season.

Twice on our drives, she pulled over at the old windmill and we took out the shotguns to wait for the doves. But when they came, she couldn't hit any. She blamed the drugs, but not like she really cared. I only aimed enough to miss, afraid what it would do to her if I hit what she couldn't. The doves could hardly have been safer, and she never mentioned the guns at home.

Mostly things were normal. Like they'd always been. Until the day she cornered me at the top of the stairs. We'd just walked past each other, me going down, her going up, when she spun me back around by the shoulder, almost tumbling me down the stairs. I grabbed the railing, already laughing, expecting something fun, but Abilene said, "So, this is what you've done the whole time? Moped around the house?"

"That's not what I'm doing," I said, looking at her in surprise. That's when I saw the first hint that the sharp angles of her face might be coming back, the buttons of her shirt maybe pulling a little less.

"Looked like you'd been awful busy at the base. All that new construction."

"Just rebuilt the mound, Ab'lene. That's all. You know that."

"Those balls look like you put them through the dailies." She leaned in at me, pressing me back against the railing.

I shrugged. "Keeping tuned."

"You were pitching? The whole time I was gone?"

I looked at her. Then away. "Sure, Ab'lene. At the base. By myself. Not on the team. Nothing like that. Just keeping tuned until you got back."

I glanced at her, found her staring at me.

"I've been out there, Austin."

"I know."

"Were you *sleeping* there too?"

"No."

She grabbed my chin, pulled my face around to hers.

I knocked her hand away. "Just sometimes, Ab'lene. Okay? I just did sometimes."

"Why?"

"Just because." I wriggled away from her, starting down the stairs. "Sometimes I'd stay too late to come home."

Abilene watched me go. "Were you doing your cheerleaders out there? Out in *our* tank?" She raised her voice as I got farther down. "Well, why don't you go out there now?" she shouted. "You don't have to sit around here waiting on me anymore!" Go!"

I leapt down the last steps and almost crashed into Mom as she scurried out of the living room, rushing to put out any fires.

I kept going right out the door, letting the screen slam behind me. I didn't turn around at all, though I could feel Abilene watching long after I'd left the house.

I stayed out late that night, and steered as clear as I could from Abilene afterward, but only a couple of days later, while Dad and I were out for the dawn game of catch, Dad caught a glimpse of Abilene peeking at us from the kitchen door. He grinned instantly, waving his mitt at her, calling, "Come on out, Abilene. Show us what you've got." He kicked his own leg as high as he could, showing off what heat he had. By the time the ball was in my mitt, even the shadow of Abilene in the door was gone.

"She won't play, Dad. The lithium."

"Of course," he answered, like he'd made a blunder anyone else would have seen a mile off.

But the next Saturday, Dad stayed home all day, and right after breakfast, Abilene still up in her room, Dad said, "Let's get out there before the sun fries us like an egg." We kept the mitts by the door and we each snagged our own on the way out.

We'd only made a few tosses when Abilene bounced out. "Well, well, well," she said, leaning over the porch railing. "What've we got here? One of those nostalgia leagues?"

Dad gave me a quick glance, but I looked down at the broken white rock he'd trucked in to bury Abilene's diamond.

"Austin and I were tossing around the old horsehide," Dad said, smiling back at Abilene. "You should see him throw."

"Oh, I've seen Austin throw." Abilene sprang off the porch and walked up beside me. "But I wouldn't say Austin's the main attraction here." She clapped her hands together, looking for the ball.

Dad didn't say anything else, and I listened to the rock crunch beneath Abilene's high-tops. "Where's 'the old horsehide' now?" she asked.

I pinched the ball tight in my mitt. "We were just going in, Ab'lene."

"Nonsense. You're still warming up. My pills don't make me blind. Or stupid."

"Give her the ball," Dad said.

I stopped short, glancing at him.

He smiled and nodded. "Go ahead."

"Or throw it, Austin," Abilene said. "Show Dad your dark one."

I glanced at one, then the other of them. She didn't even have a mitt. "I'm going in," I said.

"Fire the dark one," Dad said, still smiling. He pounded his mitt with his fist. "Come on, Austin. No quitting in this family."

Abilene leaned toward me, her breath brushing my ear when she whispered, "Fireballer."

I looked at her to show I'd been trapped into this, how I'd just been looking for an excuse to get out of it, how I didn't think it was near as funny as she did.

Abilene held her hand out for the ball. "If you won't throw it, I will."

I threw it to Dad, just a quiet lob, anything better than letting Abilene have it.

Abilene shook her head. "Now what's the good of that, Austin? How am I supposed to see what the old guy's got if you toss him candy like that?"

Darting forward, snakelike, she plucked the mitt from my hand before I could tighten my fingers inside the leather.

"Ab'lene!"

She wriggled her fingers into place, then snapped the mitt open and shut, open and shut, like the jaws of a trap. "Let's see it, Dad," she challenged. "Your best stuff."

Dad hesitated. "Are you sure, Abilene?"

She cracked one of her nicest smiles. "I think I'll be able to handle it."

Dad smiled and gave his little leg lift, putting a good bit into his throw, but going easy on Abilene, finding out what she could do now.

As soon as the ball slapped into the bottom of my glove, Abilene ripped her hand out like she'd been stung by a hornet. "Whoowee!" she cried.

Dad's smile faltered, then came back. "Now you know why they always gave me a bat," he said, like it was all in fun. Just dugout teasing. Like back in his old Lubbock days.

Watching Dad's smile, his eyes squinting against the sun, almost disappearing, I didn't see Abilene throw. But I saw the quick change in Dad's face, the sudden, startled sweep of his mitt. And I heard the thwack of the ball striking home.

Even with the wince of impact, Dad's smile was real when he said, "Take the time to warm up, Abilene. You'll hurt yourself." He wiped his forehead with his sleeve and peeled the ball from his glove. He tossed back an easy one for her.

The second he warned her to warm up, Abilene's whole body

froze into her game face. The ball barely touched her mitt before she kicked her leg chin-high, rocketing another pitch straight
at Dad.

The crack against his mitt was like a rifle, and Dad smiled,
pulling the tattered ball out of the old leather. "Nice throw," he
said, and I wondered if he thought he had a chance here, if he
thought he might be able to win her over by playing along, by
showing he wasn't as helpless as she might think. He lobbed the
ball back, and I saw his knees bend, saw him go up on the balls
of his feet, ready for Abilene's lightning return.

Both her pitches had been dead center, grooved-down-the-
pipe strikes. Not an inch difference in placement. "Ab'lene?" I
said. "Dad?" But they were all concentration.

They went on like that longer than I thought either of them
could, Dad firing back as hard as he could, Abilene going beyond
anything I'd ever seen at the base. Dad's face grew crimson,
streaming lines of sweat. No change cracked Abilene's grim determination, but I knew her arm must be on fire, throwing like
that straight from nothing, from not having touched a baseball
in months.

She bored in pitch after pitch, each one straight at his chest,
like she was trying to drive a hole right through his mitt, right
through his heart.

When she finally missed that mark, Dad nearly let the ball get
by him. But he made a wild sweep and the ball ice-cream-coned at
the edge of his mitt's webbing, almost tearing the mitt from his
hand. "Look what I found," I whispered without thinking.

Dad smiled. "Ball one."

Though I didn't think it was possible, Abilene threw even
harder next time. She grunted. I remembered how when we'd
first started the whole baseball thing, she'd throw at me like that
as punishment, punishment for a bad throw, a lapse of concentration. It scared me now as much as it had back then.

The pitch went even wider, Dad again barely making the snag, his breathing reaching new heights. For a second I thought Abilene was throwing beyond herself, getting wild, but then I wondered if she wasn't exactly as precise as ever.

"You guys," I said.

But Dad just fired the ball back. "Ball two," he said, somehow still smiling.

"Ab'lene," I said.

When Abilene rifled her next pitch, I knew she had her control back. The ball was in the rocks, exactly too far in front of Dad for him to reach, but too close to be able to play the hop. It handcuffed him the same way it always had me: Abilene's most severe lesson.

Instead of spinning away, protecting himself, Dad kept his head down, following the ball into his mitt just like you're supposed to, though on the broken rock it was suicide. Or maybe he wasn't trying to stop it, but just wasn't quick enough to get out of the way.

Instead of ricocheting into his shins, like it always had mine, the ball hit the crushed rock of the drive and wild-hopped straight up.

Dad's head snapped back as soon as I saw the ball hit the driveway, before I could quite put together what had happened. It went so fast that when Dad staggered back, his nose already pouring blood, his eyes full of tears, it almost seemed like something normal, like he'd been that way a long time.

His hands went up to his face slowly, his mitt holding his forehead, his bare hand going to his nose but stopping before it touched, like he could feel all that was broken just by having his hand so close.

"Dad?" I whispered.

"It's okay, Austin," Dad said, his voice already thick and nasal. "All part of the game. Bad hop."

I turned to look at Abilene. She was still bent low in her follow-through, her face rigid, her eyebrows scrunched down like some kind of hawk. But her face had gone white, her hair looking even redder against the blanched skin. Her lips trembled, usually the first sign that her game face was breaking. She straightened herself, the rock scratching beneath her feet. She flexed her shoulder, which had to be screaming with how hard she'd thrown. She still stared straight at Dad.

He was touching his face now, his cheeks, his chin, his lips, everywhere but his nose, surveying damage. "Bad hop," he said again, the blood staining his huge, wet, white shirt. "Just a bloody nose."

"You okay?" Abilene finally said, the same way she always did to me after hitting me that way, daring me to say I wasn't.

Dad nodded his head and I could feel how just that movement would make his nose swell and throb. He moved his fingers to his eyes, wiping at the tears. His mitt hand still held his forehead, like somehow he was holding himself up. "I'm fine," he said as he cleared his eyes, making himself see again.

He touched one fingertip under his nose, then held it out, focusing on the blood. Carefully he slipped his handkerchief from his back pocket and cupped it under his nose, as if his blood wasn't already soaking all over his shirt, as if he could still save something.

Then, having done all he could, Dad looked at us, at Abilene and me standing together. Somehow he smiled again. "I don't know what I was thinking," he said, the smile crumbling. "Playing this game with you youngsters."

Still wearing his old mitt, he took his first shaky step toward the house, where Mom would take care of him. I fought the urge to jump to help, to steady him, and stood where I was.

"Dad?" I asked, the best I could manage.

He shook his head, lifting his mitt to keep me away as he made it past us toward the house. "I don't know what I was thinking."

"It was just a bad hop," I called after him.

I listened to the screen bang shut behind him, heard him

mumble, "Sorry," the way he always did when he forgot to catch the door.

I half expected to hear Abilene's truck fire, but I could feel the heat of her standing close beside me, not moving.

"Why'd you do that?"

She didn't answer and I looked at my mitt, still stuck on the end of her wrist. I held my hand out for it, and Abilene shook it off, letting it slip from her fingers to mine.

"What lesson did you think you could teach him with the handcuffer?"

"You tell me," Abilene whispered.

"He doesn't want to learn anything new."

Abilene shifted her feet, squinting out at the bright shine of the desert.

I slapped my mitt against my thigh.

"What, Austin?" she shouted, spinning to face me. "You want him coming out for doves with us too? You want to ruin everything?"

I pinched my mitt tight to my side. "No," I whispered.

I walked across the drive, picking the baseball from the rock where Dad had left it lying. It had one deep, new scuff on it, from digging into the rock before hitting him. The smash into his nose had been too quick to leave any blood.

"Come on, Austin," Abilene sighed, calling me back. "We better go check on Dad. Mom's probably already called out the Guard—'Help us! Help us! She's gone crazy! She's trying to kill us all with a baseball!'" Abilene cried in a trembling falsetto I'd never heard from her before, a perfect imitation of Mom at her scared worst.

I joined Abilene on the porch and we went inside together.

"It was a bad hop, Ab'lene."

"Of course it was."

"Part of the game."

"You got that."

twenty-nine

Instead of checking on Dad, Abilene walked straight through the kitchen and up the stairs. I followed as far as the base of the steps, watching her go, wondering if she'd crawl out her window, almost hoping she would. Then I crept through the house, unable to keep myself from looking for a blood trail.

The washer and dryer whirred and clattered, but Mom and Dad weren't back there. I found them in the next room, the mudroom, the washer shaking the wall. Mom had Dad sitting on the little stepladder she used for the upper cabinets, his head bent backward over the slop sink. She worked a washcloth over his face so gently it seemed she wasn't touching him, but still the flowered cloth turned red.

She spun around when she heard the floor creak beneath me, her eyes wild, and all I could think of was Abilene wailing, "She's gone crazy! She's going to kill us all!"

But seeing me, Mom slumped, relaxing. "Oh, Austin," she breathed. "It's you."

"It was an accident, Mom."

She had Dad tipped back so far to stop the blood flow I could barely see his face. But he said, "Now will you believe me, Ruby? We were playing catch. The ball took a crazy bounce."

Mom looked at me.

I nodded. "I saw it, Mom. I was right there."

"But you didn't throw it."

I shook my head. "Abilene did. But it's the lithium, Mom," I said, knowing it wasn't true. "You heard her. She can't pitch like she used to. She was—"

"So this is where you're all hiding," Abilene said right behind me, making me jump, making Mom's eyes go wide again.

"I thought you'd be upstairs." Abilene held out a package of gauze in one hand, a white roll of adhesive tape in the other. "I knew you'd be playing trainer," she said to Mom.

"We had to get the bleeding stopped first," Dad said in his new, clogged voice. He struggled against Mom's hands, pushing himself upright on his tiny perch.

The pockets around Dad's eyes were already tinged purplish black. His nose, though, shone red, the skin shiny, stretched tight. He tried to smile.

"Think it's broke?" Abilene asked.

Dad shook his head. "Just a good wallop."

It couldn't have been more broken.

Abilene slipped past me with her bandages. Mom slid away, leaving him to her.

"Should probably tape it anyway. Even if it's not broken." Abilene smiled. "Keep you from looking like some old boxer gone to seed."

Before any of us could say a thing, she stripped out a bit of tape and a pad of gauze and went to work. We all watched, Abilene's hands as gentle as Mom's had been, her voice quiet and soft when she warned, "This might hurt," before pinching the bridge of Dad's nose, pulling it up and straight and then trapping it there under the strips of tape.

"Good as new," Abilene said, stepping back.

"Feels better already. Really."

"Part of the game." Abilene tapped Dad's shoulder with her knuckles. "Wear sunglasses and nobody'll know you lost your fight with a ground ball."

"Right," Dad said, but Abilene was already walking away. He called, "Thanks," after her, and I looked at the floor.

With Abilene gone, Mom stepped forward. "Did that really help, Clay?"

Dad held out one of his enormous hands, picking Mom's from the air. "I'm fine, Ruby. We're all just fine."

I gnawed at my lip, the same way I'd been chewing it since Abilene had appeared to patch things up. "No, we're not."

Mom and Dad looked at me.

"What do you mean?" Dad asked.

I tasted the blood from my lip. From the instant she'd planted her handcuffer in that one deadly spot, I knew I had to tell about the guns, but all I got out was, "I think maybe she's not taking her medicine."

Mom squinted at me, puzzled. "Of course she is. I watch her every time. Morning and evening."

"I don't know how. But watch her. Look at her." I stopped. I wanted to tell them how accurate every one of her throws had been, each one doing exactly what she wanted. Surgical. But it was hopeless. They didn't know her the way I did.

They were both staring at me, waiting. "What makes you think so, Austin?" Dad asked. "What do you see?"

His nose looked like a tomato, his eyes like holes, and he asked me what I saw.

"Nothing, I guess. I don't see anything." I turned and walked out of the room.

And though each step must have been like a jackhammer pile-driving his nose, Dad was up off the ladder before I'd gotten out of the hallway. I heard him wheezing behind me. "What? Austin, we have to know."

I blew through the screen, straight across the rock and into the desert. I heard Dad stop out on the rock, calling, "Austin! Wait! Come back! Austin!"

As I ran through the desert, I kept glancing back for the glint of sun off Abilene's windshield, tracking me down. To see, I had to wipe at the surprise of the tears that kept welling up. Part of the game? I kept thinking as I pushed through the creosote. Part of the game?

When I finally reached the base, I went straight for the tank, the Nolan Ryan ball. Picking it from its spot, I lay down on the floor, and still blinded by the sun, I tossed the ball up into the darkness, over and over. By the time my eyes adjusted I still hadn't dropped it, and after that, with the light from the door, it was just cheating, but I kept going, up and down, never once losing it.

After a long time I stopped and just held the ball, squeezing it until my fingers hurt.

I got up and walked to the door, staggered by the intensity of the light and heat, the same as always. Stumbling to the mound, squinting against the glare that came even from the ground itself, I toed the splintery rubber.

I glanced once at the tire, still as death, then looked down, into my windup before I could stop myself.

I threw so hard I screamed, not from pain, but effort. I didn't want that ball to ever stop. I stood splayed out on the front of the mound, caught in my follow-through, my eyes closed so I wouldn't see where the ball landed, hoping I wouldn't one day be searching to retrieve it. My stupid Nolan Ryan. My Fireballer.

I heard the ball hit dirt, then something crack, creosote maybe. Then, eyes still closed, I heard something else, something coming on fast, and I turned to see Abilene's truck tearing toward me down the runway, only a speck but growing fast, reaching takeoff speed.

She kept on straight at me, making my knees go rubbery, my stomach sick and flighty.

She launched off the end of the runway, screeching to a sideways hockey-stop by the mound. Her dust poured over me.

When it drifted past, the first thing I saw was her smile. She stuck a sandwich out the window. "You must be starved."

I looked at her and her sandwich. She shook it at me and I took it without wanting to.

"Where've you been?" she asked, though I was standing right there where she knew she'd find me, right on top of my mound.

I stared at her as long as I could. "You tell me."

"Right here feeling sorry for yourself."

"For myself?" I blurted. "After what you did?"

"I didn't do anything, Austin." She stared back. "Did I ask him to play? Did I say, 'Say, Dad, stand there a second while I throw you the dark one'?"

"We were just playing. He used to—"

"He used to play," Abilene hissed. "It's how he met Mom. The girlfriend of the girlfriend of the precious Vernon Klee. 'Roma Lee Agostinelli. How's that for a handle?' You think I don't know all that lizard shit?"

Her face was only inches from mine. "I didn't know any of that. I'd never heard it before."

"Well, it's an old story."

I turned away from her and took a bite of the sandwich she had made for me—enough ham crammed between the bread to feed a whole team. She watched me, making it hard to swallow.

"So," Abilene said, still leaning out her window, "what are

you going to do now? Join Mom in the death watch? Watch her mother her new baby?"

"No. He's fine."

"No harm done."

"Ab'lene, he—"

"You just said he was fine."

"He's got a broken nose, Ab'lene. Black eyes. I just meant that there's nothing we can do for him."

"So it's just like any other day."

"Why do you hate him?" I blurted. "Why'd you have to break his nose?"

"I didn't break his nose," she answered quick. "A bad hop did."

"That was a handcuffer, Ab'lene."

"Did a handcuffer ever bust your face?"

I stuffed another bite into my mouth, wishing I'd never have to talk again.

"If you can swallow that without choking, let's roll."

I glanced up.

"That's right. Nothing's changed here, Austin. All part of the game." Abilene leaned over, shoving open my door. "Come on. I've got something even better than doves."

I walked around the front of her truck, knowing I had to go with her, but feeling more tired than I ever had in my life.

As soon as I sat down, Abilene shot the truck forward, rocking me back against my seat.

"He just wanted to play catch with me is all, Ab'lene. He didn't mean anything."

Abilene looked straight ahead as if I were on another planet.

"He was just trying to remember what that was like," I murmured. "Just that one tiny part of his life."

"Let him, Austin," Abilene said at last. "But, you and me, we got our own lives to get to."

"Like what?" I said, staring out at the parched ground. "What lives?"

I could feel her staring at me, staring a long time before just saying, "You tell me," like a threat.

It was then that I saw her pills: a carpet of the yellow and gray capsules scattered across the floor of her truck. Like wasps.

I jerked my feet up off them.

"Help yourself," Abilene said. "Want to know how a voodoo zombie feels? You just help yourself."

thirty

Abilene roared silent along roads I'd never seen, finally blowing off onto a narrow little two-track, barely a scratch on the dirt. I sat beside her, knees held up high, keeping my feet from crushing her meds, afraid to move, even to glance back at the rooster tail of our dust.

I don't know how long she'd been looking at me before we drifted off the two-track, smashing through the brush. Abilene smiled, looking only at me. Her old game of chicken.

"Where are we going?" I asked, just loud enough to be heard over the crash of the truck and the desert.

She grinned even wider, and just when I thought she wasn't going to answer, she yelled, "The river!" and bounced us through a hole that launched me into the roof of the cab, driving the top button of my Pecos cap into my skull. I grabbed the door again, trying to hang on, and Abilene took a hand off the wheel and slipped it beneath my cap, rubbing away the sting. "Sorry," she said, smiling.

"The river?" I asked, her hand still on my dirty hair. The only spot where we could get to water was miles and miles from here.

Abilene nodded, dodging around a clump of straggling cholla overgrowing the path. "What's the hardest thing you can think to shoot?" she said, shouting above the rumbling roar.

I thought of the pills under my feet, how desperate I'd been to tell Mom and Dad about the guns. "Ab'lene, I don't want to shoot anything."

"The hardest thing?" she shouted. She pushed the bill of my cap down over my eyes.

I pushed it up, smiling a little. "Doves," I said, picturing their herky-jerky flight, the teardrop-bullet shape of their whistling bodies.

"Nope."

I waited a minute to see if she'd help, but she just kept rocketing along. "Jackrabbits?"

"Nope," she said again, so fast I knew I wasn't supposed to get it.

"Think, Austin! Not just what people hunt. Anything. Anything at all. What would be the hardest?"

"I don't know," I said, but she still wouldn't help.

I was about to say *People?* just for something to say, when Abilene roared, "Swallows!" grabbing the wheel tight, slithering onto a road even sketchier than the one we'd been on. "Think of trying to hit one of them."

Bodies the size of gnats, I thought, flitting up, down, left, right—wherever the bugs flew. She was right. There couldn't be anything harder than swallows. I leaned back into the rush of wind and let Abilene take me wherever she wanted, imagining the dodging, impossible flight of the swallows. We couldn't even hit a dove.

It was late afternoon before Abilene made another wild turn, bucking down a pair of gullied ruts through a hidden cut to the river. She skidded to a halt on a tiny, muddy beach, closed off with huge mesquite, their thin, pale leaves rustling in the breeze. There was even a little grass, a tiny stand of river cane; an old fire ring and the washed-out ruts were the only sign that anyone had ever been here before.

I stepped out of the truck slowly, stiff from hanging on all through the long ride. My high-tops left prints in the grimy sand. The river here was nothing like the ditch it was at Pecos; it was almost deep, a slow pool against a sheer rock wall on the other side. "You've been here before?" I asked, suddenly wondering if the fire ring was hers, if this was a hideout.

Abilene shrugged.

I followed her glance to the rock wall, the swallows' mud nests stuck all over. Now, with the fierce edge of the heat, there wasn't a trace of life. Not even over the water.

Abilene dropped her seat forward, retrieving her shotgun. She worked the pump, savoring that deadly working of steel. She threw Dad's gun to me. "First hit wins."

"Hit what?" I asked. "Wins what?"

And just then a single swallow swooped down through the mesquite, hauling up short at the nest cliff. It dodged into the tiny entrance of a mud house without landing first, flying right through a hole the size of a quarter, a nickel maybe, and then stopping dead, home again.

"Did you see that?" I marveled.

"Want to know the secret, Austin? The killing secret?"

I didn't say that I did, but Abilene said, "Watch this."

Without lifting her gun, but shooting straight from her hip, straight across the river at the cliff crowded with mud nests, Abilene fired all five shots as fast as she could work the pump. I twisted away, covering my face with my hands as the pellets sang back around us, the same way I'd always cowered from the handcuffer. In the ringing silence after the fifth shot I peeked up, seeing the big vacant holes among the surviving nests. The air was suddenly full of birds, circling everywhere, back and forth, peep-peeping.

The river, reflecting the flat, blank blue of the sky, was glossy and pale, but as I stood beside Abilene, I saw the little dark spots on its surface, the floating bodies of the dead swallows that didn't reflect anything.

"You got a pile of them," I whispered.

"I know. I win."

I looked at the drift of bodies, the slow swirl of them in the backwater eddy. "Now what?"

"Reload." Before long she was shooting again at the confused birds. She didn't hit a single one when they were in the air.

Then Abilene stared down at the scattering of her empty shells, like all of a sudden this wasn't fun anymore. She looked from the shells to the birds in the water to the nests. "Austin, do you think this is crazy?"

"What?"

"This. Everything." She waved her arms around like Dad used to, telling How All This Started. "Do you think I'm crazy?"

I couldn't think of a way to answer that. I just stood there watching the smile grow across her face.

"Thanks," she said, throwing her gun back up and firing at nothing, like I'd given some sort of answer. Then, setting her gun across the hood of her truck, she bulled into the brush, breaking up dead branches of the mesquite, throwing them toward the old fire ring.

I put Dad's gun across the seat of her truck, back in its case, careful not to scratch it. "What now?"

"We'll build a fire. Get ready for the feast. Soon as the sun goes down, this place will be swarming with bugs. With swallows. It'll be like a shooting gallery."

"It's pretty hot for a fire, Ab'lene."

She hesitated over the fire ring, her arms full of broken gray branches. "And this time, Austin, I want you shooting too. There's not much meat on a swallow. We're going to need all we can get."

I watched her throw down her wood.

"Come on, Ab'lene. I couldn't hit one of those things in a million years."

"I got a plan for that too." She veered off from her path to the mesquite, hopping to her truck, like she couldn't get anything done fast enough.

She pulled Dad's gun out again, sliding it from its case, tossing it across the tailgate as soon as she got it dropped. I winced at the metal against metal. "Careful!"

"My middle name." Abilene dug through the spare tire and junk in the back of her truck, finally brandishing a rickety old hacksaw, waving it toward Dad's shotgun.

I tried to get between her and it. "What are you doing, Ab'lene?"

"I've got a world-record idea," she said, smiling huge. "We're going to make us the ultimate swallow gun."

"Don't, Ab'lene," I begged, but she kept coming like I wasn't there, and I had to slip out of her way. "Ab'lene. Don't."

As I watched, pleading, Abilene hunched over the gun, her arm working like a fevered pump jack, the dull blade screeching and whining against the steel. In no time a chunk of barrel almost a foot long clattered against the rocks and dirt.

Abilene worked the burrs off the barrel with her pocketknife, scraping it around, running her finger inside testing for smoothness, silvery scratches winding around the end of the fresh cut.

Turning and shaking the gun between us, she cried, "We'll sweep them from the skies!"

I looked down at the chopped-off barrel poking from beneath

her truck. I picked it up, saw the scattered bright filings in the sand, glinting in the sun. Abilene had worked so fast the cut end of the barrel was still hot.

Before she could say a thing, I threw the piece of barrel as hard as I could out into the river, watched it splash down where Dad would never have to see it.

Abilene glanced after it. "Nice toss. That's some arm you've got. Loaded with potential."

I glanced at her and she winked. Then she spun the gun around on the tailgate. "It's a hair long for you too," she said, digging the saw into the wood of the stock. It was a lot harder going, the saw not meant for that kind of work, but Abilene rasped away until a little less than an inch of the dark walnut fell to the ground.

"Here." She held the gun out to me. "I pass it on to you."

I took it, wondering if I should throw it into the river too.

"What do you think?" Abilene blurted, all excited.

"He didn't mean for me to have this."

"Sure he did. He just didn't know it yet."

She stuck a fistful of shells in my face. "It's going to cut them down like a scythe, Austin!"

And as the sun set, and the bugs came out, and the swallows again filled the air, sweeping down low along the water, it did.

At the sight of the first bird, Abilene tugged Dad's mangled gun away from me, giving me hers. "We'll take turns," she promised. Then she set her feet, raising Dad's gun to her shoulder. She looked for a target in the birds whipping by and asked, "Ready?"

I hunched my head toward my shoulders, flinching before anything had happened.

Her shot scattered all over out of the short barrel, and she brought down a swallow with the first pull of the trigger. She let out a whoop and held the gun to me. "Your turn!" she yelled.

She was screaming, "Shoot!" before I even had the gun in my hands.

We took turns, one shot apiece, and we found that if we waited right, we could knock down three, four, five at a time. Nobody ever said Abilene didn't know what she was doing.

We got tons of swallows. When I knelt down, leaning to rip the shot low over the sluggish brown river, where the swallows cruised for bugs hatching out of the water, the shot cleared a swath through the little birds, leaving the air blank and empty for a second. Watching the water stripe white, the birds crashing everywhere, Abilene cheered, yelling, "It's the handcuffer!"

We got so many Abilene could barely stand it, jerking around like a marionette when it was my turn, saying, "Hurry! Shoot!" before I could even find a clump of birds to aim at.

After my last shot, Abilene jumped like I'd hit her. "Look at them, Austin!" she cried. "Look at all of them!"

I looked, the little dark bodies clotting the river.

"We got to get them!" Abilene shrieked, her voice cracking. "Get in there and get them, Austin! They're drifting away! They're getting away!"

"What?"

Abilene gave a quick, frustrated yelp and jumped into the river. I only stood on the muddy bank, watching her thrash around in water up to her thighs, throwing tiny dead birds back to shore. I had to dodge one soggy ball of feathers after another.

Then, before Abilene could get started on me, before she even noticed I was just standing there, I waded out into the warm water downstream from where she was beating the surface to a froth. I tossed the little bodies back to shore, amazed to find the birds were simply weightless, even wet.

As I worked, combing the river for bird after bird, I kept glancing at Abilene. Even after she'd cleaned up everything that hadn't drifted to me, she kept turning this way and that, panting and laughing. With the weight of the water, her shirt stuck close to her and pulled out of her pants. Right through the cloth I could see the laciness of her bra, the same way it'd looked after she broke up my ball game, busting out of her shirt while the men pulled at her. The material hid her tattoo, but I imagined the bright blaze of the word *Fireballer*. Those days seemed like something that'd happened years ago; something that'd happened to somebody else. I turned away before she could catch me gawking.

After bringing in the last of the birds, I pulled myself up onto the bank next to Abilene, onto the rocks above the mud. Water streamed from our clothes, staining the white, mud-caked stones dark. Dead swallows surrounded us.

Abilene took out her pocketknife, wrestling it from the sopping folds of her jeans. She snapped up the first bird.

I picked up one of my own, for the first time seeing a swallow close and still. In the air they were nothing but dark streaks. Now the one I held was all chestnutty and blue-black, streaked with white, with a big white forehead that somehow made it look smarter than a regular bird. And that glossy open eye.

I held the tiny bird in my hand and watched Abilene work the swallows exactly the same way she had the dove, making a little crosscut, then scooping out the insides, only her pinky fitting inside. The swallows were so fragile though, so tiny, that Abilene couldn't save the legs. Instead she broke the spine off below the breast, pinched the head and wings off with her thumbnail, leaving only the little ball of the chest.

She hurled each tiny blob of guts and parts into the river, saying, "We're going to have to come back here fishing, Austin. There's going to be a catfish in here the size of a truck. Probably already picking his teeth with your gun barrel."

Seeing how excited she still was, even doing this, I had to turn away. But as the mound of gutted little bodies grew, I finally asked, "Ab'lene? What are we doing?"

"What do you mean?"

"What are we going to do with them? With all these teeny birds?"

"Have them for dinner. Deep-fry them in olive oil. They do it all the time."

I looked at her. "Who?"

"Italians."

"Italians?"

Abilene laughed, hunching over another swallow, scooping in her pinky.

"I'll start the fire," I said, needing to get away from her. I had to pick my way to keep from squashing any of the birds she hadn't collected yet.

"Hold your horses, Austin," Abilene said, still not looking away from her work. "This is real gourmet stuff. No fire this time. We need a fully stocked kitchen."

"A kitchen?"

"Home cooking this time around, Austin."

I set my foot down, careful to avoid the carcasses. "Our home, Ab'lene?"

"Now you're thinking."

"You're going to take these back home? To our house?"

Abilene tapped the tip of her finger to the end of her nose. It left a bloody smudge above her grin, sliding off toward one cheek. "High time we start eating as a family again!"

"What are you going to say, Ab'lene? To Mom and Dad?"

"*Bon appétit!*" she cried, laughing and slapping her hand on the stones.

thirty-one

Before Abilene could get the kitchen door open, I saw Mom and Dad through the glass. Mom jumped at the rattle of the door, already looking like she wished they'd eaten earlier, that they were already safe in the living room, that they'd done anything but just wait for us. And that was before she saw Abilene.

Dad sat across from her with his patched face and darkened eyes, looking alone and resigned to whatever might sweep over him next.

Whipping the door back, Abilene marched in with the shotguns. She leaned them against the wall. There hadn't been a thing I could do to stop her.

I followed with my shirt pulled out in front of me, cradling the swallows in the bulging cloth. "Look," I said, hoping somehow to distract them from the guns. Mom and Dad barely glanced at all the tiny, naked birds crowded into my arms, each one smaller than a golf ball. The meat was dark, dark red; almost purple.

On the stove a pan of enchiladas sat ready to be popped into the oven. Abilene jumped over and in one quick sweep dumped them, pan and all, into the garbage. "Day off, Mom! We're cooking tonight!"

Mom whispered, "Austin?" but Abilene shushed her.

"Get the fryer, Austin," she called, "we got work to do." She waved the back of her hands toward Mom and Dad, shooing them away. "Go on into the living room and relax, you two. This is going to be a dining experience! Most excitement for you guys since that night in Abilene. Or maybe Austin." She gave me a whack on the shoulder, rolling her eyes to the ceiling.

Dad sat rooted where he'd been since Abilene pushed open the door. He kept staring at the guns, his big, bandaged face drooping down, the bandage stark white between his blackened eyes. His old shotgun stood beside Abilene's new one, the barrel hacked off, the splinters at the end of the stock white and raw. He looked over at Abilene and then back at the guns.

Mom stared at him, her fingers winding around and around each other.

Eventually Dad took a long, shaky breath and stood, sliding the one step over to the guns, his shoulders sagging.

Abilene said, "Careful."

But Dad picked up Abilene's gun and jacked out all the shells. Then he picked up his old gun and did the same.

Abilene stood and watched, grinning.

Without saying a word, Dad put all the shells in the front pockets of his pants. Then he leaned his mutilated gun back against the wall. "You wouldn't believe how proud I was when I first got this," he said, his voice thick and clotted.

Abilene snorted and Dad winced.

"Come on, Ruby," he said to Mom, holding his hand out to her. When she started to protest, saying something about the guns and Abilene, he shook his head, pursing his lips as if saying *Shh, shh.* He took her by the hand and walked her quietly to the living room. Even after they were gone I could hear his wheezing.

With Mom and Dad safely out of the kitchen Abilene dug in her pockets, pulling out a handful of shells, and reloaded the sawed-off gun.

When she caught me watching, she only said, "Always ready," like a joke.

After setting Dad's loaded gun beside her empty one, Abilene rummaged through all the cupboards. She grumbled about our not having any olive oil, but pulled out a can of Crisco. "There's not an Italian within a thousand miles of here anyway," she said, melting the blocky, white chunks in the biggest pan we had.

Without trying one first, or testing anything, Abilene heaped mound after mound of swallows into the hissing, spitting oil, stirring them around with Mom's slotted spoon. When she somehow decided they were done, she dumped them into a cake pan she'd lined with paper towels. The grease from the pan spattered onto the stove top, cooling into little pale, waxy drops.

After running all the swallows through the pan, she loaded them onto plates, heaping Dad's so high they kept falling off. "Come and get it!" she called, then yelled it again. Finally she strolled into the living room, still carrying her greasy slotted spoon.

I stayed in the kitchen, looking at the plates she'd set on the table, steaming into the air. I could picture Abilene waving the spoon at them, urging them on.

And then in she marched, Mom and Dad towed along behind. We all followed Abilene, pulling out our chairs, scraping them over the linoleum, sitting down around the table in our usual spots to stare at our swallows.

No one said a thing, just looked down at our plates, avoiding eye contact with Abilene, who sat ramrod straight in her chair, beaming at each of us.

At last, clearing his throat, Dad made the first move, poking at one of the swallows on his plate with his fork, trying half-heartedly to pull some meat away from the tiny bones.

"No, Daddy," Abilene said, and I could see Dad's fingers whiten around his fork.

"Like this," she said when he looked at her. She popped a whole bird into her mouth with a suddenness that made me flinch. I could hear the bones crunching as she chewed, then she swallowed and smiled. "Scrumptious!"

Mom and Dad looked like they'd been turned to stone. So I picked up a bird of my own, gulping first, trying to wet my dust-dry tongue. Then I popped the swallow into my mouth the way Abilene had. At first, just the thought of it made me kind of sick, but really it wasn't bad, the bones not much more than sardines'.

"Attaboy!" Abilene picked another from her plate, and when she was sure everyone was watching, she tossed it into the air, saying, "Peep, peep," before catching it in her mouth. She winked at Mom.

Mom stared at Abilene a second longer, but when Dad reached for a swallow, picking it up with his bare fingers, Mom scrunched her napkin onto the table beside her plate and scraped back her chair. She looked long and hard at Dad, then turned and walked out of the kitchen.

Looking after her, Abilene said, "Must be a little under the weather." She tossed another swallow into the air, catching it like before.

Dad eyed her, then eventually put the swallow he'd picked up carefully into his mouth. He bit down like he expected something to explode, some poison to leak out. Then, having survived, he began to chew. Abilene's bandage on his nose wiggled with each chomp, and I knew it had to be hurting him. He smiled a little half-smile and swallowed. "These are good, Abilene. Really."

Abilene winked at him too. "I knew you'd like them."

Turning to me, she added, "Didn't I say that, Austin? Didn't I say Dad would eat them up?"

Dad smiled the same way I pictured him in that dugout, being introduced to Mom. "I do like my meals." He put another swallow in his mouth, and even before he'd finished chewing, he said, "Maybe we ought to do more of this. All of us. Together. Trying new things." Even with his downcast, blackened eyes he had a look of hope.

"Well," Abilene said, "with that new swallow-slayer we'll be steady on swallows for a while."

She pointed right at the mutilated shotgun and I shrank back in my chair, but Dad just nodded. He plucked a piece of tiny shot delicately from the tip of his tongue and put it in his napkin. He reached for another swallow.

As soon as I thought Abilene might let me, I started clearing the table, trying to snatch away Dad's plate while it was still stacked with swallows. But Abilene grabbed my arm and I let go of his plate without looking at her, without saying a word. When I started running the dishwater, Abilene said, "We cooked, Austin. Mom and Dad clean. You know the rules."

Dad nodded. "She's right, Austin. Mom and I will take care of all of this."

Turning off the water, I studied the back of Dad's big head, the post of his neck, the hump of his shoulders.

Feeling the grease setting up in slippery white layers inside me, I said, "It's late." I tried to say something else, my lips still moving, but no words came out until I mumbled, "Well, good night."

Abilene watched me all the way out of the room, making me

concentrate just on walking, but I made it up the stairs without her calling me back. The last thing I heard her say was, "What say I give you a hand with those dishes, Dad? Mom's looking a little peaked. We'll let her get some rest."

Dad whispered, "Thanks."

I closed my door almost all the way, then sat on the edge of my bed in the dark, waiting for the roar of Abilene's truck, or for Dad's surrendering climb of the stairs, trying to guess which would come first. I thought of slipping out Abilene's window and waiting for her in her truck. Maybe stowing away. But, though I knew I couldn't let her get away again, I wasn't sure I had the courage to follow her. So I sat on the edge of my bed, grinding my fist into my palm.

What I heard next, when I finally heard anything at all, were Mom's soft steps, pussyfooting down the stairs to Dad and Abilene, the last thing in the world I'd ever thought would happen.

The fight blew up in seconds. For a minute I couldn't move; just cowered at the edge of my bed, shivering, the swallows in my stomach threatening to fly back out. I listened to the bang of the screen, then the screech and slam of Abilene's truck door, but then, instead of the blast of her engine, I heard the screen bang shut again.

For an instant I tried to put together a picture: Abilene coming back to the house for something, or Dad chasing after her, but when the shouting started again, it was Abilene's. Frozen on the edge of my bed, I couldn't make out the words. I guessed what I'd heard was Abilene taking the guns, locking them in her truck.

When I finally crept to the top of the steps, as far as I could make myself go, I heard Mom's voice, as thin and fragile as she was, pleading, "But, Abilene, it's for your own good. We're so worried about you."

Abilene laughed like crazy at that. Then there was a loud slap,

Abilene bringing her hands down hard and flat on the table. "No, it is not for my own good."

Mom sucked in a startled breath. "Abilene."

Abilene shouted, "Don't ever call me that filthy name again! Never! I'm Abby!"

"That's fine, Abby, honey," Mom said.

Abilene shrieked, "My name is not Abby-honey!"

I wondered how Mom had gotten the word *Abby* out so fast, so natural.

I kept waiting for the bang of the screen again, Abilene's truck roaring, but instead Abilene thundered up the stairs. I crouched against the hard, turned posts of the railing, and though I was in plain sight, Abilene charged right past. The slam of her door was so sharp and sudden I leapt up, afraid I might have been shot, though Abilene had been empty-handed.

I waited, but Mom and Dad didn't come after her. I pictured them standing stunned in the kitchen, but then I heard the phone lifted off the hook, Mom's quaky voice asking, "Dr. Pape?" I forced myself up, my legs shaking.

When I was steady enough to walk, I stepped to Abilene's door and whispered, "Abby?" practicing the name in my head before I spoke. I said it again.

Her voice came muffled through the door. "You can still call me Ab'lene. That's a whole different story."

"Okay." I stared at her door and whispered, "Are you all right?"

She didn't answer, so I went on, talking almost singsongy, like you would to a baby. "It's okay, Ab'lene. Ab'lene's a great name. Let's not forget it could have been Lubbock."

I heard her laugh a little, and I could picture her in there, biting her red knuckles, trying not to laugh at all.

"Are the guns in your truck?" I asked.

She did laugh then. "Yes. They were trying to steal them."

I didn't know what to say.

Abilene waited a minute, then said, "Good night, Fireballer."

"Good night," I said, just loud enough she'd hear me. I said it again, even softer, then tiptoed down the hallway and sat again on the edge of my bed, waiting for the slow ascent of our parents, the quiet slide of Abilene's window.

thirty-two

It was hard, from my room, to make sense of all the sounds that night. Abilene paced and thumped in her room, at one point knocking something big over, a clattering spill, her bookshelf maybe. She laughed afterward, and now and then I heard her talking fast, all alone in there. Once, clear as glass, I heard her say, "Oh, no, you don't!" Another time she shouted, "No, I don't think *you're* coming along," and I heard a quick, hard rip of cloth.

Holding my head in my hands, I whispered, "Who, Ab'lene? You're alone."

I strained to hear Mom and Dad come upstairs, hoping they'd go straight to their room. I prayed they weren't bringing Dr. Pape out.

But downstairs Mom was on the phone again, her whispering murmur sifting up through the floor.

The screen door screeched once for sure, though there was no slam; somebody being careful. I got up then, crouching to peek out the corner of my window, and saw Dad standing beside Abilene's truck, just standing at the driver's door, hands on his hips, like he was having a little talk with Abilene, chatting about the drought, though I could still hear her stalking around her room.

As soon as Dad went back inside, I slid my window open, to hear better out there without letting anyone know I was listening.

Abilene laughed again. Something smashed against her wall.

I lay back on my bed, my feet still on the floor. I had to stay with Abilene, but if I went downstairs to stow away in her truck, Mom and Dad would stop me. If I went to Abilene's room, she wouldn't let me in, not even to use her window. I almost convinced myself there was nothing I could do.

The night fogged with Mom's whispering, Abilene's frightening laughter, Dad's sneaking about, and I nearly dozed off, bolting upright only when I heard a heavy crack, a collapse somewhere of glass.

I blinked in the darkness, then slid back off my bed to the window. The baked-dust smell of the desert wrapped around me as I crouched, and something, someone, a quick shadow, slipped by below me. I heard the screen. The pale wash of moonlight flattened the yard, making everything look like cardboard cutouts. I remembered the sound of glass, but then wondered if I'd really heard it, if I'd really been awake.

I stayed crouched by the window a long time, but nothing else moved out there. Downstairs everything grew quiet; even Abilene, for the moment, was still. I wondered if she was looking out her window too.

Then, at last, Mom and Dad came up the steps, the same heavy footsteps, Mom whispering one last thing before their door clicked shut behind them. I let out a breath it seemed I'd been holding all night, since the moment we walked in the door with those guns, those swallows.

Abilene, I figured, would make her break soon now. I sat

staring at the truck. If she crossed the white rock, I'd see her. I'd whisper, "Fireballer," magically stopping her long enough for me to finally do something.

But I watched the truck for what felt like hours, my eyes dry and tired, my stomach flighty, my legs cramping. There wasn't a sound from the house, from either Mom and Dad or Abilene, and I thought maybe this was somehow all blowing over, another blue norther that brought no rain. I crept back to my bed, sat down on its edge.

Maybe Abilene had learned to control it now without the meds. Maybe she could pull back from that edge now, the way she'd hoped, now that she knew what lay beyond it. I didn't know. Maybe we'd all be all right.

But I knew that there was more to safety than hope, and at last, feeling in the back of my mind that Abilene really wasn't going to leave that night, I found the courage to sneak out of my room, on my way to her truck. I carried my pillow with me, determined to spend the night out there, if only to show Abilene that I wasn't going to let her go off alone again, that I hadn't been absolutely crippled with fear.

Opening my door, I peered down the hallway in both directions, first toward Mom and Dad's room, then toward Abilene's. There wasn't a sound, not even the odd creak and groan of the house settling, its slow collapse back into the desert.

I peered toward Abilene's door, which looked like it gaped wide open. It was impossible to tell in the dark. I stepped that way, past the stairs, the door yawning black and empty before me. "Ab'lene?" I whispered.

The quick, hard slap of the screen stopped me cold, caught me trapped out in the hallway, my stupid pillow dangling from my hand. Hearing the charge that could only have been Abilene—a kitchen chair clattered over in the darkness, a three-or-four-steps-at-a-time blind rush up the stairs—I shrank back against the wall, trying to make myself smaller, invisible.

Whipping herself around the banister, flinging herself head-long into Mom and Dad's door, batting it open with her forearm, a smashing jolt that would have raised the dead, Abilene never glanced my way.

I couldn't imagine how she'd gotten out of her room without me hearing.

For a moment after that slam there was silence, and I pictured the moonlit staredown, Mom and Dad both shocked straight up in bed, Mom clinging to the sheet, Dad raccoon-faced, the white blob of the bandage murkily visible, and Abilene, trembling at the foot of their bed, tall and furious, out of her mind.

Then, after that second, Abilene shrieked, "Where are they?"

Mom stammered something, and I heard Dad's feet hit the floor before Abilene bellowed, "Where?"

Her fists slammed down on something soft, or padded. The foot of their bed, I hoped.

"Where are they, Daddy?" Abilene howled.

"Abby," Mom started, and I heard a whack. Though I'd never heard it before, I knew right away it was the sound of a hand against a face, and I squeezed myself even tighter to the wall, my shoulder blades pressed flat against the cool plaster.

There was more shouting then, not words, just shouts, and in a second Dad staggered out of the bedroom with Abilene pinched in his giant arms. The hallway light flashed on, catching all of us for a second in its sudden stark glare. Abilene, her hair torn loose from her braid, flying all over her face, all over Dad's, thrashed like a broken-backed rattler, but she didn't have a chance against Dad's size.

Dad staggered toward the steps, his face twisted away from me, from Abilene, protecting his nose from the thrashing blows of her head as she fought.

Mom stood alone at the light switch, fumbling to turn them all on, to light Dad's descent down the steps.

As Dad took his first uncertain step down, Abilene finally

worked her screams into words. "Motherfucker!" she shrieked, battering at his shins with her heels. "My fucking guns, you cocksucker!" She was trying now to hit him with the back of her head, Dad ducking and weaving as she hammered backward at him, her arms pinched under his.

They went down the steps in a rush, one long fall, Dad somehow keeping his feet under him, yanking her toward the kitchen, kicking her legs out from under her whenever she got one planted on the floor.

Mom was right behind, all the lights on, as if the darkness held some new terror. She stopped beside me just long enough to say, "We're taking Abby to town, Austin." She had tears running down her face. "I'm sorry we have to leave you alone."

She looked at me a second longer, touching my face with her shaky hand, and I studied the bright pink outline of Abilene's fingers on her cheek.

I followed her downstairs, then watched from the doorway as she slipped behind the wheel, Dad still fighting to get Abilene's hands and feet folded up long enough to squeeze her into the backseat. He fell in there on top of her, and as soon as he wrestled the door shut, Abilene broke her torrent of swearing to shout for help. "Austin!" she kept yelling, her mouth pressed to the gap at the top of the window, Dad holding on to her, pulling her back. "Austin!"

I stood just inside the screen, still clutching my pillow.

When the car was long out of sight, when I couldn't even make believe I heard it anymore, I eased open the screen and slowly walked out to Abilene's truck. Her door was wide open, the keys dangling from the lock, the back of the seat still thrown forward, just the way Abilene had found it.

Not until I stepped around the door did I see that the window wasn't rolled down; it was smashed in, bits of it glittering across the seat, the floorboards, sparkly among her discarded pills. I took a step back, more of the glass crunching between my feet and the broken rock of the driveway.

I wrenched the keys from the lock and stuffed them into my pocket. My eyes burned, and swiping at them, I said, "Why didn't you just go to bed?" I slammed the truck door and turned back to the house.

I could just hear Dr. Pape's soft voice telling them, at all costs, to get the guns away from Abilene. At all costs. The stinging fall of glass as Dad broke the window of Abilene's truck. And louder still, my own voice telling Mom and Dad that we were not all right, that Abilene was off her meds.

I trudged back into the kitchen, slowly pulling myself up the railing to Mom and Dad's room, the house still lit up like an operating room. I swung open their closet door, sifting through Dad's suits, Mom's outfits, behind the shoe boxes up on the shelf. But the guns weren't there.

They were in the basement, not hard to find, just behind some boxes and the carpet roll, stashed away with the rest of Dad's life. He'd hidden each one in a length of PVC, leftover pipe from the septic tank. The white tubes lay side by side, along with a whole garbage bag of Abilene's shells. They must've been in her truck too.

It was a ridiculous hiding spot. If Abilene hadn't blown up like she had, we'd be out right now, doing nothing more dangerous than pumping the night full of holes. Maybe a few bats too, at worst.

I duct-taped the ends of the PVC shut, holding the guns inside. Then, shouldering the sack and pinching the guns under my arm, I started into the moonlight for the base.

thirty-three

The trip out to the base that night was deadly. Steering by the glimmer of moonlight on the hangar walls, feeling my way through the shadows of the mesquite, I punctured my leg on a shin dagger before finally reaching the runway, limping down its long stretch with my load. Then, after finding our broken shovel, I went to work hiding the guns and the shells. The moon was down, the sun coming on strong before I finished. The rough, dried wood of the shovel handle had stopped just short of blistering my hands, and straightening up, I hurled it back into the desert. Then, the guns safe, I turned to face the bloodred east and started back down the runway, the day's heat gaining on me.

At home, Mom and Dad still gone, I went in for a garbage bag, then sat down in Abilene's truck, picking up every single pill, every last piece of broken window. I threw the bag into the back, with the rest of the junk.

I went in the house then and sat down in the kitchen, the shin dagger's dried trickles of blood crinkling my skin, the swollen stab wounds throbbing, but I couldn't stand the stillness. I walked upstairs, through all the rooms, ending up in Abilene's. I twisted the lock shut behind me.

The crash I'd heard last night had been books. Abilene's mostly empty bookcase stood shoved up against her window, as if she'd been afraid somebody was going to come into her room that way.

Sinking down on Abilene's bed, I leaned close, taking a deep breath of her pillow, but her smell was lost in the detergent Mom used on the sheets, which only made Abilene seem that much more gone. I lifted my face, and walking slowly to the window, I pushed the bookcase aside, back to its place.

I started stacking the books back onto their shelves, putting everything back in its place; all her old baseball coaching manuals, her pitching guides. Even my old kids' book: *Nolan Ryan: Fireballer.*

But as I picked up the books and could see the floor again, I found what they'd been tipped down on top of. Crumpled at the bottom of the pile was a baseball uniform, *Pecos* emblazoned across the chest. The shirt was torn near in half, and for just an instant I thought it was mine. But it was the old style, the letters slanted and purple, and I knew it had to be Abilene's, stolen and hidden away all those years. *I don't think you're coming along!*

I picked up the shirt and put it carefully on a hanger. I stood looking at it in her closet, and as I turned away, I caught a glimpse of a sliver of dirty wood hidden behind her clothes. Reaching between the legs of some jeans, I found Dad's old baseball bat. I pulled it out, swung it by the knob at the end, the pine tar still tacky. She must have found it downstairs with the shotgun. But what, I wondered, was her plan hiding it away up here?

I spread my feet, bent my knees, holding the bat up high,

waggling the tip the way Dad had. He'd looked pretty menacing, but I knew Abilene with this would put ice into anyone's heart.

I was still standing there, the least-feared batter in all of Texas, when I heard the car. I dropped the bat down to my side and glanced out the window, watched Mom park, both of them climbing slowly out of their seats.

I lay Dad's bat across Abilene's bed, out in plain sight. Maybe it'd be just one more thing for them to worry about, but maybe it might seem like something nice: Abilene's caring enough to want that memento of their old life for her own.

I met them at the stairs, me at the top, them at the bottom, peering up. Back from town, they were still in their pajamas, fragile-looking that way. Dad seemed exhausted, nodding a little greeting, rubbing his hand along the side of his face, careful to avoid his nose. Mom shadowed him, smaller than ever.

"What are you *both* doing back here?"

"They've got her knocked out," Dad said. "Dr. Pape practically insisted we come home. 'You'll need your rest,' she said."

"We're back to square one," Mom added. "Everything all over again."

"They'll restart her meds," Dad said. He leaned in against the newel, as if it took all he had left simply to stand. "How did you know, Austin? How did you know she'd stopped taking them?"

"Anybody who knew her could have seen it." I shook my head, looking down at them. "Why didn't you ask me first before taking the guns?"

"You must see Abilene can't have guns," Mom said. "Not now. Look what she did with just a Coke can. What happens next time? With a gun?"

I was so near to tears I couldn't look at them. Couldn't face anybody. "We only shot some swallows." My voice caught and I looked away. "One lousy dove."

"Austin, honey. Abilene is so sick."

I stared down the hallway at her open, empty door. Below me Mom and Dad just stood there, side by side, probably scared for me now.

"I found where you hid them," I said at last, pushing myself away from the railing, dragging my feet down the hallway toward Abilene's room. "Abilene would've found them there in a second."

Dad started to say something, but I interrupted.

"I moved them. They're safe now." I knew that even downstairs they heard the twist and click of Abilene's lock between us.

thirty-four

Days crawled by without Abilene, then weeks, Mom and Dad never letting me know when she was coming home. The way they talked, the hospital was her home. They spent every spare second over in Midland, seeing Abilene, working with the doctors. They tried talking me into going with them, saying it was only for Abilene, only for her good. Which, I figured, Abilene would say was so much lizard shit.

Dad tried and tried to get me to tell him where the guns were, but I was done telling them anything. I just shook my head, saying, "They're safe. They're gone. No one will ever find them again. I promise."

He studied me. "You understand how serious this is. If she gets depressed again?"

"I'll be the first to know," I answered.

———

When school started, I piled on the credits, the way Abilene had wanted me to, the same way she had. I was too late to graduate any more than half a year early, but it was all I could do. After one of the first days back, I trudged out to the base, but it was so full of Abilene, all the mistakes I'd made with her, I left before I even reached the tank. I could hardly breathe out there on the frypan-hot runway, thinking of that dead soldier, *Because Somebody Talked,* remembering that I'd actually thrown away the ball she'd driven across all of Texas to get signed for me.

Getting home that evening, late for dinner, Mom and Dad worried, I slumped into my seat. They watched me, not saying anything until Dad practically whispered, "Were you out at Pyote? Working on your pitching?"

I stared at the edge of the table, unable to believe I'd even told him about the base. I shook my head.

"Abilene asked to see you again," Mom said.

"I doubt that," I muttered.

"She's doing much better, Austin," Dad said. "The lithium levels are back up. They think last time the antidepressants may have pushed her over into a manic phase." He stammered a little. "And then she went off her lithium."

"I know."

"She's really much better," Mom said. "You should think about coming in with us. She wants to see you. You're all she talks about."

"Abilene would hate me seeing her locked up anywhere."

Dad shook his head. "Maybe when she's manic, but that's not Abilene. Not really."

I looked straight at him. His nose was its normal size again, a little crook in it up by the bridge, only the last streaks of purpled blood below his eyes. I pictured Abilene where they'd locked her, crouched in the corner of some bare room, her own eyes like bruises in her white face, her wild hair bright against the soft, pale walls.

"Lizard shit," I said.

Dad's face sagged and Mom sighed. "It's hard enough, Austin," she began. "It's hard enough on all of us without having to fight you every inch of the way. What Abilene needs now is understanding. What Abilene needs now is you."

I glared at her, always after me, like this was all my fault. "Lizard shit." I stood half up, leaning over the table into her face. "Lizard shit. Lizard shit. Lizard shit!" I was shouting.

Without leaving his chair, like he was too exhausted to deal with any of this anymore, Dad reached out and gave me a shove, getting me away from Mom.

That's all he was doing, getting me away from Mom. I'm sure of that. But I wasn't expecting it and I went sprawling, bashing into a chair, then the floor.

I braced myself up on an elbow, surprised, the floor cool beneath me. I tried out a laugh. The legs of the tipped-over chair stuck out at me like a lion tamer's. Dad gave me a glance, then slid out of his chair to hold Mom.

Mom held her hands up to her ears, whispering, "Stop it, stop it, stop it!" like we were shouting, though no one was saying a word.

Stop what? I wondered, and I asked it out loud. "Stop what?" When nobody answered, I said, "And once we start stopping, where do we stop?"

Dad glanced at me. "Be quiet," he said, hardly sounding mad. "Just be quiet. Just get out of here."

I really wanted to know about the stopping, but I scrambled up, pushing the tipped-over chair away from me. "No problem there," I said. "I'm gone."

Just before the screen slammed I heard Mom sob my name. Then came the same old rattling bang as ever.

Though it felt as wrong as anything I'd ever done, I went straight to Abilene's truck, throwing myself behind the wheel, tugging the keys out of my pocket, where I'd kept them like some kind of talisman, since the night they'd taken her away. As I cranked it over, then spun backward out the drive, I saw Dad at the door, watching.

Slamming it into first, I thundered down the gravel alone in Abilene's truck, turning the radio up full blast, till it was nothing but static and distortion. The rooster tail of talc-dry dust went up behind me, a lonely kite's tail.

Till I hit the interstate, I didn't have any idea where I was going. But I turned east onto the four-lane, toward Odessa and Midland, the sun a big, low ball behind me. Abilene was locked up somewhere ahead of me, but there was no way I could face her like that.

After more than an hour of hot, blasting wind I hit Odessa and kept on for Midland, drawn to her despite myself. Maybe I had to see her. Maybe break her out. In Midland I followed the path of the white *H*'s on blue signs. I was slicked with sweat, my throat growing tighter every second, wanting to turn away, turn back, but not knowing if I could.

Then I saw the Tattoos sign, a bright, green, neon glow in the dusk, and I thought of the *Fireballer* on Abilene's chest, how it had lighted her up, how she'd done it all for me.

I let off the gas, coasting to a stop in the middle of the road.

There was a screech behind me, a honk, and I nearly stalled it out pulling over. Opening Abilene's door before I could think, I stumbled into the tattoo place.

A skinny guy wearing an old-man T-shirt glanced up from a desk. You could hardly see skin through the tattoos. "What can I do for you?"

I swallowed. "I need a tattoo."

He stubbed out a cigarette. "Any one in particular?"

The walls were tacked over with examples. File binders full of designs littered his desk. "Got any paper?"

He shoved some across his desk.

"Pencil?"

He flipped one down.

I stooped over, sketching out a drawing of Abilene's tattoo, the big, bold word, the underlining baseball comet. "Can you do that?"

After barely a glance he straightened up, eyeing me and grinning. "On you?"

I looked away from him, then back. "I'm a pitcher."

"I bet you are," he said, still smiling like we were both part of some barely secret joke.

"Can you do it?" I asked again, wanting to bolt back out the door.

"You bet. Practice makes perfect. If you got the money, we can do it right now."

"You've done this one before?"

Standing aside and waving me to his chair with a big stagy flourish, he just kept grinning. "Every tattoo of mine is an original work of art."

"Have you? On a girl? On her chest?"

"On a girl's chest?" He pulled at the few scraggly whiskers on his chin. "Let's see. How many of those have I forgotten?"

He thumped the seat of the chair. "Come on, kid. You come for a tattoo today, or just this little chat?"

I looked away from all his tattoos, his blue-green skin. "I want it."

"Arm?"

"Chest."

He whistled. "Whole hog." He motioned for me to pull off my shirt and climb into the chair.

He stenciled awhile, getting the design stuck to my chest, then he turned on his machine. It sounded so much like a dentist's drill I wanted to run. But I figured Abilene had done the same for me, and I dug my fingers into the arms of the chair and lay back. Gritting my teeth, I watched the cool blue swirls of his cigarette smoke, concentrating on its hot stench. But when he started, it wasn't that bad. Stung some, burned a little. As he went on and on, hours' worth, I started reeling through Nolan Ryan's last no-hitter, distracting myself batter by batter, pitch by pitch.

When the guy was done, Nolan Ryan was in the eighth inning, mowing down Blue Jays, everybody being careful not to say, "No-hitter." No one jinxing anything.

Glancing down to my chest, all I could see was a big patch of white. A bandage. "I usually use Saran Wrap," the guy said, "so you can show it off right away. But I'm out. So don't go ripping this off, showing your buddies. Keep it on a day. Then keep it clean."

"Did it work?"

"Sure. You're the Fireballer from hell."

"It looks just like the drawing?"

"You're a walking, talking Xerox."

With my chin down on my chest, like I could see through the bandages if I only tried hard enough, I couldn't help but pick at the corner of the tape. Abilene and I were the same now.

Tattoo knocked my hand away. "Leave it alone."

"It looks all right?"

"Fantastic." He held my drawing out to me. There was a little stain on it, which might've been ink, but looked more like blood.

I took it and sat up, edging off his chair.

He told me how much it cost and I dug in my wallet. Almost everything I had.

Folding the bills and sliding them into his front jeans pocket, he said, "Okay, kid, I can't stand it anymore. Tell me."

"What?"

"You're just so in fucking love, or what?"

I stared at his chest.

He could hardly keep from laughing. "You think this is going to sweep her off her feet?"

"What are you talking about?" I was sweating. I licked my lips.

"The fireballer chick." He couldn't keep the laugh in any longer. "You think a little skin art is going to make the two of you a team?"

I stood there staring at him. "I'm a pitcher," I said. My chest burned.

He laughed harder. "That chick is full-time fucking nuts, kid. Even if you two already got all sweaty, which I doubt, there's no way you're going to hold her."

"You don't know shit," I blurted, just to stop him.

Tattoo quit chuckling long enough to actually look at me. "How old are you? Don't tell me. The Fireballer popped your cherry. Oh, kid. Holy fuck. You thought the two of you had something? That you just had this one special thing that made her fall for you? Oh, fuck, kid."

I backed toward the door. "Listen!" I shouted. "You don't know a single thing!"

"Oh, fuck it, kid. That chick is legend material. She's not going to hang with you. You think I wouldn't have done her if I could?" He swung his arm behind him toward this chair. "She was lying half-naked, right there in that chair. Hell, by the time I was done with her tattoo, I let *her* tattoo *me*!" He started toward me, lifting his shirt, wanting to show me the mark Abilene had left on him.

I dropped the stained drawing of our tattoo as I fumbled for the door, fought to get it open and get out.

"Forget her, kid. She comes and goes anyway. See her around awhile, then nothing. No telling if she'll ever be back."

As I squeaked outside, he shouted, "You think *I* haven't looked for her?"

I threw myself into Abilene's truck and jerked out onto the road, fumbling for the lights, screeching to get away before he could tell me one more word.

I peeled into a U-turn, out of town, back into the desert,

farther and farther from Abilene every second. My chest felt like one gigantic raspberry, and I rubbed it against the steering wheel, squeezing back the tears. Marked for life.

I goosed the gas, making the engine roar, the truck leap. I picked at the line of tape I could feel through my shirt, wanting to strip it off, to see what had happened to me, wishing I could scrape it all off.

It was nearly midnight by the time I reached Abilene's overpass; the thin band of Pecos's lights stretching north ahead of me. Traffic was as dead as ever, and I pulled over, walking out to the same spot where we'd hung so far out over the huge, empty road.

For a long time I just looked down at the railing, at where we'd hooked our bellies, then, slowly, I leaned over, feeling all wrong about being here without Abilene, about ever letting her come here without me.

Tiny chips of rock in the bleached pavement flashed back the lights of a single passing truck, and I leaned even farther, barely hanging on, the raw skin stretching and stinging. All I had was a big scab on my chest, ink mixing with blood, something I could never lose. I leaned over the cold steel edge into nothing, where Abilene thought she could fly. Stained just like her, I thought of her topless, laughing, hunched over Tattoo, his whining ink gun in her hand, and I felt further from her than I ever thought I'd be.

When I got home, I killed the engine and the lights, coasting into the driveway as quiet as I could. I sat behind the wheel of Abilene's truck, staring at our house—Dad's great deal—not knowing what to do next.

The kitchen light was still on, and I checked how my T-shirt hung on me, hoping the bandage would be invisible, and cracked open the door of the truck.

Inside, the dinner plates were cleared, the table cleaned, my plate no longer left set and waiting. The house was still and quiet, another dim light seeping into the hallway from the living room. My chest itched.

Then Dad flashed out from the living room. He was throwing my mitt at me before I even saw it. It bounced off my chest, making my eyes water. I reached down for it. "What?"

He had his own mitt on already and he never slowed down. As he went by me, he clamped on to my biceps and just kept going, dragging me out the door. I staggered after him, trying to turn around, get my feet straightened out, knowing how Abilene must have felt trapped in this grip.

"What?" I said again.

Dad shoved me out onto the driveway. He ducked his head through Abilene's missing window, flipping on the headlights. Then he opened his own car door, and Mom's, turning on all the lights.

I squinted against them, but Dad held up his ball for a second before throwing it at me. A real throw. Everything he had in him. I could barely see to catch it. "What?" I shouted.

But Dad just kept staring right through me.

So, as soon as I found the seams, I kicked my leg to my chest and shot one back that should've taken off his head. It was insane in the jangled shadows, the blinding beams.

But Dad snagged it, the ball cracking into his old glove. "Whole different game, isn't it?" he snapped.

I stayed on the edge of the light, bent at the knees, ready for his next shot. "What do you mean?"

"When you turn everything into weapons." He kicked his leg up, rifling another one at my chest. I stepped aside, letting the ball bounce into the rocks behind me, ricocheting off into the night.

"Who do you think you are?" I asked him. "Ab'lene?"

He kept staring at me, but when I stomped by him, tossing my mitt back at him, he let it bounce off him down onto the rock.

Then he whirled after me, catching me in that iron-hard grip once more, spinning me around, jerking me up against his chest, scraping my tattoo, his face in mine. His whole body shook.

"I brought those mitts out here, that ball, because it seems that's all you understand." Even his voice trembled. "I brought them out here to keep me from beating some sense into you."

I didn't say a word. Just looked below his eyes, at his chin, too close to focus on. He'd never hit anyone in his life.

"You ever pull another stunt like that with your mother, there won't be mitts and balls." He shook me once, hard. "Do you understand?"

I kept trying to focus on his chin.

He shook me again. "Understood?"

I nodded, felt him tightening his grip even more. "Yes."

He pushed me away from him then, out onto the chilly white rocks where both our mitts lay, where I stood watching him return to the house.

He was just at the door when I said, "She is so fucked-up, Dad."

Dad whirled, leaping down the steps.

I staggered backward into the dark. "Abilene! Abilene! Not Mom!"

Dad stopped. He couldn't see me behind all the headlights. "She's sick. Abilene is not fucked-up. She's sick."

The words sounded so odd coming out of him I only watched him squinting into the lights.

"She's sick," he said once more, then again turned and walked into the house.

I waited out in the darkness a long time before going to each car and shutting off the lights.

thirty-five

After that night I slipped around our house like a stranger, a thief. Half the time the house would be empty when I got home from school, everyone in Midland, and I'd sit alone in the kitchen, watching the cloudless evening settle down around me. Even when they were home, Mom and Dad let me slide by, didn't come chasing after me anymore, didn't come begging me to go into Midland with them, to go see Abilene all locked up.

About two weeks after I got my tattoo, something I could barely bring myself to look at, I walked up our road and saw their cars parked out front, both of them home early. My steps slowed, knowing I'd have to eat with them, fill another dinnertime with silence, a few grunted yeses and noes.

I trudged into the kitchen, but it was empty, and I thought I might make it up to my room without getting caught. I eased past the living room without a glance and had a hand on the banister, swinging myself up, when Dad stopped me with "Austin," too loud to pretend I didn't hear.

I stood holding on to the post, looking up the stairs, waiting. He didn't say anything else, forcing me to say, "What?"

"Come here please."

I closed my eyes, took a big breath, and shoved myself backward. "What?" I said again, stepping into the doorway.

The TV was on with hardly any sound, Mom and Dad on the couch. Across from them sat Abilene, facing the door. She gave me a tiny smile. "Hey, Austin," she whispered.

Mom was half out of her seat, but Dad reached over, holding her down.

Abilene was heavier again, a little puffy, but there were no dark eyes, no vacant stare. "Hey, Ab'lene."

"It's me," she answered, still with that tired smile.

Dad and Mom eased over to me together. Dad touched my arm, "Let's get something to eat," he said.

I stared at Abilene.

Dad tugged me toward the kitchen. "We expected you quite awhile ago."

I pulled my arm away.

"You want to pitch a game, Ab'lene?" I asked, forgetting that she wouldn't, but just wanting to get her out of that room.

Abilene's smile stayed the same. "Not just yet, Austin. I'm more than a little rusty."

"Sure. Of course." I couldn't tell if she was looking at me or not.

I was too stunned to keep Mom and Dad from steering me to the kitchen.

"We didn't mean this as a surprise, Austin," Dad said.

"We thought you'd be home in time for me to tell you," Mom added. "Tell you everything before Dad got home with Abilene."

I stared at both of them. They spoke in whispers, Abilene so close again.

"It's going to take a while to even out her medications," Dad said. "To find the proper level. They're trying Tegretol along with the lithium now. It's supposed to be more effective for rapid cyclers."

"First she's a magnet," I said. "Now she's a rapid cycler?"

"The mood swings, Austin. The period between highs and lows," Mom said.

"But she's fine, Austin," Dad said, sounding as if he truly believed it. "She's tired is all. This has been pretty tough on her."

"Coming home?"

"Well, yes. Of course. She's been gone a long time."

I saw them watching me, hoping I'd be calm. I wondered if they worried whether Dad would have to pinch me in his bear hug now, haul me off for reconditioning or whatever. I turned and walked back into the living room.

Squatting beside Abilene's chair, I whispered, "Hey, Ab'lene." I could feel Mom and Dad stop in the entrance, watching.

"Hey, Austin."

"You want to go upstairs? Want to go to your room?"

Abilene nodded, but didn't budge. "In a minute maybe." Her voice was still all flat and breathless. "I just got here."

"Ab'lene, it's just upstairs."

She nodded. "In a minute maybe." She just sat there, not really looking at anything.

I glanced down to Abilene's chest, my own tattoo burning—*that chick is legend material.*

I turned to glare at Mom and Dad. Waving my arms wide, I asked, "You want to brag about this now too?"

Abilene really was just tired that first night, and though she didn't stay that flattened the next day, she didn't rise up much either. We all stayed home again, like we had when she'd come home on her own, but there was no laughing this time, no Abilene teasing us about clumping together around her. She just sat around, staring off at nothing. Catching lint, she would have called it once. Half the time she was parked in front of the TV with Mom, which I knew would kill her when she came back enough to realize it. I'd sit down with her, whispering until I talked her into getting up, at least going up to her room, or out to sit on the tailgate of her truck.

I don't know if she wasn't allowed to drive, but she never even asked about her keys. Her truck sat as dead as when she was gone. I asked if she wanted to go for a ride, but she breathed slow and said, "I don't think so, Austin. Too hot."

When she said things like that, I wanted to check her head for scars.

I went off to school the next day, unable to sit there with the three of them for another second.

When I got home that afternoon, Dad was sitting on the tailgate of Abilene's truck, his mitt in his lap, ready to play ball the way we had when Abilene was missing. I wondered if he'd sat out there all day, just so he'd be that ready when I showed.

I walked past him, saying, "She's not *missing* anymore."

Dad reached out, snagging my hand, pulling me back, but not like before, gentle this time, letting me stay out at arm's length, keeping my hand in his, but not just to capture me.

I looked down at our hands until he let mine go.

"You've got to be easy with her. As hard as this is on us, it's worse for her."

I stared at him. "You think I don't know that?"

Dad nodded. "Just don't push her. Let her find her own way back."

I looked out to the desert, then back to Dad, then away again. I bent down, picking up one of Dad's white rocks, whipping it out into the creosote. "Aren't you afraid she won't ever make it back?"

"Of course," Dad said. "I've never been more frightened in my life."

We looked at each other. "Do you want to get your mitt?" he asked.

I thought, then shook my head. "I'm going to check on Ab'lene."

Every day after that, no matter when I came home, no matter if Abilene was home or off to the doctor's with Mom, Dad would be sitting out there, his mitt in his lap, like some huge dog waiting for its dead master. He must have been working half-time or something, even more worried about Mom stuck out here alone with Abilene than he was about medical bills.

He never said a word when I walked past, just sat there, letting me know he was ready when I was.

Most afternoons I could talk Abilene into moving outside. We didn't drive anywhere, only sat on the tailgate after Dad went in, usually not even talking, just staring out at the evening. I'd look at her, at her quiet stare, and know I should have gone to see her in the hospital. I could have done something before it got this far. Even if it was just breaking her out.

Before I could convince myself I shouldn't, I reached out and picked Abilene's hand from her lap. I whispered, "I'm sorry I didn't come see you, Ab'lene."

Abilene just smiled. "I don't think I would've wanted you seeing me there, Austin." She squeezed my hand, lifting it and letting it drop against her jeans before working her fingers free. "Watching me doing my crafts. Joining in on group."

I picked at an old pitching callus with my thumbnail. "You sure you don't want to go for a ride?"

"Yeah. Things'd move too fast for me now." Abilene turned

and looked at me. "But, you know, Austin, you could take my truck. If you need it for anything."

"Without you?"

"Sure."

It'd be like me breathing for her, I thought, my heart pumping her blood. I stood up. I couldn't just sit there. "You want to take a walk, Ab'lene? You want to go out to the base maybe?"

"The base. That's a haul, Austin. Too far for me."

"Too far? We used to go there all the time. Every day, practically."

"Used to." Abilene smiled again.

"We could go to the tank, Ab'lene. Remember how cool it is in there? You're always saying it's too hot."

Abilene wiped at her puffy forehead. She sweat all the time now. "I'd burn up before we got there, Austin."

"Okay."

But I gave it one last try. "Want to play catch, Ab'lene? We could take it as easy as you want. We could do it right here."

She didn't say no right away.

"Only a couple of tosses," I pleaded. "Get the feel of it again."

"I'm not even sure I could get it to you on the hop, Austin," Abilene said with a little bit of a laugh. "No, my pitching days are over."

"No, they're not! I'll get the gloves! I'll get the ball!"

"No, Austin," Abilene said, looking at Dad's white rocks beneath her feet. "I couldn't. I can't."

"Just hang on, Ab'lene. I'm going to get the mitts."

I took off before she could say anything, running so fast I was on the stairs before the screen banged shut.

Even so, by the time I collected my mitt and found a spare for Abilene and leapt back down the stairs, she was in the kitchen, sitting at the table, staring at her fingers.

"Ab'lene?"

She looked up, gave her same smile. "Hey, Austin."

I held up the gloves. "Come on. I got everything."

Abilene shook her head. "You know I can't. Not after the way I used to be able to."

"Maybe some other day," I answered, but looking at her washed-out face, her dulled red hair pulled back in the simplest braid, I doubted there'd ever be some other day.

thirty-six

It became my ritual, every day asking Abilene if she wanted to go for a drive, if she wanted to walk to the tank, if she just wanted to toss the ball around. But every day she said no, not yet, some other time, too hot. Sometimes, when I went up to where she was sitting, she'd turn to me with that quiet new smile, and instead of dropping down beside her I'd just say, "Hey, Ab'lene," and swerve away.

For more than a month Abilene drifted through the house all quiet, not shouting at anyone, not laughing at anything. She'd talk when I talked to her, but never went much beyond that. I'd sit beside her, trying to think of something new to say, trying not to see how when she wore any of her old clothes her new weight tugged at her shirt buttons, the spaces between starting to gape, revealing dark glimpses of her shadowed tattoo.

When I saw that, I brushed my fingers across my shirt, as if I could feel the letters staining my skin underneath. I was tempted to show her, to shock her into doing something, but I could only picture Abilene sprawled in Tattoo's chair, and I kept it hidden. I got dressed in the dark now as much as I could, so I wouldn't have to see it myself.

Finally, on a Friday night, a whole empty weekend yawning before us, when Abilene again refused to go for a drive, adding, "It just doesn't sound fun, Austin. Bombing around the desert," I snapped.

"Do you know you don't even have your keys anymore!" I tugged them out of my pocket and dangled them in her face.

Abilene glanced at me, raising an eyebrow. Just that lifted eyebrow put me into a sweat, but the flash of the old Abilene was gone before I could swear I actually saw it.

"Go ahead then," she said.

I stared a moment more, then shouted, "Okay, I will!" and spun out the door. But even as I threw myself behind the wheel of her truck, I knew there was no place I wanted to go. Not without her.

I cranked the key anyway, stomping the gas, chattering backward over the rocks, but when I reached the end of the drive, I only stood on the brakes. After a second or two trying to decide where I might go, I turned off the engine, everything silent after the quick roar of Abilene's truck. I slammed my fists against the wheel.

So I sat there, parked at the end of our driveway. I picked at the tear in the vinyl, pulling out bits of hardened foam. I ran my hand back and forth over the softly frayed ends of the seat belts Abilene had cut out, remembering the first case of baseballs she'd brought home for me, how they'd taken up all my legroom, how I'd had to ride with my knees in my chest.

As dusk came on, the whiteness of the house and our driveway seemed to brighten for a minute or two against the graying drabness of the desert, the deepening purple of the sky. Then it went as flat and dull and lifeless as everything else, night coming on.

And that's when I noticed at last. The sky.

To the north a creeping wall of gray ate into the dusky blue, blotting it out. I twisted in my seat to stare, then quick leaned over, cranking open the passenger window. The breeze came right through and out Abilene's broken driver's window, the curls of freshening wind brushing my face, carrying the first traces of water it seemed I'd ever known. I could barely keep myself in the truck. All I wanted to do was rush in to see Abilene, but I couldn't make myself move. I couldn't bear it if the norther didn't touch her.

With whole spaces of stars blanked out by the storm, night fell fast, and still I sat in the driveway, watching the house, knowing they were all inside. I barely breathed.

The windows lit up, one room at a time, the brightness streaming toward me but falling short. I could see them pass back and forth. Mom and Dad and Abilene. I watched them sit down to dinner. Get up and leave the kitchen.

I listened as the wind gained strength, as it cut around the interruption of our house, the truck, impatient about it. Not long after the lights in the house began to wink off. Then the real wind reached us, rocking the truck like a cradle. A true blue norther.

I remembered how I used to wait, nights like these, my blankets pulled tight to my chin, for the slightest trace of sound, the first creak of my doorknob, never knowing if Abilene would come for me, or if I'd have to go to her. Then Abilene would slip in like a ghost, the door never opened any wider than she was, whisked shut as soon as she was through. "Austin?" she'd whisper as she slid to the window, pushing it up, the creosotes' sharpness filling the room.

I'd already be holding the blankets up, the cold flooding

around me in the moment before Abilene dove in. Then we'd shiver, our arms tight to our chests, our legs dancing against each other's.

Our laughing would stutter through our chattering teeth for the moment it took us to get warm, and then Abilene would say, "Listen!" and we'd lie still and feel the norther. "It's going to be a whole new world tomorrow, Austin. You just wait and see."

We were only kids.

I woke with a start, my teeth chattering even as I opened my eyes. It took me a second to realize where I was, still behind the wheel of Abilene's truck, my arms pinched against my chest, my knees tight to my chin. The house still sat before me and I blinked and rubbed at my face. A shiver racked me and then set up steady, my arms and shoulders dancing.

The first trace of dawn already streaked the horizon, the sky seeming low enough to touch. I opened the door and stumbled outside.

The wind stung, throwing bits of sand and dirt against me, though I was so cold I heard it more than felt it. I held my arms out, sucking the wind into my lungs, the whole world still almost as dark as a coal. I turned circles in the driveway, letting it touch me everywhere.

I shuffled stiff and tight and shivering to the porch and climbed the steps, easing the screen open and shut behind me.

Abilene was already at the table, wearing Dad's old satiny blue pajamas, and I stood long minutes with my back against the door. She sat alone in the gloom, gazing out the window, as if she couldn't understand that I was there too. She clutched a steaming cup between her palms. A jar of instant coffee sat open before her, a spoon jabbed into it. The stink of scorched dust haunted the air, the coils of the electric heater glowing red in the wall. I wanted to crawl up to it, but instead I only watched Abilene and listened to the house. The only sound was the norther though, everything it knocked against us.

Finally, I whispered, "Hear that wind?"

When Abilene didn't answer, I said, "It's going to be a whole new world."

"I've been listening."

"We've got ourselves a norther."

"Where did you go?" she asked after just breathing for a few seconds.

"Nowhere. I never left."

"Oh, really?" Abilene said, just enough of a hint of smile in her words that I felt a little shock of the old Abilene charging the air.

I reached for the light switch, but Abilene said, "No!"

I stopped. "I just wanted to see your face."

"Same old face, Austin."

In the darkness even her old voice was back. I thought of her pills stacked up somewhere new now, hidden away, yellow flashes scattered under the creosote like blossoms. I wondered if even I'd been fooled this time.

I squinted, peering to see her face, her eyes, trying to see if this was the real Abilene back at last. I whispered, "I think this norther's for real, Ab'lene. It's got to bring rain."

She nodded and whispered, "I was listening to it."

"Were you waiting for me?" I listened to her breathe. "We're always together for northers, Ab'lene."

"We are together, Austin. We'll always be that."

I stepped toward her. "Really? Are you sure?"

"We're too old now for some of that, though. Remember? Running off to each other's bed."

"You want me to open the windows, Ab'lene? Want to have the norther right inside here with us?"

"No. I don't need that."

"I do," I said, and I pushed open the first window. I walked across the room, pushing open the next. The curtains billowed in in hard waves, snapping like sails, turning the room to ice. I soaked it in, the wind charging the room, rustling everything loose. "I've been out all night in it, Ab'lene. Remembering all that, how we used to be."

Abilene nodded.

I stepped to the table, trying to catch a glimpse of her, see if the norther had really shaken her awake at last. But what I saw was her cup, filled with steaming water. Plain water.

I rubbed my face, slumping into the chair beside her. The pot on the stove barely whispered. "Looks a little weak, don't you think?"

Abilene turned to me. I pointed at her cup. She looked, then smiled. "I got watching the wind."

Abilene reached for the coffee jar and stirred the crystals into the water. After taking a sip, she said, "Not much difference."

"Ab'lene, this norther's better outside. It'd be better to be inside it, inside the storm."

"Always is."

I looked hard, but she seemed pretty much the same. Her cheeks still had their puff, the sharper angles missing, the game face buried somewhere inside.

"Want to drive into it, Ab'lene?" I asked, barely daring to breathe. "Find where it's raining?"

She looked down at her coffee.

"Not too hot now, Ab'lene. Not anymore. Not with a norther."

She kept watching her cup, the wisps of steam.

"You're not even sweating, Ab'lene."

"No. No, I'm not."

"Why don't you get dressed, Ab'lene?"

Abilene blew out a long, slow breath. I closed my eyes, covering them with my fists, but then Abilene whispered, "Okay, Austin."

I dropped my hands to the table. "What?"

Before she could answer, I heard footsteps upstairs. "Come on, Ab'lene. We've got to go now."

"Do you mind driving?"

"Mind? I'll drive you to Canada, Ab'lene! But we got to go."

Abilene nodded, her face going flat as Dad thumped down the steps. "As long as you drive, I suppose it might be nice to get out of the house a little," she said, suddenly loud, Dad sure to hear.

"I suppose so," I said, trying not to stare at her as Dad walked in, Mom right there with him.

Dad looked at us. He shivered and hugged his arms around himself. "Cold as Eskimo toes in here." He circled the kitchen, slamming the windows down. He twisted the heater's knob all the way around. "What were you thinking?"

Abilene stood up. "We're thinking we'll take a drive," she announced, like she wasn't saying anything more than that we were going to have breakfast. "We're going to have a look at this storm."

Mom and Dad glanced at each other, then at us, at me. I shrugged.

"Austin's going to drive," she said as she left the room.

We listened to her climbing footsteps. When we couldn't hear her anymore, Dad asked, "Where are you going to go?"

I shrugged again. "Don't you think getting out would do her some good? Getting out of here for even a few minutes?"

They looked at each other again. "Clay?" Mom whispered.

"I don't suppose there's any harm," he started, but sounding less certain, he added, "Be careful, Austin. Don't try to rush things."

"Rush what?"

"Anything."

Mom said, "Nancy is afraid you're——"

"Wait a second," I said, loud enough to stop them. "We're

just going for a ride. She hasn't been out of this house since she got back."

"I take her to Midland twice a week for blood tests," Mom said.

"Besides that," I said, trying to keep this from blowing up before I could pirate Abilene away. "All we're doing is taking a ride. Seeing the storm. Getting out."

Dad nodded. "You'll take it easy, Austin? Really?"

"She asked me to drive. How tired can she get looking out the window?"

Abilene stepped into the kitchen then, dressed like she used to, jeans and a faded button-up shirt. She poked an arm into her old jean jacket with the inside pockets, flipping the collar up. "I'm ready, I guess," she whispered. As she slipped past Dad, she reached out, brushing her fingers along his arm. "We'll see you all in a little while, all right?"

"All right," Dad said.

I felt like I was on my first date, like I should ask when I should have her home.

I held the door open for Abilene. Touching her elbow, I guided her through. I pinched the door behind us so the last thing Mom and Dad saw was my face. I could barely keep from shouting, *I win!*

Then I clapped the door shut and Abilene and I stepped across the driveway stones. I opened the door for Abilene and ran around the front of the truck, hopping behind the wheel. Opening a door for the old Abilene was something that could get you killed.

Barely keeping myself from shouting, from laughing, I roared the engine, backing out of the drive without looking.

Slamming on the brakes and shifting into first, I bashed my open hand against the dash. "We are out of here!" I cried.

thirty-seven

Though I rocketed through the gears, winding the speedometer out, so fired up I could only say, "We are out of here!" Abilene didn't say a word. When I looked her way, she gave me a quiet smile, like what we were doing just barely gave her a tickle, and I had that queasy feeling again, like she knew all the secrets.

The air was heavy with rain yet to fall, but the dust still plumed behind us, a thin rooster tail, nothing like an off-roader, but a rooster tail all the same. Grinning, I jerked a thumb over my shoulder. "No moss, Ab'lene," I said, just loud enough for her to hear.

Abilene's smile widened for a second, but she didn't bother looking behind us.

Though it was cold outside, I had no window to roll up and the air rushed in around us. To the north, just off the road, I could see rain dragging down from the clouds. I slammed my hand against the wheel, bouncing in my seat. Just to keep from bursting, I shouted for Abilene to roll down her window too.

I glanced over and saw her big hand and thin wrist poking white from the rolled-back cuff of her jacket as she slowly wound the crank around. The tan I'd never seen her without had disappeared without my noticing, the scars on her wrist fading along with it.

As the wind tugged at her, pulling at her hair, Abilene kept smiling, a regular old this-is-nice smile. Like an undertaker might put on a corpse: all-right looking, but not like anything from a person's real life.

Pulling her old trick of not watching the road, I turned to see Abilene full on. She watched me back, her expression not changing a speck, not a blink of an eye.

Her skin really had gone pale. Her hair, starting to whip loose in the rush of wind, framed her white face like fire. "Ab'lene!" I shouted.

She looked at me.

I waved a hand to everything outside her truck. "It's going to rain!"

She stared back at me until I had to glance at the road, losing the game. I half expected to hear her making chicken squawks, but she stayed quiet.

I drove a little longer down the road, but couldn't stand it anymore. Shouting, "Hang on!" I dashed the wheel to the right, plowing through the ditch and pitching back up into the desert. The barbed wire sang, whistling like bullets as we shot through the fence, something I'd never done before in my life.

Abilene stayed in her seat as if glued, but now our rooster tail was a full-blown white tornado climbing the dark skies behind us. Grabbing Abilene's shoulder, twisting her around to see, I shrieked, "Look, Ab'lene! No fucking moss!"

Abilene smiled, but instead of the laughing I'd hoped for, the slow winding up until she was doubled over, gulping for breath, she seemed to be searching me for some answer I knew I didn't have.

So, to keep her from asking anything, I hammered down at the gas, making myself laugh, pretending this was all as good as it used to be.

I drove us harder than we'd ever gone, barely able to steer, but refusing to let up off the gas. I dodged what I could and drove over the rest, but I never saw the cut of the creek bed until we flew over its bank, smashing into the gravel bottom and flying back into the air.

When we bounced down again, I got the truck turned up the dry bed, just dinging the far bank. "Ab'lene!" I shouted, but she didn't answer, and I couldn't take even an instant to look her way.

My left foot hovered over the brake, but I was afraid what might happen if I gave up and used it. So, my mouth dry as bone, I put everything I had into keeping us off the rocks.

When I lost it at last, skittering through a sharp curve, ricocheting off the edge of the cut, grinding up the side of the truck and blowing a tire clean off its bead, I finally let off the gas and we lurched to a stop, all the dust billowing in with us.

It was a long time before I could just unwind my fingers from the wheel, crack open the door, and get out. "Sorry," I said, looking at the new dents and scrapes. "Sorry about your truck, Ab'lene."

She opened her door and peered out. "It's all right. I never thought I was invincible."

I blinked a couple of times, not looking at her, my mouth even drier than before. "Your truck, you mean?"

She stepped down onto the pebbly hardpan. "Well, I never thought it could fly, anyway."

I thought of her tearing takeoff runs down the old Rattlesnake runway. Looking away from her, I asked, "Are you okay, Ab'lene?"

She gave a quick, tiny laugh. "Just what I was going to ask you. Did you survive the landing, Austin?"

I nodded.

"And the rest of this whole crazy flight?"

I nodded. "Got my wings now. Just soloed."

She studied me so intently I had to turn away. I wanted to ask her so much, but I pointed to the sky, the rain flushing the horizon. "Ab'lene," I whispered. "We probably couldn't be in a worse place than this creek right now."

She stared at me. "Wouldn't it be sweet to think so?"

But at last she looked away, giving the sky a glance and saying, "You're right. If we stay here, we'll get flash-flooded clear to the Rio Grande. Flush out at Brownsville."

She reached into the truck bed for the tire iron, and I bulled the spare tire up over the side of the bed, holding it there as I watched Abilene fit the iron over the first lug nut. It screeched as she bore down, forcing it loose.

I dropped the spare beside her, keeping my hands on it as it bounced. "Why, let me tell you about the night in Brownsville!" I said, trying to get it just right, the way she used to imitate Dad.

She stuck the jack beneath the bumper.

"We were young!" I belted out. "Newlyweds! And you know how that can be!"

Abilene steadied the jack, tightening it up.

"Now, of course our boy Brownsville was stillborn. But there were those other nights! The one in Abilene! The one in Austin! Our stars! How all this started!"

Abilene cranked at the jack, trying to smile. "Thank God for stillborns," she whispered.

"How'd you like to have to call me Brownsville all the time?"

Abilene cranked harder on the jack handle, lifting the flat tire up off the bits of rock. She was out of breath, just pumping the jack handle.

Watching her, her hair falling around her face, waving like water with each pump she gave the jack, I suddenly missed the stillborn brother I'd just made up, missed him so much it hurt. I wondered what another of us would have done, how he would have changed things.

I pulled the old tire off and wrestled the new one up over the bolts. Abilene handed me the nuts one at a time, watching me as I hand-tightened them. I wanted to ask about Brownsville, have her help keep the story going, but suddenly I remembered her baby, her whole "procedure," and I froze, pinching the last lug nut tight, my fingers thick with dust.

"Ab'lene," I stammered. "I'm sorry. About that whole dumb story, about——"

"You clear?" Abilene said fast.

I stepped back and Abilene gave the jack a quick kick and the truck shot down, bouncing and rocking. She heaved the jack into the bed. It bounced and scraped against the metal and paint.

Then she was back at the nuts with the tire iron, wrenching them in, her shoulders hunching as she threw herself down against the iron. Then she stood fast, tossing the iron in after the jack.

"Ready?" she asked.

I lifted the flat tire and dropped it in with the rest of our tools. "Ab'lene?"

She hopped into the passenger seat and slammed her door. "Let's go. But no more flying."

I walked around the truck and sat behind the wheel. "You sure you don't want to drive?"

"Go ahead. You're doing fine."

I inched the truck forward, looking for a place to get out of

the creek bed, looking anywhere but at Abilene. Rain was dragging down all around us, and I pictured the frothy brown roar
channeling through here, sweeping us away.

"How about there?" I pointed at a steep break in the wall.

Abilene shook her head. "Never make it." I drove a little
faster, Abilene still shaking her head. "How'd I ever let you get
us stuck down here?"

Then, before I even saw the gap, Abilene pointed. When I
turned toward it, she said, "Go," and I put on a little gas.

But Abilene whipped her foot around the stick and pinned
my foot to the floor on top of the gas. We rifled up and through,
the tires skipping at the crest, throwing back rock but skittering
us over, up into the safe, flat desert. "And you were worried,"
Abilene said, wriggling her leg back around the stick, giving a
little smile.

We zigzagged across the desert, first toward one squall, then
the next, never catching the rain. But when lightning began flickering and flashing in a thunderhead north of us, Abilene reached
out, nudging the wheel till we pointed that way. We headed
toward it like a needle to a magnet.

The storm moved toward us at least as quick as we headed
for it, the collision faster than I expected, the darkness sudden,
the whole world turned the glossy black of wet chalkboards. The
pounding of the fat, screaming drops on the roof made me duck
my ears to my shoulders. Coming through the window, they
struck as hard as hail. If I hadn't turned to see, I would never
have known Abilene was laughing. She looked like a silent movie,
black-and-white, the color stolen from the air by the storm.

It was impossible to see where we were going and I stood
on the brakes, the truck sliding to a stop in the suddenly slick
mud. I realized I didn't even know if Abilene's windshield wipers
worked, and I started to smile. "Abilene," I shouted. "Do your—"

Then the lightning struck. The thunder clapped against me at
the same instant, stinging, then rumbling, like a huge, roaring

truck passing right through me. The instant of white light caught
Abilene frozen, her loose hair standing on end like a bristle of
splinters, as though she were caught in the middle of some terrible accident.

Abilene stuck her head out the window, her hair flattened in
a split second of the frantic rain. She looked sleek again, something you'd expect to see sliding up out of a whole river of
water.

When the lightning struck again, just as close, making it hard
to breath, the ozone thick in our noses, on our tongues, Abilene
slipped farther out, till she was sitting on the edge of the door,
only her legs inside the truck, her jeans spotting dark with drops.

I scrambled through my own window, up and out into the
deluge. But though the storm was blinding, I could make out
enough of Abilene across the width of the cab to see that she
wasn't shaking her fists at the thunder, wasn't screaming into the
storm, wasn't letting the lightning know who was in charge, who
had come back; none of the things I had imagined. She just sat
there smiling, her face tilted back, letting the rain drum down
on her eyes, her cheeks, her throat. I sat down against my door
and watched.

As soon as the rolling crash of the rain began to slack off, the
lightning moving behind us, the thunder lagging behind the flash,
Abilene slid back into the cab, her jacket nearly black, water
running from the sleeves. I followed just a second behind, my
soggy shirt sticking to the seat, crawling up my back.

The storm kept moving off, even a little slip of sun coming
through, a long way out in front of us.

Abilene wiped her hands against her face, squeegeeing off
water. "Rain. Can you believe it?"

"Are you okay, Ab'lene?"

She smiled again slowly. "You've got to stop asking me that,
Austin."

"I just—"

Abilene glanced out to what was left of the storm. "You know what they say, Austin, about how much of our brains we use? About ten percent. The average person only ever makes use of ten percent of their brain's abilities." The storm raced farther and farther away. "For a while there I was using ninety percent. A hundred. A hundred and ten. So, am I all right? Am I okay?"

She glanced at me. "I don't know. But I miss that, Austin. Stuck back at ten, I miss it so much."

"Your ten's like anybody else's ninety."

She tried to smile, but her lip quivered and she looked away.

"Are you still taking the pills, Ab'lene? That's what I—"

"My stillborn pills? Every day, Austin. I have to. Even a hundred and ten percent isn't worth what comes in on its heels."

She looked like she might break down right there in her truck, her fortress, and before she could, I said, "Remember when I was a kid?"

"You're still a kid. With any luck, you're still a kid."

"Remember the time you caught me in my room, posing like my Nolan Ryan poster?"

"Fireballer," Abilene said slowly, like something she barely remembered.

I fingered the bottom of my soaking-wet T-shirt. "Remember how we called ourselves that? Fireballers? How that's who we were?"

"Of course I remember, Austin. I haven't forgotten our whole lives."

I kept staring at her, wondering if that was true. I tugged at the wet, clinging cloth of my T-shirt, lifting it till my Fireballer was bare. "Me too, Ab'lene. I won't forget."

Abilene leaned forward, like she couldn't see what she was staring at. But she only looked like she might cry. "Oh, Austin. What happened?" She sounded less like Abilene than anyone I'd ever heard. She sounded like Mom.

"Nothing *happened*. I did it. For us."

Abilene kept staring at my tattoo, the blazing legend, like I was the mutilated survivor of something too horrible for words. I saw the slow crumple of her face, heard her whisper, "Oh, Austin. You didn't have to do that."

But I was barely listening. I couldn't help but grin. I lifted my face to Abilene's. "*We're* the Fireballers, Ab'lene! Only us. Forever now."

Abilene nodded, biting her lip. Reaching out, she wrapped her arm around the back of my neck, tugging me toward her. I tipped forward, Abilene pressing my face into her chest. She rubbed the back of my neck, whispering, "Fireballers," into the top of my head.

I took a deep breath. "We're going to be all right, aren't we, Ab'lene?" I whispered.

"You got that," she answered, mean and sure, just like always.

She held me that way a long time, her face down on the top of my head, before finally relaxing her grip and easing me back up straight behind the wheel.

"Where to?" I asked.

Abilene bit her lip, not looking at my chest. "Austin," she started, but she shook her head and turned to look away from me. "You have to tell me where the guns are, Austin."

I pushed the truck into gear, lurching forward and sideways in the greasy, unfamiliar mud.

"Mom and Dad told me you took them. I need to know what you did with them."

I quick slid us around in a turn like I was only going to chase the storm. But when I straightened out, we were pointed straight toward the bomber base.

"Austin . . ."

"They're safe. Ab'lene. They're safe."

thirty-eight

I drove straight ahead, feeling Abilene studying me as if I were some totally new person. The crack of the lightning so close was like nothing compared to that.

"Austin," she whispered.

I glanced her way. "I took them, Ab'lene. They weren't right to steal them. We weren't doing anything wrong. We weren't doing any harm." I smiled. "Unless you're a dove. A swallow."

"But, Austin—"

"You're not dangerous!" I shouted, slamming my fists against the wheel. Into the shock of silence, I said, "All right, Ab'lene? You're not."

Abilene kept quiet, letting me drive her to the base, the truck slithering in the mud until the tires finally gripped the runway's old pavement. I turned the key then, letting us coast to a stop. The rain was past us, but the base was soaked, the runway shiny, pearly looking where it wasn't broken by cracks and weeds. The tank glistened. Even the old tire, hanging dead in the stillness after the storm, looked glossy and new, like we'd just hung it up, like we were only here to play our first game.

Abilene blew out a long breath. "Pretty, isn't it?"

I nodded. Before the drought we'd always gone out after rains, just to see how different everything could be.

"Dad said he looked out here," Abilene said.

"He checked every inch of the tank. I saw his footprints. But he won't find them in a million years."

Abilene sat quiet, looking out at the tank.

"They're not in the tank," I said.

Abilene waited. "You tell me," she said at last, but not the way she used to say it. It was a command now.

I opened my door and stepped down to the wet runway. Without cracking her door, Abilene watched me walk out to the pitcher's mound.

I stood on the wooden plank of the rubber and stared down at the new-looking tire, holding my hands at my waist, like I had a mitt, like I had a ball. Like I was just waiting for the catcher to give me the sign. Like I could somehow carry the both of us back to that time.

I heard Abilene get out of the truck and crunch across the gravel to me. "One is for the fastball," she coached. "He's calling for pure heat."

I nodded. "They always do out here."

Abilene waited another second. "Where are they, Austin?"

I stared at the little round hole of wet desert in the middle of the shining black ring of tire. "Remember what you always used to say, Ab'lene? About hitting? How hitting a round ball with a round bat was the most difficult thing of all? How, if we practiced, we could push it way past difficult? How we could make it pure impossible?"

"Where are they, Austin?"

"Do you remember any of that, Ab'lene?"

"Every word, Austin. But you have to tell me now."

I raised my arms, stepping into my windup. Lifting my leg and then letting it fall, I drove myself toward the tire, rocketing in my pitch of nothing. My left foot slipped in the mud and I had to skip forward to keep myself from falling flat. I turned to look at Abilene. She jerked her hand out, the strike sign. I couldn't stop a little smile.

Smiling back, Abilene stepped onto the mound. She held a baseball out to me, holding it deep in her palm, her fingers following the curve of the stitching. "Use a ball, Austin. Makes it a lot easier for the ump."

I looked at the sun-faded, cracked-leather ball, wondering where she'd found it. It was dry, not something that'd been caught out in the storm. Twisting her fingers, feeling for the right grip, Abilene rolled the ball in her hand.

I tried to remember the last time I'd seen her with a ball. Maybe when she broke Dad with the handcuffer. I reached for it, but Abilene pulled it away.

She hopped it in her hand. "Trade you for it." She wiped her tangled, wet hair back from her forehead.

I glanced at the ruined ball Abilene slapped from hand to hand. She had her feet set for a pitch, her right foot braced against the edge of the plank, her left out front, pointing toward the tire. Just standing there talking, she was still that ready to pitch, something she said she'd never do again.

I stepped back, giving her a clean path to the tire. "Go ahead. Show me what you got."

Abilene smiled, but shook her head. "I told you. My pitching days are over."

"I just want to see that again. Just once more."

She didn't budge. "Some things you'll just have to remember."

I pictured her motion, the clean, high leg kick, the whip of her body around the ball, and couldn't believe it was something I would never see again.

"Where are they, Austin?"

"They're safe, Ab'lene. They're safe. Okay?"

Abilene eyed me, and then suddenly she smiled. She lifted her foot and stamped down on our pitching rubber. The ring of her foot against the plank was just less than solid.

She stared at me, smiling sadly, shaking her head. "That's beautiful."

I watched her slip the ball into her pocket, then pry back the edge of the plank, watched the wet dirt resist the pull on the spikes more than it ever had dry. When she bent down to pull out the first PVC tube, she whispered, "Were you afraid too, Austin? Were you afraid of what I might do?"

"No," I lied.

"I was."

Abilene pulled the duct tape off and slid the ruined sawed-off into her hand. The sun was on us now, the mud drying.

"They're as good as new," she said softly.

She pulled Dad's old gun completely out into the sun, turning it this way and that, the splinters at the end of the stock disturbingly white, the damage still obvious. Opening it, making sure it was unloaded, she turned it toward herself, looking down the empty, dark tube of the barrel. "And to think some say black holes are just a theory."

I almost said, "What?" but the last thing I wanted was an explanation. Instead I looked at the thick mud already drying on her jeans, caking her fingers. "I think I should keep them."

Abilene glanced up at me. She shook her head. "Neither one of us should. It's not in our history."

"Well, what then?"

Abilene looked down at the wreckage of the mound. "We have to fix this."

"Ab'lene."

"We have to, Austin!" Her sharpened voice was a shock in the wet air. "You don't have to help, but I'm not leaving it like this again."

I watched her a second, then reached out a foot, shoving a pile of muddy dirt back into the hole.

"Go find the shovel."

I walked off, circling through the desert around her.

When I found the shovel and brought it back, Abilene was on her hands and knees, scraping dirt like it was sand on some beach.

"Hang on, Ab'lene. I'll shovel."

She shook her head, slowly and carefully pushing up dirt, patting it down. "I've got it." Her hair dragged in the dirt, the splintering plank beside her, the spikes sticking up into the air.

I tamped the last of the dirt down with the back of the shovel as Abilene positioned the plank. Taking the shovel from my hands, she drove down the spikes, the sharp ring of the blade against the spike heads striking out into the desert.

Handing the shovel back to me, Abilene scooped up the shotguns and carried them back to her truck. She eased them down in the bed.

I followed after, but when I moved to climb behind the wheel, she held me by the arm and slipped past me, saying, "I'll drive."

She flipped on the headlights, the day almost gone without our having noticed.

thirty-nine

Abilene drove us rattling down the runway, past the hangar walls, the crumbling, old housing foundations, and turned for home. She didn't say a word and I could only sit and watch the dim glow of the dash lights against her skin, her game face visible again even through the bloat of the pills.

When we rolled up into our drive, she jumped out of the truck and pulled the guns from the back, leaving the PVC tubes behind. One in each hand, she climbed the porch steps. "I'll take care of these."

"This isn't where they should be, Ab'lene," I said, but she was already in, slipping like a shadow down the hallway, and I chased after her.

She caught Mom and Dad in the living room, walking straight in with the guns before I could stop her. They looked startled, but somehow not worried, and I hung back in the doorway.

"I told you I could get them," Abilene said, soft enough I knew she didn't want me to hear.

Dad stood up and she held the guns out to him. He took them one at a time, checking their empty chambers the same way Abilene had at the base.

Then Abilene just said, "I'm done. I'll see you all in the morning." She walked past me and I listened to her move up the stairs.

Dad still stood there with the shotguns.

"I didn't tell her where they were," I said. "She found them. I didn't want her to have them again. But it was her idea, bringing them here."

"You're right," Mom said. "It was her idea."

"We'll take them now," Dad said. "We'll get rid of them."

Mom stood up, taking a step toward me. "How was she, Austin? Did she seem all right?"

For the first time ever they knew more about Abilene than I did, and just the calm, soothing way Mom asked those two tiny questions made me think I might cry. "I don't know."

Mom reached for me, but I took a step away, then turned and bolted for the stairs.

Abilene was sitting at the head of the stairs, the same place I'd kept watch during the night of the swallows. Instead of looking at me, she kept peering down the stairs, like she was waiting for something else. But before I could slip by, she reached up and patted my chest.

"Fireballer," she whispered, her hand still on my chest, not looking at me. "The one and only."

I started to deny that, but then only twisted away, leaving her alone as I shut myself into my room.

I stretched out on my bed, thinking Abilene might follow me in, but what I heard instead was the trudge of her feet as she went back down the stairs, back to Mom and Dad. Then I heard voices, Abilene and Mom and Dad talking. Talking, not shouting.

Talking for a long, long time, about me now, I guessed, the way Mom and Dad used to talk about Abilene.

Lying in the dark, I wondered if I shouldn't slip off in the night by myself.

I fell asleep that way, across my bed, all my clothes on, listening to them talk.

Then, in the heart of the night, something woke me. Woke me when I didn't even know I was asleep. I rolled over quick, peering into the pitch-black of my room, breathing hard, wondering what had happened.

But the night was black and still, the clouds blocking even the starlight. I couldn't see a thing. I eased back down, hoping I'd only been dreaming. It wasn't until my breathing slowed that I heard the soft breathing of someone else in my room, someone standing close.

I froze, sweat popping out all over. Then, quietly, out of the absolute blackness, Abilene said, "Why'd you do it, Austin? Why'd you do that to yourself?"

I didn't answer.

"To be like me? Did you get that done to yourself just so you could follow me?"

It took me a second to realize she was only talking about the tattoo. "Sure, Ab'lene. I mean, we're Fireballers."

Abilene took a big breath, a shaky one I could hear emptying the room of all its air. "Austin, I was out of my head. I didn't even know I'd done it till things slowed down, till I felt its burn. I was too afraid to even look."

"But you said . . ."

I could hear Abilene rubbing at her face. "You've spent your whole life trying to be like me, Austin. And now I take pills to be somebody else."

I pushed myself up onto an elbow. "We're still the Fireballers."

"We're nothing but a snake eating its tail."

"No, Ab'lene, we're—"

Ignoring me, Abilene asked, "You want to know the only good part of How All This Started?"

"What, Ab'lene?"

"The night in Austin."

The floor creaked beneath her, and I heard the gentle way she had of closing the door, even turning the handle so the latch wouldn't bump over the catch.

After Abilene had spirited in and out of my room like that, sleep didn't have a chance. I sat on the edge of my bed, staring out into the blackness of the night until my eyes ached. I felt as if I'd never slept, and never would, and when dawn crept into the sky, I was still on the edge of my bed, my clothes stiff and wrinkly from the storm and the night. I was trying to see the color seep into the sky, concentrating so hard to catch something so gradual that I didn't hear a trace of Dad until he cracked open my door.

I spun around as he poked his head in. "I thought you'd be up," he said, slipping in, leaving the door open behind him.

He was already dressed, like he might go to work today, Sunday. "I couldn't sleep either," he said, his voice cracking different from the way mine did; more like he hadn't spoken in years, instead of something changing inside him.

I stood slowly on the side of the bed away from him, still looking out the window. The day was gray, the air wet with the storm, which was gone now, leaving behind the cold and the damp.

Dad walked up beside me. Both of us looked out the window instead of at each other.

"Austin . . ." His voice cracked that way again. "I think what you're trying to do is the bravest thing I've ever heard." He cleared his throat. "Abilene . . . she told us about your tattoo."

I couldn't keep from lifting my hand to my chest, like I could still keep him from knowing. I didn't say anything, just waited for whatever he'd do.

"I was never so proud," he said.

I glanced at him. "The whole thing was a mistake," I whispered. "I wished I'd never done it."

"No, it wasn't a mistake. But we can't follow Abilene now. None of us can. Not even you."

"I can try."

Dad put his hand on my arm, pinching it the way he used to when I was little, asking him to feel my muscles. "You can't go with her through this. I know you want to, that you'd do anything for her, but you won't survive it, Austin. We can't even be sure Abilene will. All we can do is hope."

I stood beside him staring out the window, not knowing what to say, until I began to feel eyes, someone else watching. I turned around.

Mom was standing in my door, the house black around her, but even so I caught a glimpse of a bigger, taller shadow behind her. Abilene. Caught in the darkness, she was no more than a ghost really.

She put a hand up on Mom's shoulder. "I have to borrow Austin now, Dad."

Mom and Dad didn't say anything. I didn't move.

"Come on, Austin," Abilene said quietly. "We've got places to go."

I glanced at Dad, expecting him to plant me in place with a look, maybe even jump between us. But he only nodded, trying to smile.

I took a staggering step toward Abilene, like my feet were somebody else's. I wondered if she'd really come into my room last night at all, if that was an Abilene I'd only dreamed.

Though I could hardly believe it, Mom stepped aside for me too, and I followed Abilene down the stairs, out into the cold, gray dawn.

forty

Following Abilene out to her truck, I asked, "You want me to drive?"

Abilene shook her head. "I'm in the driver's seat."

I slid into my old spot and Abilene turned the key. But then she just sat. I followed her look up to my window and saw Mom and Dad standing there, watching us. Abilene lifted her hand out in a wave and slipped the truck into reverse.

They waved back and I couldn't believe they weren't doing a thing to stop us.

Abilene slowly built up speed, driving carefully, not stopping or saying another word until she pulled into Pecos for gas. Even then, all she said was, "Fill it up, Austin. We've got big miles ahead."

When I climbed back in, she said, "There's an extra jacket behind the seat if you're cold."

"I'm fine," I said, but I couldn't keep from shivering.

Abilene twisted to reach behind the seat herself, wrenching her coat out, dropping it onto my lap. I shoved my arms through the sleeves and pulled it tight across my chest.

Abilene drove out of Pecos then, back the way we'd come, but taking the old road leading to her overpass. Finally I asked, "What're we doing, Ab'lene?"

"Major road trip." She didn't take her eyes off the highway.

We flashed down the road, the bridge looming ahead, its steel and concrete the only thing cutting into the sky from the flatness around us. But instead of slowing, Abilene kept flying along. I sat up, watching Abilene, but she kept her face straight forward. The hiss of the tires sang on the surface of the bridge, and I pictured the interstate shooting away beneath us. I wanted to ask Abilene if she remembered hanging over the side, the dizziness of standing straight again. But I knew she remembered.

Once we were across, we turned, heading right into the rising sun. If it hadn't been so cloudy, we'd have been blinded. I snuck a glance at Abilene, wondering how much she had told Mom and Dad. Why they'd just let us go.

"Where are we going?"

"East." Abilene looked away from the road long enough to give me a quick smile.

"How come Mom and Dad let us go?"

"You think they could stop us?" Abilene sounded surprised, but fake surprised.

"Do they know where we're going?"

She tensed for a second.

I looked out the side window. "If you already told them, you might as well tell me."

Abilene watched the highway a long time. She slowed to swing south on a paved ranch road I'd never been down. Once she got back up to speed, she said, "Open the glove box."

I looked at her.

She didn't say anything else.

The latch had been broken forever—Abilene's security system—so I thumped my fist on the dashboard, the door of the box dropping open.

The box was full of the usual tangle of papers and empty shotgun shells, but nested in the middle was a wrecked old baseball, one of the lost ones, cracked and faded. I was reaching for it when I saw the writing, so far gone I nearly missed it. I took it out, rolling it in my hands, reading Nolan Ryan's name out loud. "My partner on the Express," I murmured.

"Must've been one wild pitch," Abilene said.

Holding tight to the ball, I pictured Abilene out in the desert, roaming around the abandoned base, somehow knowing she had to search for this. I rubbed the ball in my palms. "It's the worst thing I've ever done," I whispered.

Abilene gave a small laugh. "What I'd give for a conscience so clear."

"No, it's not like that."

"Austin, it's the same as if I threw it out there myself." She reached to push her hair away from her forehead, but it was all still tight in her braid. She put her hand back on the wheel. "I'm only surprised you didn't throw it any farther."

"That was as far as I could."

Abilene looked at me. "Maybe so."

I kept rubbing the ball. While she was looking at me, for the quick second I could see her eyes, I asked, "You did tell them where we're going, didn't you?"

Abilene started for her hair again, but let her hand fall onto the seat between us. "Yes."

Even though I already knew, her saying so stole my wind. "Are you going to tell me?" I whispered.

Abilene looked down the road. "We're going to get a replacement for that ball."

I glanced at it in my lap. "You said you went to Nolan Ryan's house for this. That you had him sign it himself."

"See what I mean about a clear conscience?"

"I don't know what you're talking about, Ab'lene."

Abilene slapped her forehead. "The ball, Austin! I stole it from a set of them at Wal-Mart. It was autographed by some machine."

"But it was signed to me."

"I wrote that myself. 'My partner on the Express.'"

I glanced again at the ball. "But the Fireballer. It's exactly right."

"How do you think it was such a perfect match? What do you think, I went to Nolan Ryan and ripped my shirt open so he could copy my lousy tattoo?"

I looked again at the ball, the scratches of her pen faded more than the signature. She didn't have her tattoo when she gave me this ball, like she'd still only been building herself up to that day in Tattoo's chair.

"So you never went to Alvin? You never met him?"

"How close do you think I'd've got, Austin? A punk kid trying to get an autograph? How many of those do you suppose he turns down every day?"

None like Abilene, I thought.

"No, Austin." She blew out a big breath. "I never went to Alvin. I never met Nolan Ryan." She gripped and regripped the steering wheel. "It was all just lies."

I swallowed. "But you never told me that, Ab'lene. You never told me you went there. I asked, but you never actually said. So—"

"It's the same thing, Austin, letting you think that."

I watched the dash, the blur of road above it. "So you stole it for me. That's okay. Where? Midland?"

Abilene nodded, closing her eyes for a second. I watched the road for her.

"So that's where we're going? To Midland? To get a new ball?" She'd turned off that road a long time ago. We were going the wrong way.

Abilene chewed her lip. "I'm doing it right this time, Austin. We're going to Alvin. Somehow I'm going to make him give you the real thing. Like I should have right off."

I sat back in my seat, taking small breaths. Going to Alvin. To meet Nolan Ryan himself. Only Abilene could ever pull that off. But as we zipped along, picking up the interstate out of Fort Stockton, I kept looking at Abilene, at her stare locked on everything still in front of us.

"I don't want to, Ab'lene."

"What?"

"I don't want another ball."

"That one is a wreck. We ruined it."

"It's perfect."

Abilene kept driving, not saying anything else.

"Really. I don't want to go to Alvin. I don't want to have to tell him How All This Started."

"I don't think we'd have to go into that, Austin," she answered, a trace of a smile haunting the corners of her mouth.

After we'd gone a few more miles, the tires droning on and on, I asked, "How far is it?"

"Alvin?"

"Uh-huh."

"Just about forever. All the way to Houston."

"Houston. I wonder if Mom and Dad ever made it that far. Back in the newlywed days."

Abilene forced a smile. "Don't tell me we got another stillborn?" Her voice was dry. "Not Houston?"

I nodded. "The whole state's littered with them."

"Texas is a pretty big place, Austin."

"It'd have to be."

Abilene shook her head. "Newlyweds," she muttered.

I picked at the baseball's faded stitching. Abilene kept driving. After a while, I said, "So they know where we're going? Mom and Dad?"

Abilene looked like she hadn't heard, like she'd forgotten I was there.

"You've been talking to them?"

She turned the wheel slightly, guiding us through a long, steady interstate curve. "Yeah, Austin, I guess we talk some. Who'd have ever believed it?"

I looked at her, at her braid lying straight down her shoulder, at her jaw shut tight.

"I can't remember the last time I talked to them," I said. "Except for shouting about you. Trying to keep them away from you."

Abilene shook her head like a boxer sagged against the ropes.

"I guess it was when you were gone. Dad took me into the basement, trying to show me all his old things. Trying to showing me he had a life before us."

"He did that to me once too." Abilene laughed a little. "I told Nancy it was his facts-of-life talk."

I watched her as we roared down the highway. "What else did you tell her?"

"What else? All we do is talk. Mostly about us. Our family."

"About me?"

Abilene kept looking down the road, driving carefully.

"Was Mom there with you? When you and the doctor talked?"

"Sometimes."

"Dad?"

"Not as much."

I rubbed at my pitching calluses. "And you talked about me? You and Mom and that doctor?"

Abilene bit her lip, then let it loose. "Some, Austin."

I nodded and watched the highway roar past. "Did Mom tell her about when I was a kid? When she told me how handsome I was? Did she ever tell about that?"

Abilene puffed out her cheeks, blowing out another tired breath. "No, Austin. I don't think so."

"Remember how Mom used to wear perfume? I remember her holding my head in her hands, her face close, that way she smelled."

Abilene didn't say a word.

"She said, 'You are my handsome little man, Austin. The girls at school are going to just die for you.'" I tried out a laugh. "I told her I didn't want anybody dying for me."

Abilene kept looking straight ahead. "I'd die for you in a heartbeat, Austin," she whispered.

"I don't want anybody dying for me!" I shouted.

Abilene squinted, as if the sun had flashed out, though the day was just as gray as before.

I watched her a long time before saying, "She said how when I was grown-up, I'd be glad to have those girls after me. She said I'd marry somebody beautiful and have my own family."

I waited again, long enough that Abilene turned to me. "And?"

"I told her that wasn't ever going to happen. I said, 'I'm going to marry Ab'lene, Mom. We'll always stay here.'"

Abilene squinted even tighter.

"That was before I decided you were going to marry Nolan Ryan."

Abilene didn't even start to smile. "What'd Mom say?"

"She laughed. But when she saw I was serious, she said, 'But Abilene's your sister, honey. You can't marry your sister.'

"'I'm going to,' I told her."

"But Mom said, 'Abilene will have a husband all her own by then.'"

Abilene held the steering wheel like it was trying to get away from her. Her mouth was clamped shut, her lips gone white. "Why in the world did she have to tell you that?"

"I thought getting married just meant staying together, Ab'lene, having all your stories together, like Mom and Dad. It was before you gave me your own facts-of-life talk. Before I saw how they'd shut themselves away in the desert and didn't have anything left *but* those stories."

Abilene kept shaking her head, her eyes flicking along the dull road, nothing but mile markers breaking the endless stretch of mesquite and creosote.

"But before then I used to like those stories," I admitted, barely loud enough to be heard over the gush of the wind, the whine of the tires. "I used to love them. Especially How All This Started. It made me feel like we were part of something huge. I thought if we got married, they'd just go on and on."

Abilene didn't say anything and we drove on in silence until I said, "But it just got to seem so pathetic, you know? How they'd driven around to all those towns, thinking everything in the whole world was still out there in front of them. Not knowing that when we came along it was already all over."

I didn't think Abilene was going to answer. But then she said, "That was me, Austin. I made you think that way. There's nothing wrong with Mom and Dad. They're just so ordinary. I wanted more for you and me."

I shook my head. "Now I just can't believe that they gave it all up for us. You know how long that honeymoon of theirs was? The newlywed days? I did the math. Six years. That's what they called their honeymoon. Everything before us."

Abilene looked lost, the road endless before her.

"Once I figured that out," I went on, "I couldn't stand that story because it made me feel so bad. I thought maybe Dad told it just to rub it in, like he was saying, 'See what you've done to us?'"

"He never did that. That was me. Mom and Dad, they still believe the whole story. They really think we're the best things that ever happened to them."

Abilene's voice was falling apart, and when I looked her way, I saw she had tears streaking her cheeks. She swiped at them, ducking her head, trying to see the road.

I looked away. "I really don't want to go to Alvin."

Abilene acted as if she were someplace else, miles from me.

"Don't you see, Ab'lene? Nolan Ryan's *our* story. We started him ourselves."

"I don't know what I see anymore, Austin," Abilene said, wiping her cheeks dry with the sleeve of her coat, sounding even more tired than Dad had looked that morning.

I turned the baseball round and round in my fingers. "What do you think we'll find in Alvin, Ab'lene? An old retired guy putting around on a riding mower? An aspirin salesman? I don't want to see that." I waved the ball at her. "This ball's a hundred times better than one he'd sign just to get rid of us. He's not even the Fireballer anymore, Ab'lene. We are."

Abilene's voice cracked when she tried to answer. She cleared her throat, but then just reached to take the baseball from my hand. I gave it to her, and she found her fastball grip. She thumped the ball up and down on her thigh. "What do you think that's like, Austin? Your whole life over and done, just sitting around wondering what's going to happen next? Wondering if there'll be anything at all?"

I shrugged. "What else does anybody ever do? Don't you wake up every day wondering what's going to happen?"

"I wake up dreading it." Abilene took her foot off the gas and we coasted along the flat road. As we lost more and more speed, she eased onto the shoulder.

"When you told me to come with you this morning, you know what I thought?"

Abilene didn't budge.

"I thought, at last she's leaving for good and taking me with her."

"It's no place you want to go, Austin." She stared at the center of the wheel.

"Dad told me it'd kill me if I keep trying to go with you."

Abilene gave a tiny snort; a laugh, a sneer, I couldn't tell which. Lowering her forehead to rest against the curve of the wheel, she whispered, "What am I going to do without you?"

"I'm going to stay with you." Making myself smile, hoping to make her smile, I said, "Hasn't killed me so far."

"No, but I wonder what it *has* done to you."

I looked down at the floorboards, then out the window. "Hasn't done anything to me I wouldn't do again."

Abilene shook her head and I watched her until she sat back straight in her seat.

"Can we go home, Ab'lene?"

"You can." She tossed the Nolan Ryan ball to me. "You're going to wake up every day wondering what's going to happen next, wondering how many strikeouts you're going to get, how many no-hitters."

"But what about you, Ab'lene?"

"I'll be wondering the same thing, believe me." She threw the truck into gear and stomped the gas, whirling us through a giant U-turn, bucking through the interstate's center strip and onto the long, empty lanes heading home.

"But what about *you?*" I asked again, watching her white-knuckling the steering wheel.

Abilene finally smiled. "You tell me."

forty-one

Abilene didn't say anything else. She just drove and drove, silent. By the time we reached the turn at Fort Stockton, it was dark, the rare stretch of highway lights bright in the sky. As a kid I loved how the windshield turned the lights into long beams, latching onto the glass and swinging us forward to the next. But after we'd flashed through the last of them, there wasn't anything to guide us but Abilene's dusty, bug-smeared headlights.

Every now and then a jackrabbit would dodge in front of us, but Abilene never flinched, never braked or sped up, steered at them or away. Just kept barreling along.

We made it almost all the way home, following those dim lights, never hitting a single jackrabbit. But when we reached the last turn to our house, the turn where the school bus dropped me, Abilene pulled over instead of making the corner. We sat there idling. After so long blasting along, the stillness took some getting used to.

Finally Abilene said, "Have you been eating your carrots?"

"What?"

"How's your night vision?"

"What do you want, Ab'lene?" I asked, afraid of what she might answer.

Abilene smiled. "What I was asking, Austin, is how's your night vision?"

"It's fine, I guess."

"Make it home from here?"

"Sure. It's just down the road. But——"

"Get out, Austin," Abilene said.

"Out? What are you talking about?"

"Get out. I've got things to do."

"It's the middle of the night."

We watched each other in the dim reflection from the headlights, the slight glow of the dashboard. Abilene looked silver, like some kind of statue. She was still smiling.

Then she leaned forward, toward me, and before I knew it, she had her arms around me, squeezing me in a hug that stole my breath, as much out of surprise as from the strength of it. I tried to untangle my arms to hug her back, but before I got my arms around her, Abilene reached past me and popped open my door. The bent metal screeched, the desert naked-cold behind me. "Go on," she whispered, her mouth so close I could feel the heat of her words on my ear. "I have to do this on my own."

"What, Ab'lene?"

She retightened her grip on me for another instant, but I was too scared now to hug back. I breathed in deep gulps of her, her smell already overwhelmed by the creosote. "You can't just leave."

"I'll let you know where I am," she promised, straightening behind the wheel.

I reached one foot out into the empty space, the darkness. Suddenly I wasn't at all sure I'd be able to find my way without her, and I turned back to Abilene. "You can't just leave me."

"Don't make me push you."

I stepped down, my feet scraping the packed and graded gravel. Before I could turn, before I could open my mouth to beg her to stay, or to take me with her, her tires spun and she was gone, the cab light spilling out my open door until she leaned over and pulled it shut. Even over the roar of her acceleration, I could hear that screech and slam.

I watched until there was nothing left, not even the wash of headlights against the sky. Nothing at all. Then I turned down the road and started the awful, slow shuffle home.

There were no stars, but the clouds were stretched thin, glowing in places with the light of the moon behind them, plenty bright enough for me to make it home. Once I heard the heart-stopping rattle of a snake, and I froze until I heard the slick, dry slip of scales as it retreated.

The lights were on in the house, though I'd hoped it was too late for Mom and Dad to be up. I lowered my head, not letting the lights blind me, and trudged on, wondering what I'd tell them.

In the driveway, my head still lowered, I almost walked into a truck. I pulled up short in its shadow, breathing fast, wondering how Abilene had gotten around me, how she'd beaten me home. But once I gave myself time to think, I saw that though the truck was a beater, almost as old as Abilene's, it wasn't hers. I wondered who could be here this time, who wanted some piece of her now. For a second I was almost glad she wasn't here.

I swung open the door and took one step inside the kitchen, blocking the light with my hand. Mom and Dad were sitting together at the table. There wasn't anybody else, no one waiting for Abilene.

Mom whispered, "Austin." Dad stared at me.

I squinted back. When the light's sting faded, I realized they weren't searching frantically over my shoulder, weren't asking about Abilene.

"She's gone."

Dad nodded. Mom kept staring right at me. Her chin quaked for an instant. She tried to smile.

"I don't know where she went."

"She wouldn't tell you?" Mom asked.

"She wouldn't even drive me home."

"You walked?" Mom said, seeming even closer to breaking down.

"Just from the road."

Dad cleared his throat, trying to smile too. "Did you get a chance to meet Nolan Ryan?" But he shook his head right away. "No. No, of course not. You're back too soon for that."

"What happened, Austin?" Mom said, pushing back her chair and coming to stand next to me. She touched my hand and I flinched away. I couldn't help it. Abilene had even told them about Nolan Ryan.

"I didn't want to go," I whispered. "I didn't let her take me there."

"But, Austin," Mom said. "Abilene wanted to. She wanted to do that for you more than anything."

"What for, Mom? To see some guy whose life is already over?"

Mom stopped reaching for my hand. I watched the end of the table, feeling them looking at each other.

I walked around the table, but at the end of the kitchen I stopped and turned halfway back toward them. "Do you know where she is? Do you know what she's doing? Did she even tell you that too?"

Dad cleared his throat again. "Did you see your truck in the drive?" he asked. "Mom and I spent all day looking, until we were sure we found a good, reliable—"

"She's trying something new, Austin," Mom said, touching Dad's arm, giving a tiny shake of her head. "She's going to stay away from us. She's going to see how she does on her own."

"You knew? You knew she wasn't coming back?"

"She wanted to say good-bye," Dad said.

"Well, she didn't. She didn't tell me anything."

Leaving them there, I crept up the stairs and went straight into Abilene's room. Even with the lights off I knew there wasn't a thing missing, that Abilene had gone with only what she had in her truck, like I'd always guessed she would. I sat down on her bed, then lay back, putting my arm over my eyes. I couldn't believe she'd left me in this house alone with Mom and Dad; all the things she always said she couldn't wait to get away from.

Lying there on Abilene's bed, I went through all of Dad's stories, everything that had brought us this far. And after all that, what I pictured was the bombers he'd told me about out at the base, rows and rows of them stretching as far as anyone could see, their time passed, every one of them worn-out and useless. And I remembered how Abilene always made me imagine the *Enola Gay* soaring into the sky out of here, when really it was just one more chunk of metal parked in the scrap pile.

Somehow, with the way she always ran down Mom and Dad, she'd made that one bomber seem more alive to me than she'd ever let them seem.

And, for a few minutes, squeezing my arm down tight over my eyes, making the red swim behind my eyelids, I was afraid that this would be the story of my life, what I'd someday have to tell my kids. "When I was young, you know, your age, your Aunt Abilene and I spent all our time in an abandoned airplane boneyard." I pictured myself as an aging, retired ballplayer, another Nolan Ryan, just like Abilene had always wanted. "Your aunt taught me to pitch out there. She made me throw until my fingers bled. She once used a baseball to break your grandpa's face." I pictured their looks, their rolling eyes, how they'd try sneaking away to keep from hearing my ancient stories. "She slapped Grandma. She stole Grandpa's gun and sawed it in half." But then, lifting my arm off my face, I pictured myself spinning around, telling them in an excited whisper, "But then she brought the gun back. She gave back everything she'd taken from them. From all of us."

I opened my eyes to the just-less-than-black darkness of Abilene's abandoned room. I ran back through that scrap of waking nightmare: me reeling out my own stories; Dad's and Abilene's haunting me.

Sitting up with a shiver, I wondered what Abilene's story would be. But as I pictured her with a lap full of kids, telling how she had soared out of Pyote like her old bomber, I remembered that Abilene would have no kids, no one to bore with her stories. I pictured Dad booming out, "We were only in Abilene for the night!" to an empty, echoey room.

And with Dad's voice ringing inside my head, Abilene's children vanishing before my eyes, I heard Dad's intro to the other half of that story, the half that kept *me* from vanishing: "We were only in Austin for the night too!"

But I realized now that they'd bought this place just before Abilene was born. They settled down here to have her. "Built our nest," Dad always said.

It didn't fit at all. Their traveling days had ended with Abilene, with this place. Suddenly I knew that there had never been a night in Austin. They'd made it up. For me. Just to make me feel part of something so great they'd given up their whole lives for it.

I sat there long after the night sounds settled, feeling a big gap yawning open in me, as if I'd suddenly found out that I was adopted. I realized I wanted to be part of their story, a real part, and I could hardly believe I'd come to want such a thing.

The house silent around me, I stood up at last. Slipping down the hallway, I crept to Mom and Dad's door. Swallowing the knob's rattle in my fist, the way Abilene had taught me, I un-latched their door and eased it open.

The same gray light filling Abilene's room filled theirs too, and I stood in their doorway listening to them sleep: Dad's quiet rumbling; Mom's little slips of breath.

I listened to their breathing a long time before finally stepping to the foot of their bed. Tipping my head back the way Abilene had to feel the rain, I threw my arms out wide and turned a big, silent circle, encompassing, I saw at last, the place I'd always belonged.

forty-two

For a long time I didn't see Abilene at all. Though she'd only moved to Midland, into some sort of group home the hospital ran where she could try going it on her own, she said it was easier not seeing anybody, even me. She said it was better that way for both of us.

For the rest of that fall, and on into winter, I didn't touch the truck Mom and Dad had bought for me. It felt too much like a trade for Abilene. But by February, with baseball practice keeping me late, it only made sense, and I started driving it in to school. Without Abilene, nobody talked anymore about me graduating early.

After practice I rarely drove straight home. Some days I'd make a run out to Abilene's overpass, hoping for a chance to see her, but at the same time afraid I might find her truck alone there, empty. Other days I drove out to the base, but she was never there either.

All I had was Abilene's post office box. Though Mom and Dad knew where she lived, they said she asked them not to tell me, not until she was ready. So I sent her letters. Abilene hardly ever answered with more than a line or two, but I kept sending them. I let her know I was pitching again, that I was on the team. I told her how each of my starts went, batter by batter, pitch by pitch. She sent a note after my first win, just a blank post office card with "Pure heat!" scrawled across the back. About midseason she sent another: "Why no no-hitters? Bear down." I pictured her compiling my stats and wished it would lure her back, that she wouldn't be able to stand not coaching me.

I got into a habit of skipping school the afternoons of my home starts and screaming down the one hundred straight, flat freeway miles to Midland. Then I'd cruise a different section of the city each time, a kind of grid search for her truck, without ever really expecting to find anything. It took most of a day to get my game face on, going over all Abilene's old coaching, filtering out the odder parts, and that long drive into Midland became one of the biggest pieces of it.

So when I saw her parked truck that spring, a few weeks before divisionals, I didn't know what to do. I just stopped and stared, my truck idling in the middle of the little street.

Eventually I pulled over, my hands shaking on the steering wheel. I looked around, guessing at which place was hers. But it was hopeless, all the buildings apartments, old duplex and fourplex type things. I wound up just picking one and going up and hammering at the door.

A man answered, and I stammered a moment before I could say, "I'm looking for somebody." I pointed out toward Abilene's truck. "I found her truck."

The guy stared at me. "Abilene."

I nodded.

I was wearing my uniform shirt, like we did every game day, and the guy seemed to take a long time reading the one word—

Pecos—across the chest. "Austin," he said quietly. "I'll tell her you're here."

I started to follow, but he turned and said, "Wait here." He shrugged apologetically. "I can't let anyone in without an okay from the resident."

"What?" I asked, and the guy stepped back, explaining that he was a kind of house parent. "There are four residents now. Abilene's been here the longest. Longer than me. She's incredible, you know. I can hardly imagine the place without her."

I nodded and waited.

He was back in just a few seconds, smiling. "Upstairs. Second door."

I was trembling, covered with sweat before I got to the top of the steps. Abilene's door gaped open before me, and I stood still, practicing my breathing before stepping into it.

Abilene stood in the center of the room, just stood there staring at me, like she didn't know if she should slam the door and hide or what. That fast I knew I'd never ask anything I'd thought I might, nothing about doctors or therapy or medication, about what she was doing now.

Looking past her into her tiny room, I whispered, "Hey, Ab'lene."

Then, at last, Abilene grinned and said, "Hey, yourself." Like we saw each other every day. She stepped back, inviting me in.

Her room was bare: an old couch, a tiny table, one chair. Nothing on the walls, nothing to let you know who lived here.

Abilene caught me staring. "Figured I'd get myself a personality before I gave this place one."

Then I saw it, sitting on the planks she had propped up for a kind of coffee table, the only thing I could see that she didn't absolutely need—a cracked old baseball I didn't have to look at to know how it was signed.

"Souvenir," Abilene said.

I nodded.

"From the old days."

I just kept looking at that beat up old ball.

When the quiet grew too long, she said, "So, Big Spring again tonight. Should be a good one."

"They're always tough." I was surprised, even with all my letters, that she'd know my schedule.

We looked around each other until Abilene asked, "Do you still throw out at the base? Coach let you do that?"

I nodded. "Though I'm not sure how much he really knows about it."

Abilene smiled and I wondered if she'd been out there, if she'd snuck up the tiny wash to watch me pitch. I wondered if she'd seen that the tire had fallen down, pulling the power pole's crossbar down with it. Or if she'd seen that I'd rolled the tire into the tank and stole a pitching net from school, saving me all the time of searching through the desert for the balls.

"So, you were just cruising around? Just decided to drop by and say hello?"

"I drive out here every game day. For luck. Kind of looking for you, I guess."

"Wouldn't a rabbit's foot be easier?"

I shrugged.

"I can imagine this is really going to help your concentration today."

"Yeah. Probably not."

We stood there until finally I said, "I wanted to see you. I just—"

Abilene reached forward and touched my jersey. But rather than touching me, it felt like she was feeling the cloth, remembering the uniform. She shook her head. "Things are okay here, Austin. Really. No matter what it looks like."

"All I do is think about you, Ab'lene, but playing baseball was always the plan. I'm just doing what we always talked about. I'm not—"

"I know, Austin. I know." She held her hand flat against my chest. "I'm going to college again. Back at Midland CC. Can you believe it?"

"That's good."

"They've got a journalism degree, with a broadcasting emphasis. I'm thinking of sports announcing. How about that? Following you around, calling all your games. Making my living telling everyone what a star my little brother is. I'm going to call the first twenty-seven-strikeout perfect game ever."

I couldn't help smiling. "You might starve."

"Not a chance." She was still brushing my uniform, tracing the letters with her fingertips. I didn't know if she was only imagining my tattoo under there, or if she was trying to put herself in this uniform again, make herself the pitcher they all pinned their hopes on. "Mom told me about the scout," she whispered.

I'd left that out of my last letter on purpose, not sure, after everything, if I wanted Abilene putting her old phenom twist on me again.

"The Baltimore Orioles." She smiled. "Lots more money than wins."

"He was just passing through. I think Coach might have called him."

"The first ant. Next thing you know it'll be a steady stream. Then a swarm. They've got the scent now."

"I know Coach called some guy he knows at UT."

"Austin in Austin. Where All This Started. Has a certain poetry to it."

"He hasn't even come out yet, Ab'lene."

"Dad tells me you're into the ninety-mile-an-hour range."

I turned my face away from her, hiding the blush I felt rising in my cheeks. I hadn't told her that either. It was still so far from her dreams of one hundred. One twenty.

298 * Pete Fromm

"They're all going to want you, Austin. Everyone in the world. It's your pick, not theirs."

"I didn't come out here to talk about my baseball career, Ab'lene."

"What else is there?"

"You. I wanted to see you. I wanted—"

She waved her hands down her sides. "Voilà. A work in progress."

"But what—"

Abilene tapped the back of her wrist. "You're going to be late for your start."

I could only look at her.

"You better go. Get a couple extra warm up throws in. Get yourself settled."

I stepped back to the door, and when I said good-bye, Abilene waved. "Low and fast. Nobody can hurt you low and fast."

I drove straight to the field and sat in the dugout, holding my face in my glove until the team showed up, nerves twisting my insides like never before. Thank God there weren't any scouts at that game. I got pulled in the second.

The rest of that season I drove to Abilene's before every start. But I'd picture her in that empty room, interrupting me every time I tried asking anything about her, about anything beside my own pitching, and I'd drive by without stopping, almost used to being by myself now.

That summer, Abilene moved out of the group home. She sent me a card announcing her change of address, a form card, like one from a box of hundreds. Across the back of it she wrote, "What am I supposed to do with the rest of these cards?"

I drove by her new place the same day I got her card, but her truck wasn't there, and again I didn't stop. Even if it had been, I didn't want to see another naked room, hear Abilene talking about not having a personality. And, though I hated to even think it, I'd kind of gotten used to just knowing she was not too far away, that we were supposed to make our own way now.

From right there in Midland I sent her a note on the plain white post office cards she used. It only said, "I think your house parent was in love with you." It came back a few days later with "What do you mean *was*?!" slashed across the top.

She came out to the house twice, once that summer, and again in the fall. But both times I was out at the base pitching. It was like she tried to miss me. Standing sweaty and dirty in the kitchen, I yelled, "Didn't you tell her where I was?"

Mom and Dad nodded. "Of course we did, Austin. But this is still her call. Let her decide."

"But she sent me her new address. Why would she do that if she—"

Dad lifted his hands in a shrug. "It's up to her."

So I scribbled out another card. "Rattlesnake Bomber Base. Would you like directions?"

This time her return card was a Smithsonian picture of the *Enola Gay,* sitting firmly on the ground: "Sorry, Austin. But cold turkey is still best. For both of us. Besides, aren't you supposed to be in Baltimore by now?"

So for the next year all we had was our steady stream of one- or two-line postcards. During the season the scouts started trickling, then pouring in, just like Abilene had said. She'd scribble a line about each one: "Big farm boys playing Little League," about Sul Ross, the state university south of here. "Whoa dude, surf's up!" for Southern California and UCLA both. For Houston she only said, "Nolan Ryan might come to a game, but too humid."

It was the same with the pro scouts. "Winners, but they're

still the Yankees." When the Rangers got serious: "It'd be Texas anyway, but Dallas?" For the Marlins she only wrote, "Don't you dare!"

I didn't actually see Abilene until the final game of the divisional championships. The stands were pretty well jammed, and I didn't see her till after my half of the fifth. I was throwing like mercury pours, only giving up one hit, a Texas leaguer, and the crowd was clapping after I struck out the side. Somehow, jogging to the dugout through all that, without even looking, I picked her out, the only person not clapping, not moving at all. She was just sitting there, all alone in that crowd, staring out at the mound as if I was still there, still throwing.

I sat in the dugout all that half-inning, not opening my eyes, not seeing a single one of our hitters. At the base Abilene had taught me how I had to block out the crowd—the whole world—till there was nothing but me, the catcher and the ball, but I had to dig deeper than ever to block out Abilene.

Coach left me in for the whole game. A shutout. A complete game. I gave up a couple more hits, though, one opposite-field single, and a two-out double off a change-up the guy must have been waiting his whole life for. At the last out, a dribbling grounder the first baseman picked off unassisted, the crowd leapt to their feet. We'd finally knocked off Big Spring. Before the team could swarm me, I lifted my mitt to Abilene, but I couldn't find her. I searched the stands even as they started tackling me, but she was gone.

We didn't get far at state, and I don't know if Abilene came to the games or not. I never let myself look. During my one start, a one-to-nothing nail-biter we won, I just imagined her up there in the stands, willing me on.

I didn't get up the nerve to see her at her new place till the day I left for college. Though I knew Mom and Dad must have told her right away, I wanted to tell her in person about the full ride to UT, where Roger Clemens had pitched. Clemens wasn't Nolan Ryan, of course, but Nolan never went to college—straight from high school to the Mets.

I'd only be in Austin, I wanted to tell her. She'd be able to stay with me anytime she wanted.

Mom and Dad helped me pack, Dad lifting my suitcase into the back of the truck while Mom gave me a hug. After shaking my hand, Dad pressed his old first-baseman's glove into my palm, folding my fingers around it. I tried to say something, but he smiled and shook his head. "Tell Abilene we say hello."

I hadn't told them I was going there, but I nodded and said, "I will."

I slipped into my truck, setting his mitt down beside the shoe box with Abilene's steel spikes. Then, as I drove away, I pushed the rearview mirror up toward the ceiling so I couldn't look back at the two of them standing alone again at last on their white-rock driveway.

Abilene's place was only a few blocks from Midland Community College, and again her truck was gone. I rang the bell anyway, and it wasn't a second before she was there. "Mom called." She glanced at her watch, something I'd never seen her wear before. "What did you do, drive a hundred miles an hour?"

"Same as always." I glanced back to the street. "I didn't think you were here. Didn't see your truck."

"A friend's using it this morning." She stepped back and waved me in. "If Mom hadn't called, I'd be helping them move right now."

Her new apartment was as old as the other place, but not a bit empty. There were posters on the wall, one of an old guy in a broadcast booth above a baseball field. "Red Barber," Abilene told me when she saw me looking. "A legend."

On the opposite wall was a poster of Nolan Ryan. There was no *Fireballer* on this one, no words at all, just Nolan, looking so dangerous, peering over his kicked-up leg, all that pent-up energy about to be cut loose.

"Him you know," Abilene said.

"Did Mom and Dad tell you? About UT?"

Abilene nodded.

"I came to tell you that. I wanted to let you know myself."

"It's a good choice, Austin."

We just stood there a second, looking at each other. "I didn't know if you wanted me to come here at all."

"Neither did I."

"Mom and Dad told me I had to let you decide."

She nodded. "But I'm glad you did come. I'm through the worst of it, I think, just still a little afraid to introduce the old life and the new. I guess it's time to see how they get along."

I kept looking at her. She finally laughed and took me by the arm, starting me down the hall. Taped to the bathroom door were two ragged pages torn from a magazine or maybe a catalog. Colored pictures of pills.

"Hey, you guys, this is Austin. The one you've heard so much about." She smacked her finger down on one picture. "Austin, this is my friend lithium." Then the other. "My pal Tegretol."

She laughed a little. "After a year or two of that, you start to wonder about your friends."

She laughed again, maybe catching my uncertain glance. "Really I just put those up so I don't forget to take them. I can't ever forget to do that."

Walking back out toward the living room, I noticed what I hadn't before, a *Pecos Enterprise* picture of me on the mound— last year's no-hitter.

Abilene caught me looking and turned around. She snapped her finger down on that picture too. "I haven't forgotten you, Austin. Just had to have a little time out to kick-start my own life here."

We walked the rest of the way to the living room, and Abilene asked, "So, you want to go out for dinner or cook up something here?"

I stopped behind her. "I can't stay, Ab'lene. I told you. I just wanted to see that you're all right."

"Right as rain," she said. "But don't tell me you can't stay. After all this time. We have to have some sort of send-off."

"I have to go, Ab'lene. I do. You can come to Austin whenever you want. You can stay with me. You—"

"I bet your roommate would love that."

"He'll think I'm the luckiest guy in the world."

"Must be crazier than I am."

She smiled, but I couldn't.

"Ab'lene, I don't even know if I have a roommate. I have to go and register, find out all that stuff. I have to go—"

Abilene laughed. "All right! Go then! See you in the big leagues."

I started backing toward the door, but Abilene said, "Wait. I suppose you ought to see this."

"What?" I asked, but just the way she said it made me pretty sure I didn't want to see whatever she wanted to show me. I thought about interrupting her, asking her if she still had the Fireballer ball, if I could take it with me.

Abilene took a step back, away from me. She was wearing a T-shirt and she fiddled with the bottom edge. "Just a sec'," she said, disappearing back down the hallway.

When she came back, Abilene was wearing a button-front shirt, the buttons undone. She held it closed in a fist. Then, slowly, she pulled the shirt open just enough to let me see the tattoo. Or what was left of it.

The sides of her chest, beginning just at the rise of her breasts, were patched with smooth, fire-red scars, like she'd taken a belt sander to herself. Between the destroyed skin, the remnant of her Fireballer tattoo read "rebal."

"I thought about leaving that, but people would just think I'm too dumb to spell."

I swallowed and cleared my throat but couldn't get out any words.

"They have to do it in stages. You can't take too much at once."

"I don't think you had to do that, Ab'lene," I murmured.

"You wouldn't know," she said, for once sounding like she was just saying what was true, instead of daring me not to believe her. "There are other things that means for me. It's not you I'm erasing."

She pinched her shirt shut, working the buttons, and we stood there not looking at each other. "There are things I want to forget, Austin. But, believe me, you are not one of them. And I'm not pulling a Dad on you, either. I'm not going to lock up everything that came before now. I'm not making that mistake. There is no way my How All This Started is going to be my lithium prescription."

I brushed my fingers across my shirt, my tattoo. "What am I going to do with mine now?"

Abilene flashed a smile. She slapped her hand against my chest. "Live up to it."

I nodded, but then neither of us could think of another thing to say.

Finally Abilene said, "So you're going to be a Longhorn. Decided against going straight pro?"

She was just talking to stop the silence, but I said, "I figured I could use a little more time."

"Just to play." Abilene nodded. "Get back all that childhood you missed."

I made myself laugh. "I got more childhood crammed in than any kid," I said, wishing I could make her believe that.

She shrugged, turning to face anything other than me. Then suddenly, with me just standing there staring at her, Abilene's smile grew big. Without saying a word, she cocked back her arm and threw her leg up, holding me in her gaze an instant before pretending to wing a high, tight one at me.

I ducked backward before I knew what I was doing, but then, even though she was only a few feet away, and I was even taller than she was by then, I charged the mound, ducking my head in under that smooth Nolan Ryan move of hers. She jacked her fist around in a slow-motion version of those old lightning-fast uppercuts. All bent over with my head beneath her arm, I watched her fist, her fingers soft now and gentle, but still coming toward my mouth, my nose, my eyes, still always stopping just short.

With my ear pinched tight against her ribs, I closed my eyes and listened to her heart, remembering all the northers that had parted around us, leaving us this close, untouched.